Praise for Ann Major:

"Want it all? Read Ann Major."
—Nora Roberts, *New York Times* bestselling author

"No one provides hotter emotional fireworks
than the fiery Ann Major."
—*Romantic Times*

Praise for Christine Rimmer:

"Gifted storyteller Christine Rimmer weaves
an emotionally intense romance with top-notch characters,
easy tempo and a touch of intrigue...."
—*Romantic Times*

"A talented storyteller, Ms. Rimmer makes the most
of multi-faceted characters, solid conflicts,
smooth pacing and unbridled passion."
—*Romantic Times*

Praise for Karen Rose Smith:

"...powerful characterization, balanced emotional moments,
and a tense, compelling story line.
—*Romantic Times*

"Dynamic, skillful and refreshing, Karen Rose Smith's writing
keeps the reader turning pages and begging for more.
Ms. Smith's near flawless style, realistic characters and
tension-filled plots make for a satisfying experience
every time you read one of her books."
—*Cataromance.com*

Don't miss Signature Select's exciting series:

The Fortunes of Texas: Reunion

Starting in June 2005, get swept up in twelve new stories from your favorite family!

COWBOY AT MIDNIGHT by Ann Major

A BABY CHANGES EVERYTHING by Marie Ferrarella

IN THE ARMS OF THE LAW by Peggy Moreland

LONE STAR RANCHER by Laurie Paige

THE GOOD DOCTOR by Karen Rose Smith

THE DEBUTANTE by Elizabeth Bevarly

KEEPING HER SAFE by Myrna Mackenzie

THE LAW OF ATTRACTION by Kristi Gold

ONCE A REBEL by Sheri WhiteFeather

MILITARY MAN by Marie Ferrarella

FORTUNE'S LEGACY by Maureen Child

THE RECKONING by Christie Ridgway

Signature Select™
COLLECTION

ANN
MAJOR

CHRISTINE
RIMMER

KAREN ROSE
SMITH

Secret Admirer

Silhouette Books

Published by Silhouette Books
America's Publisher of Contemporary Romance

Special thanks and acknowledgment are given to Ann Major, Christine Rimmer and Karen Rose Smith for their contributions to the SECRET ADMIRER collection.

SILHOUETTE BOOKS

ISBN 0-373-28519-1

SECRET ADMIRER

Copyright © 2005 by Harlequin Books S.A.

The publisher acknowledges the copyright holders of the individual works as follows:

SECRET KISSES
Copyright © 2005 by Harlequin Enterprises Limited S.A.

HIDDEN HEARTS
Copyright © 2005 by Harlequin Enterprises Limited S.A.

DREAM MARRIAGE
Copyright © 2005 by Harlequin Enterprises Limited S.A.

This edition published by arrangement with Harlequin Books S.A.

® and TM are trademarks of the publisher. Trademarks indicated with ® are registered in the United States Patent and Trademark Office, the Canadian Trade Marks Office and in other countries.

Visit Silhouette Books at www.eHarlequin.com

Printed in U.S.A.

CONTENTS

Dear Reader,

I feel very lucky to have been asked to write *Secret Kisses*. The idea of an anonymous love letter being published by a mischievous, elderly editor in a small-town newspaper and that letter wreaking havoc among the gossipy denizens appealed to my imagination. There are all sorts of brokenhearted people in the world, as well as meddlers, who are looking for just such a declaration of undying love from the person who "did them or theirs wrong."

I grew up in Texas and spent a lot of summers in just such a small town. I could easily identify with my hero and heroine when they are swept into a romance because of this letter and some busybody friends and relatives.

Enjoy,

Ann Major

SECRET KISSES

Ann Major

To Patience Smith

Prologue

Saturday

"It's time for drastic measures," Ol' Bill muttered to himself as he drove down Main Street. He glanced toward the sun that was just peeping over one of the distant red hills that gave the village its name.

The trouble with a town the size of Red Rock, Texas, was everybody thought he was something on a stick. All those Texas-size egos buttin' heads used to make for lots of interestin' doings.

Used to. Lately the town had gotten downright boring.

Six in the morning was too early for most of the town's strong-minded citizens to be up meddling. Ol'

Bill Sinclair was the exception to that rule. Seventy-two and feeling it a little more than usual, he drove with care. Despite his caution, Ol' Bill's "Spring Fling juices" were flowing like a riptide rushing up to a placid summer beach to wreak havoc on kids building sand castles. He felt bright and chipper and damnably mischievous on this particular May morning.

This was 'sposed to be Spring Fling season, but there wasn't a speck of trouble brewin'. If a concerned citizen didn't think up some devilment fast, there was the very real danger the town that prided itself on its Wild West heritage would bore itself to death.

Bill was a cowboy at heart. Not that he was spry enough to ride out and seek adventure. These days he got most of his kicks by organizing the town archives at the library and by working at the *Red Rock Gazette*. Sometimes after one of his features on politics or religion appeared, folks stormed the *Gazette* and told him he should do the town a favor and retire. Helen Geary had even gifted him with a colorful ceramic tile that read, "Silence is the best substitute for brains."

Fans like Helen were a rare and treasured thing to any writer. It was thrilling to know that people were out there, reading him, appreciating him. He was so proud of his tile, he'd hung it above his toilet, so he could pay it a visit on a regular basis.

The big sky was turning all colors of pink when Bill stomped on the brakes and his battered blue pickup skidded to a halt at the last blinking red traffic light on Main Street. Just in the nick of time to miss an eighteen-wheeler whizzing past on the San Antone Highway.

Whew! His old heart raced a little faster.

Good thing he'd rolled to a stop when he had, or he'd have been roadkill for sure. For a second or two he wondered what tasty potluck dish Helen Geary would have brought to his wake to celebrate his permanent retirement.

Slowly, carefully, he made it through the light onto the highway. A few blocks farther down, he turned into the parking lot of his favorite breakfast nook, the Dairy Café.

He bumped across the familiar potholes of the empty parking lot with gleeful pride. Yes sirree, bobcat, just like always good Ol' Bill was the first customer at Red Rock's favorite dairy café. Just like always he was wearing the favorite overalls his wife kept trying to throw away. Just like always he had a briefcase full of letters to the editor to mull over while he sat in a plastic booth and swigged black coffee out of one of those tiny white foam cups he detested. Ah, what he wouldn't give for an old-fashioned, thick ceramic cup and saucer.

If he hit pay dirt, one or two of the letters would be provocative as all get out. If he hit a dry hole, he'd have to pen his own…maybe throw in a little political advice to excite his fans. One way or the other, he intended to stir up a hornet's nest to get folks in the proper mood for Red Rock's annual Spring Fling.

The Spring Fling, which was always held on the town square on May 15, was usually a time of mischief and mayhem. If he didn't act fast, this year's Spring Fling would take place without even a hint of disaster or scandal.

Dwelling on that dismal thought again, Bill ordered his coffee and sat down. One sip of the strong black liquid set him to reminiscing. Why, only last year sweet Megan Holston had made two dates for the dance. Who would have thought she had it in her? For weeks leading up to the Fling neither date had known about the other. Then at the Spring Fling, when the two beaus discovered each other and people had started laughing, there had been one helluva shoot-out.

Beau #1 had shot off the tip of his big toe, and Beau #2 had been knocked out cold from the kickback of his gun. Meanwhile, as that pair of love-struck fools had wrestled each other through the night, sweet Megan had eloped with her one true love, Johnny Ambush, and lived happily and boringly ever after.

The year before, somebody had spiked the punch at the Fling with something so powerful the entire town had ended up skinny-dipping in Lake Mondo—even the big-haired and blue-haired old biddies, much to the joy of a tabloid reporter who'd shown up. The reporter had taken pictures of the old biddies' boobs hanging to their navels and had made Red Rock the laughingstock of Texas.

Not that that was the first time lewd photographs had caused a stir during Spring Fling season.

Years ago, whew, now this *had* been a spell, brash young Matt Harper had set the town on its edge with a few amateur masterpieces. People had begun to think Matt, who'd been a mere senior in high school at the time, had finally settled down. Then he'd gone and pulled that low-down stunt.

Ol' Bill rubbed his forehead, trying to remember. First, Matt had asked shy Jane Snow, who'd had a crush on him for years, to the Fling. Of course, she'd said yes, and the romantics in town had been pleased as punch for Jane. Then Jane had broken their date and nobody had known why until the night before the Fling when young Matt plastered the football locker room with poster-size pictures of her in a revealing wet T-shirt.

The poor, beautiful child had always been embarrassed by her voluptuous figure and had always done everything she could to hide it! She'd fled Red Rock the next day. The Snows enrolled her in a prim, all-girls' school in San Antonio, and she'd stayed out of town for years. Matt had been expelled and had had to repeat that semester.

Yes sirree, the first weeks of May leading up to the Spring Fling should bring out the crazy in all true Red Rockians.

Something was definitely wrong this year.

Hell, maybe somebody had put something in the water.

Maybe it was too many tame city people moving to town.

Funny thing, after years of both of 'em being gone, Matt Harper and Jane Snow had both moved back to town. Rumor had it, they'd even kissed under the mistletoe last Christmas. What was going on?

The hard plastic seat cut into Bill's skinny rump and spine as he forced himself to begin reading the letters. Much as he wanted to pan gold, the first twelve letters he read were dryer and duller than dirt. He was about to give up, when the thirteenth letter fell on the floor just as an eighteen-wheeler pulling a load of cattle rumbled by so fast the entire building shuddered.

Bill felt a premonition in his bones. He even shivered as he picked up that thirteenth letter from the floor. Was the paper rumpled from tears that had fallen when the writer had drafted it? Yes, the ink was definitely blurry.

Hell, maybe he was desperate, but the first corny sentence stirred the mischief in his old soul. As he read on, the words that followed fanned the flames of his troublemaking instincts.

My Only One,
    From the moment I saw you, I fell in love with you, and my feelings grow with each passing day. I know we belong together, and I'm sorry I haven't told you what's in my heart.
    My behavior may not have always been per-

fect. Please believe me, I would give anything to turn back time before the moment I hurt you. I've been a complete idiot. Nothing is as you imagined, and I've always been too proud to explain or say I was sorry. And because I didn't, I lost you.

No matter how bad things seem between us right now, there has never been anyone in my heart except you. I may not have shown you or told you the true depths of my love. But that's going to change—because I want to spend my life with you and only you.

So, here I am—confessing my love in the *Gazette*—publicly. If you give us a chance, I know we can find happily-ever-after.

I love you always.

Perfect!

Not that it couldn't do with a little editing. Rare is the written masterpiece that can't be improved by judicious cutting.

In this case all that was required was scissors to snip off the signature.

The nosey citizens of Red Rock would storm the *Gazette* to find out who wrote it. Folks would see secret admirers behind every cactus, red rock and mesquite bush, in every smile, wave or handshake.

He'd run it Monday!

He read the letter again and thought of any number of star-crossed couples the letter could apply to. Most of all he thought of shy Jane Snow and Matt Harper, who were all grown up—and still single.

Yes sirree. This'll light a fire under the town, sure as a shootin' match.

Chapter 1

Jane Snow's long, slim fingers flew over her keyboard as she typed in the finishing touches to the in-depth report she was scheduled to make this afternoon on corporate branding. Pushing her glasses up her nose, she read over her statistics and beamed proudly.

Am I good? Or am I good?

Good enough to be the director of market research, a little voice in her head chirped smugly.

Better than hunky Matt Harper. Way better.

She rubbed her hands together and blew on her fingertips. Then she stabbed her red pencil through the tight knot of platinum-blond hair at her nape.

Smugness and pride were failings of hers. But she'd

worked hard for those failings. Too hard. Nothing had ever come easily for her the way it had for Harper, who'd been born smart, popular and sure of himself.

"Top that, Harper, Mr. Most Handsome. Mr. Most Likely to Succeed," she said aloud as she punched the print button. She was a little shocked by the sound of her normally soft voice ringing with vengeance throughout her silent house.

She shivered. All that anger. And repressed passion. Not to mention plain old fear…about a man who didn't deserve the time of day. Even so, her teeth began to chatter as she thought about what was at stake and what Matt might do to best her.

The promotion to director of market research meant everything to her. Here was her chance to be respected in this town—for what she could do. She wanted to be known for more than her big breasts and the bizarre circumstances of her birth.

She felt as if her whole life depended on this promotion—which was ridiculous. Deep down she was still that needy, shy, insecure little girl. The girl who'd been laughed at as much because she'd been born on a pool table in a pool hall and ogled ever since she'd developed in the fourth grade when all the other girls had still been skinny sticks.

She had too much to live down in this town. So, much as she loved her family, after college she'd moved to Atlanta, Georgia. She hadn't returned except for brief holiday visits until her mother had gotten sick. Then her mother and her sister, Mindy, had said things that had made her rethink her priorities.

So, here she was living in Red Rock, working for Fortune TX, Ltd. in San Antonio and competing for the same job as Matt Harper.

Matt would kill to be director of market research.

Not literally. Winning simply meant everything to him. It always had. Beating a woman at her game, beating her, *especially her,* whom he probably considered so far beneath him, he'd take it as his due.

Her lips trembled. He'd been nice lately, ever since Christmas. But she didn't trust him. She of all people should know he was full of dirty tricks. There was no telling what surprise punch he might pull at the meeting this afternoon. He was good. But she was better.

His sweet attentiveness is getting to you. You're a bundle of nerves.

You knew he worked for Fortune TX when Ryan talked you into applying for the job there, now, didn't you?

But I didn't know we'd end up butting heads—for the same position.

The man's ruthless. Smooth. And good.

But handsome.

Jane hated these conversations with herself. Since elementary school, she'd never talked to herself about anything other than Matthew Harper. Because he'd been three years older and male, he'd had huge advantages over her back at Red Rock Public Elementary. For one thing he'd easily been the best-looking and the most popular kid in school. He'd been brash and fearless and recklessly full of himself, always besting the teachers and getting away with it. Just the kind of smart-mouthed boy to make an impression on a shy tongue-tied girl.

Back then his family had been richer than hers. In high school he'd been a football star and had dated the prettiest cheerleaders. Jane had been poor and shy and a bookish, straight-A student. When she was mentioned, people only seemed to talk about her birth and her breasts, so naturally she hadn't wanted to call attention to herself.

He'd been a natural-born show-off. He still was. Then there was that incredible smile and that deep laugh that could melt her insides.

Was the arrogant, macho, Neanderthal going to be her nemesis all her life? Why couldn't she just forget him? Why did the thought of him sneaking up on her, and taking those sexy pictures of her when she'd been fifteen and then exhibiting them in the locker room to humiliate her still torment her dreams?

That was back in high school, for Pete's sake. He'd thought it was a joke.

A cruel joke that had crushed her.

She'd deliberately gone out of state to college. To Colorado, even though she'd hated the mountains and cold weather. He'd moved to L.A. for a while, so she'd gone East. Then her daddy had hit the gusher that made the Snows rich. There was nothing like oil money to improve one's status—at least in Texas.

Then last year her mother had become ill, and Jane had decided to move home. Ryan Fortune, the owner of Fortune TX, Ltd., had wooed Matt back to Red Rock to work for him.

Suddenly when she least wanted it to, Matt's image sprang full-blown in her mind, causing her to shudder. At thirty-five, he was lethally tall, dark and cliché gorgeous. He had a hard jaw and a permanent tan. He was powerful and sexy, his body hard and lean. Except for his loud ties, he knew how to dress. He had heavy black hair and compelling, green eyes. Lately those eyes seemed to stare deep inside her and make her too conscious of him. He laughed a lot, too.

She licked her lips as she remembered his beautifully sculpted mouth. His mouth was to die for.

Don't ever, ever think about his mouth.

She'd thought about his mouth more than she should've—ever since he'd pulled her against his muscular body and kissed her under the mistletoe at a family gathering last Christmas. Every time she thought about those gentle kisses and how she'd instantly melted and become breathless in the sweet fire, a little lightning bolt would slither through her and make her feel as if all the air had gone out of her tummy.

Other people had thought about the kiss, too—

mainly her mother, who wasn't about to forget it. As a result, the townspeople gave Jane sly glances anytime Matt's name was mentioned, just as they had after the discovery of those sexy pictures in the locker room.

Matt's parents and hers, who ran in the same circles now, thought bygones should be bygones. Her mother kept telling her that the pictures were nothing more than a boyhood prank.

"He was a photographer. He had a natural interest in the opposite sex. You shouldn't have gone braless in that T-shirt and let your sister spray you with the hose."

Right. Blame the victim. "We were on our own property tanning our legs, Mom! It got hot."

"Your father pulled a few pranks to get my attention in our younger days. Matt's different now, and so are you. I think he likes you…or he would…if you'd let him."

Jane wished her mother would mind her own business.

One might as well wish for rattlesnakes to become extinct in the Texas hill country.

When the printer stopped spitting out pages, Jane arose and did a few stretches and told herself she simply had to quit thinking about *him*. Willing herself to concentrate on her presentation, she opened the curtains and stared out at her backyard just in time to see a brand-new Texas sun peeping over the cedar fence. A lone mourning dove cooed as the live oak trees turned red.

Pretending not to hear the taunting coos of the dove, Dennis, her cat, ambled lazily up to the glass door and gave Jane *the* look. Thank goodness he didn't have a mouse or a lizard this morning. Jane hated it when he killed things. She let him in. After a brief appreciative swish of her legs with the tip of his tail, Dennis headed straight to his bowl in the kitchen.

She gave the backyard a final wistful glance. Difficult as it was facing her past here, not for anything would she live in the city. Yes, she had to drive twenty miles from Red Rock into San Antonio on a daily basis, and yes, the traffic on the interstate seemed to get worse every day, and especially since the NAFTA treaty.

When she sat back down at her desk again, she lifted a folder concerning the fund-raiser she'd volunteered to chair that would raise money to benefit after-school day care for needy children. She checked over her to-do list and was pleased to find everything in order.

At least Harper had not volunteered for the project as she'd feared, so she didn't have to deal with him at the booth she was setting up for the silent auction Wednesday night at the local high school's baseball game. Although fund-raisers weren't his thing usually, she'd thought he might volunteer just to tip the scales in his favor about the upcoming promotion. He was the last person she wanted at the event when she auctioned her cooking services.

Jane glanced at her watch. Her Honda was in the shop for routine maintenance, and her mother, who had errands in the city, had talked her out of renting a car and had promised to drive her to work today. Since her mother, who was an artist and a fortune-teller, could be forgetful, she was about to call her and remind her, when the phone suddenly rang.

"Happy birthday," her younger sister, Mindy, chirped the instant she answered. Mindy was the wild sister, the loud sister.

Jane pulled the pencil out of her hair. "I forgot. I can't believe I forgot my own birthday."

"You work too hard."

"Thirty-two," Jane said a little sadly. "I'm old. Maybe I wanted to forget."

"Age is a state of mind."

"That's easy for you to say. You're not thirty yet. You know, I can't remember when I last went out on a date."

"Because you turn everybody down."

"Maybe because the right man doesn't ask."

Mindy hesitated. "Hey, Mom just called."

"Did she remember she's picking me up?"

"Yes. But that's not why…I mean…I thought I'd better warn you. She's on one of her tears."

"Oh, dear. What's she up to now?"

"Have you seen the paper yet?"

"Mindy, I have a very important presentation this afternoon. I'd—"

"Helen Geary called Mom first thing as soon as she saw it. She was very upset about it."

Not good. Helen had been Mom's best friend since

first grade—and they were very bad influences on each other. Helen had the biggest beehive hairdo in all of Texas and that was saying something. She was also Red Rock's most opinionated gossip and a prime meddler, if you didn't count Ol' Bill Sinclair.

"So what did Ol' Bill do to get Helen's tail in a knot? More politics?"

"Ol' Bill ran a love letter."

"I don't understand."

"He snipped the signature off the letter, and he won't tell Helen who wrote it. Our mom had ideas of her own about the author, and she's been talking to Matt's mom."

"Already?"

"Mrs. Harper thinks he's definitely interested in you. Mom wants me to read you the love letter to see if it rings any bells."

"Don't tell me Mom thinks Matt wrote it."

"Duh-h-h."

"Well, she can just forget it. He's not the literary type."

"You shouldn't have kissed him last Christmas at the Harpers' party. And kept kissing him."

Jane felt her face redden as it always did when she thought about those kisses. "He's the one who kissed me under the mistletoe."

"How well we remember the cherished moment."

"He would have kissed anybody if she'd been standing under the mistletoe."

"Not like that. You both looked plenty smitten. And once you two started, you couldn't seem to stop."

"I—I was too flabbergasted and outraged."

"All anybody remembers is how you both looked pie-eyed the rest of the night. You couldn't look at each other without turning red. He is so cute. And hot. I don't get why you still hate him. Those wet T-shirt photos were flattering. I'm still jealous because he didn't take a single one of me."

"I'm going to hang up if you don't shut up about this."

"Okay already."

"Besides, he's been going out with Carol Frey."

"I rest my case. Look who's keeping up with his love life. But for the record, you'll be glad to know, Mom says that's off. *As of last night.*"

Jane's racing heart leaped into her throat. For a long minute she was unable to swallow, much less answer. Finally, she managed to say, "Look, I really do have to go."

"Not before I read you *his* love letter."

Against her will, Jane listened. Of course, after the first word, when she got to thinking it really might be Matt, she was spellbound. Certain phrases like *I would give anything to turn back time before the moment I hurt you,* made her go hot all over and catch her breath as she dreamily remembered Matt's lips clinging to hers.

"So, what do you think?" Mindy asked when she'd finished.

Jane's heart was racing at an even more frightening

pace as she pondered the phrase *there has never been anyone in my heart except you.* Soon it became difficult to breathe.

She remembered the warmth and eagerness in his eyes after their Christmas kiss. The next day when she'd refused to wave or speak to him on the town square after he'd waved, he'd looked so strange and hurt. Since then he'd been awfully nice. Not that she'd responded.

"I—I think I'd better get dressed now," Jane said quickly.

"Okay, be that way. But don't forget, I'm taking you to lunch on the river—for your birthday."

"I've been starving all week so I can eat three crepes and a chocolate dessert. It's not often that you pick up the check, little sister."

"Can I help it if I have issues about growing up? Unlike you, I never sprouted big boobs to console me."

Jane sighed. She hated her figure. "You're sure Mom won't forget about picking me up?"

"As sure as one can ever be about a mom who paints her fingernails and toenails with shiny blue paint and consults astrology charts before making the simplest decision."

"She'll probably talk about that ol' letter the whole way into town," Jane said.

"One way or the other, she'll get her licks in."

"How's she feeling?" Jane asked, her voice softening.

"Stronger every day since she stopped the chemo."

"I'm glad I came home…even if she reads our fortunes and meddles to make them come true."

"I know. Mom may be trouble but she's fun."

For no reason at all, at the thought of trouble and fun, Jane thought of Matt, and smiled.

Chapter 2

Matthew Harper's alarm blared at him from the kitchen counter of his ancient blue trailer. God, he had the hangover from hell. He'd slept with the cat from hell on the mattress from hell in a trailer that was hotter than hell. The air-conditioning had bummed out months ago, which shouldn't have mattered since Jerry Keith should have had his new house built way before May. Hell, J.K. had sworn he'd be finished way before March. But little brothers weren't so hot at keeping their promises.

Sweat rolled off Matt's forehead. Hell and damnation, but the heat was fierce! The sun was barely up, and the sheets were plastered to his damp body. So was his crazy cat. Tonight after work he was definitely install-ing his new window unit.

He'd have time since Carol had broken their date for tonight—broken all their dates for that matter, even their date to the Spring Fling. When he'd said he wasn't ready for marriage, she'd broken up with him—period.

The phone began to ring, but he fought to ignore it. Nobody in Red Rock but a lunatic or a bothersome woman who wanted an engagement ring would call a man before he had his coffee. He let the phone ring and tried not to listen when his machine picked up.

"Matt, this is Lula Snow. I need a big favor. It's about Jane. Pick up."

Jane? Lula? Carol he could handle. But it was way too early for a man with a hangover to wrap his mind around the Snow women.

Beads of perspiration rolled off his forehead. For the first time he realized his baby brother, Jerry Keith, who was also his unreliable building contractor, had been right on when he'd advised him they should finish the house first and build the garage last instead of vice versa.

What about a freak hailstorm? A man had to house his car, not a car really, a Porsche Carrera GT.

"An air-conditioned garage for a toy?" J.K. had taunted.

"For my baby. For my wheels. She's a real racing machine."

Hell, maybe if he'd listened to his brother, he

wouldn't be sleeping on this lousy couch in his lousy, ovenlike, hunting trailer, suffering phone calls about Jane from Lula.

Maybe he should have said yes when Carol had demanded marriage. She was perfect for him. Beautiful, complacent, smart, and smart enough to hide it. Other men envied him when he took her out. Jane, on the other hand, wore glasses, hid her figure and flaunted her intelligence. She had a bad habit of holding on to grudges, too.

As he thought about Jane, which he'd been doing a lot lately, a vision of her lovely mouth, not Carol's, arose in his mind's eye to taunt him. The mouth, a familiar demon, was huge and red and absolutely luscious.

Next, that male organ he normally took such immense pride in arose underneath the sheets and said, Hi, here I am, darlin', to the giant mouth. It didn't take much guessin' to know what *that* excitement was all about.

"Damn!"

Never drink too much when you've got to go to work the next morning.

He'd been so happy last night when he'd gotten home and seen Jerry Keith along with a full crew at the house actually hammering and nailing, he'd invited the guys to dinner. No sooner had he started grilling thick slabs of beef when Carol had called to ask if he'd forgotten their date. He'd apologized and asked her over to have dinner with the guys. She hadn't liked that. Somehow she'd launched into the subject of marriage. The rest was history. Or rather they were history.

Which was why he'd sat out on the big flat rocks on his land with the guys until all hours watching his pet armadillo, Dillard, dig for grubs in the moonlight. They'd all gotten to bragging about women, telling dirty jokes and drinking—mostly drinking. Everybody had wanted to hear the old story about how he and Jerry Keith had snuck up on the Snow girls right when they'd been tanning their legs behind their house that fateful afternoon the year he'd asked Jane to the Spring Fling. Too bad for him the girls had started spraying each other with hoses and Jerry Keith had grabbed his camera and started snapping pictures. But if Matt lived to be a hundred, he wasn't likely to forget how good Jane had looked with that wet cotton plastered against her breasts.

He rubbed his head where it hurt. The trouble with being a bachelor was the time gap when there wasn't a good woman to nag you into living sensibly. Carol would have stopped him on beer number three.

All of a sudden the damn alarm clock had his brain throbbing so hard he could have sworn it hopped off the counter straight into his skull. Jane's red mouth dissolved into the mists of his mind. Groaning, he jammed pillow number three over his head, rolled over onto Julie Baby, who stuck several claws in his chest. When he screamed, she jumped from the bed to the lamp, knocking it over and shattering the bulb.

"Damn your hide, cat!"

Although he wasn't much on rules, a man should know better than to sleep naked with an untrustworthy female whose nails were too long.

Matt sat bolt upright and glared at Julie Baby, who stared back at him serenely. Did cats ever blink? Growling, Matt threw a pillow at the clock, which hit the floor and mercifully died beside the jagged bits of lightbulb.

The phone rang again.

Lula again.

Later.

The trailer, what he could see of it from the tattered couch, would've made a pig oink with pride. The sink overflowed with last night's dishes. The garbage can brimmed with several days' stinky leavings.

Later. After he got the window unit installed and washed his Porsche tonight, maybe he'd vacuum. Even he could see it was time.

The phone stopped ringing. Lula didn't leave a second message.

If and when Jerry Keith ever got his ranch house finished, Matt intended to be neater. The trashed trailer, which was supposed to have been temporary lodging, would go back where it belonged—to his hunting lease.

The trouble was Jerry Keith was bad about working for other people instead of for him.

"Have to build clientele. Marketing. That's your

game, ain't it, Big Bubba? You're up for director of
market research, am I right? Same as Jane Snow? Afraid
she'll beat you?"

Matt knew he'd been way too patient with the brat,
but his kid brother did have a few things on his plate—
a pregnant wife, for one thing.

At least with no AC and open windows, Matt could
hear doves cooing outside and a whippoorwill. The
faint breeze that smelled of cedar and grass nearly
lured him outside, only the phone rang again, and he
picked up.

"Lula, darlin', you aren't gonna quit, now, are you?"

"How'd you guess it was me?" She sounded pleased.

"I'm psychic."

"Like me? Then you probably know why I called."

"Let me guess. You want a favor."

"Jane's car's in the shop. Could you drive her to work?"

Jane. She'd barely spoken to him since she'd gotten
him expelled his senior year. He'd been forced to resign
as president of his high-school class, and several honors he'd earned had been stricken from his transcripts.
He'd been in the doghouse with his folks, too.

"If she calls and asks me herself, I'll consider it."

Silence.

"Lula, are you still there?"

When Lula still didn't answer, he began to think
about the promotion Jane and he were competing for.
If Jane needed a ride, why not scope out the competi-

tion? She was a tight-ass if ever there was one. Surprises, especially from him, unnerved her.

"Do you take the *Gazette?*" There was a note in Lula's voice he knew better than to trust.

"Am I a red-blooded Red Rockian or what?"

"There's an anonymous love letter to the editor you might find very interesting. A little birdie told me it was written *to you.*"

Jane's mother wouldn't be talking about Carol. "Are you saying Jane wrote it?"

"Why don't you drive her to work and ask her yourself."

The luscious, enormous mouth came back to taunt him. The red lips puckered. He squeezed his eyes shut, but the mouth, Jane's mouth, stayed right where it was—tempting him.

He'd kissed that mouth.

The lips puckered seductively. Hell, he could almost taste her. He remembered exactly how satiny and slick those lips had felt on the outside and how wet and hot and honey sweet they'd been on the inside. He still couldn't quite believe she'd let his tongue through the pearly gates without chomping it to bits.

He thought about her hot body, and his number-two brain got so excited it tented the sheets beneath his waist. Good thing the cat wasn't watching or she would pounce for sure.

"Oh, and one more thing, Matty." He gritted his teeth

at his kindergarten nickname. "My Janie doesn't have a date to the Spring Fling."

"Because she's so damn picky, she's turned everybody down who's gotten up the nerve to ask her. Who's she waiting for—Prince Charming?"

"Could be, handsome," her mother said slyly. "So, you keep up with my Janie's love life?"

"With our nonstop gossip grapevine buzzing day and night, I'd have to be brain dead not to know everybody's business, including hers. How'd you find out Carol broke up with me last night because she's moving to Houston a week earlier than she thought?"

"She broke up with you because you wouldn't propose."

"Damn, you're good."

Lula laughed.

"It was pretty late when she called me," he muttered.

"To be exact, it was 8:30 p.m. 'Cause you stood her up."

"Next time I want to know what's going on in my life I'll call you."

"If you're driving Janie, she's expecting me at 7:30 a.m.—sharp! You know how grumpy she gets if she has to wait even one second."

"I know how grumpy she is—period—any time I come around."

"That's just because she's afraid to let you know how much she likes you."

"Right!"

"Trust me. Her mother knows. Remember, I was the one who had to put her back together after you kissed her under the mistletoe."

"Goodbye, Lula."

"Just read her letter. It made me weep."

Chapter 3

A devil bit him in the tail when Matt saw *her* street sign and realized he was almost to *her* house. He finger-combed his inky hair. He adjusted his red tie with the pink flamingos. Hell. Maybe the thing *was* too loud. He ripped it out of his collar and tossed it behind him as he yanked his collar open.

What was it? Every time he got around Jane, he got like this.

Maybe the big sexy mouth that had haunted him ever since he'd gotten up this morning had him a little crazed. Maybe it was the thought of her perfect yellow house with its perfect white shutters and a picket fence, yes, a real picket fence, damn it, the kind that made a man think of kids and a future and a sweet, alluring woman waiting for him at night, that unnerved him. Or maybe it was just her.

Not to mention *the* letter.

Had she written it?

Whoa! He wished that phrase that kept replaying like a broken record while the big, neon-red lips puckered would stop. His head hurt just thinking about it. He'd popped two aspirin, but they weren't cutting the pain.

...there has never been anyone in my heart except you.

How could this be when she ran from him instead of to him that night. People who kissed like that and couldn't stop belonged in bed together. He'd been a coward not to go after her. But after some of the hurtful things she'd said, Matt knew he'd done damage and should leave well enough alone.

As if this helped his current predicament, he thought gloomily. Without having a why for the childish insanity that getting anywhere near her brought out in him, he stomped on the gas pedal so hard the powerful engine roared. It was 7:30 a.m. sharp when Matt skidded into her driveway, leaving a trail of black marks just to prove he was the big grown-up brat she thought he was. Next he honked. Just a couple of light taps just to make her mad.

She had ears like a lynx. She'd hear him.

Her front door opened immediately. The second he caught the merest glimpse of her slim, curvy body in the shadowy doorway, a hot bolt zapped him. As always, she hid that perfect figure under one of her dull conservative black suits and high-collared blouses. As always, every pearl button was securely fastened. As usual, her long, platinum-blond hair was tied back in that odious little knot in an attempt to downplay her looks.

Oddly, the severe hairdo served to accentuate the high cheekbones and the classic lines of her exquisite face. And it was exquisite—a perfect oval. Everything she did just made her more attractive, at least to him, which was probably why she did it—to annoy him. She'd been annoying the hell out of him since she'd been a first-grader, so she was an expert at it by now.

Her blue eyes swept over her perfectly manicured lawn, the row of potted geraniums and the well-tended ivies hanging in her oak trees before zeroing in on him. Pushing her stylish, if thick, metal-framed glasses up the slender bridge of her nose, she stepped onto her porch. Her blue eyes, which were fringed by long, inky lashes, widened before they narrowed—on him. Her beautiful mouth, the mouth of his wet dreams, opened and closed with distaste.

"Your mom said you needed a ride," he yelled. She pivoted on a single high heel and slammed the door in his face.

"Good morning to you too, darlin'!"

Okay, so he shouldn't have honked.

Gripping the steering wheel, he waited a minute.

When she didn't come out, he got out, finger-combed his hair again, and then climbed her steps two at a time. Before he could knock, she opened the door.

She was on her cell phone now. "Mom! *Mother!* I know you're there." Abruptly Jane snapped her phone shut. With her eyes glued on his pink shirt, she said, "She hung up."

"Happy birthday, darlin'." He bowed low.

She didn't smile.

"We'd better go," he said.

"I'll just be a minute," she said icily, and true to her word, she was back in seconds with her briefcase and purse. He helped her into the Porsche, and in no time, they were zooming out of her driveway.

"Sorry about this," she said. "My mother—"

"Mothers like ours are forces of nature."

"She should have called me first, not you."

"It's a done deal now, darlin'."

"It's not that simple."

"It would be, if you'd let it," he said. "You always complicate everything."

She inhaled deeply. As he sped down the familiar, oak-lined streets, she turned her back to him and stared out her window gloomily. "It's just that I hate to owe a man like—"

"Me? A man like me? What do you think a man like me will exact as repayment—a pound or two of your delectable flesh?" He grinned at the back of her head. "You can relax. No hidden camera today."

She whirled around, her face red. "See—this is why I always dread being anywhere near you. You make light of things that matter a great deal to me."

"I was just teasing," he said softly.

"I don't like it."

"Sorry. I grew up with brothers." He paused. "You smell good. Like jasmine."

"Would you stop?"

"I can't tease. I can't compliment you. What does that leave?"

"Nothing. I want absolutely nothing to do with you other than a civil relationship at work."

"Why?"

"Why? We have this awful history, for starters—your stupid camera."

"Before that you had a crush on me in grade school."

"I did not!"

"Did too. Okay, I know I should have ripped the negatives of those pictures to bits."

"You shouldn't have plastered them all over the locker room!"

He scowled at the bitter memory. "I paid for it."

She lapsed into silence. His temples were throbbing when she finally spoke to him again. "I don't want to talk about it any more than you do. I just think we would both be happier if we never had to see each other—except at work."

"I wouldn't be," he muttered.

"Don't start."

"What?"

"Doing what you probably do with *every* woman."

"Is *that* it? You're jealous?"

"Hell, no. But we're competing for the same job, for one thing. We have to work together. But on a personal level we can't…"

"We can't what?"

"I—I don't know." But she did know. As always, ever since she'd come back to town, there was a hot spark of electricity between them. She hated it and hated him because of it.

She continued to stare out the window. Her hands that were folded tightly in her lap shook.

"Your mother told me to read the letters to the editor this morning," he said. "Did you happen to see that anonymous love letter?"

She blushed furiously, guiltily, and then shyly.

His heart leaped. Had she written it? Did she feel that way about him but was so repressed she couldn't face herself or him? This possibility was incredibly exciting.

"That…er…anonymous person…is living with a lot of regret," he said smoothly.

She flashed him an odd look that seemed both vulnerable and desperate. "I don't feel comfortable talking about it."

"Why the hell not?"

"Because. Just because. I…I can't believe it's taking this long to get out of Red Rock."

Frankly, he'd been too absorbed with her to notice where they were. He'd never been this close to her for this long. She always ran. In his eagerness, he spoke before he thought. "Your mother said you don't have a date to the Spring Fling. Well, it so happens that I don't either."

"My mother should mind her own business!" she snapped.

"A lot of people in Red Rock should do that." He hesitated, grinding his teeth. "I was trying to ask you to go with me to the Spring Fling."

"What? Us? You and me?"

"Why not us? Maybe we could get past the past if we did that—show the town we've buried what happened in high school."

She turned and her eyes narrowed on his face. "Did you ask me because you and I are both up for director of market research?"

"Hell no." He felt himself getting mad, too.

"I don't believe you," she said. "You asked me before when we were kids deliberately to humiliate me."

"I did not."

"You snuck up on us and took those pictures. Then you—"

"Like I told you then—I didn't."

Like always when he defended himself, she glared at him.

Damn it. He hadn't. He clenched the steering wheel, remembering the stupid misadventure that had caused both of them so much pain when they were kids.

J.K. had lured him into the cedar-brush country right behind the Snows' place with the promise of some exciting wildlife. J.K. had been toting his .22-caliber rifle and Matt had his camera.

"I don't see anything worth wasting good film on," Matt said when J.K. grabbed his arm and pulled him down behind a huge red rock.

"Just you wait."

Sure enough, it couldn't have been more than five minutes before they heard the Snows' back door close. Next, leaves crackled in the direction of the Snows' property. They heard giggles and a dog barking. Then the branches parted and Jane and Mindy Snow and their chocolate Lab, Grizzly, stepped out into the sun. The girls wore white T-shirts, and maybe, hell maybe— nothing else! A guy could hope, couldn't he? Mindy was dragging a gushing hose, which she tossed into a bed of roses.

Matt liked the way the wind blew the girls' hair, especially Jane's. When they opened their backpacks and pulled out two towels, the wind caught hold of the towels so that they flapped like orange and purple flags. Slowly, the threesome ambled over to some flat rocks sheltered by a high limestone cliff. The girls positioned their towels and then lay down on them with their legs in the sun and their heads in the shade. They began to read. Meanwhile, Grizzly ran about, sniffing rocks and chasing rabbits. Once when the Lab raised his leg on a rock not far from the boys, they were sure the dog would catch them. Fortunately, they were downwind from the beast, and the Lab trotted back to the girls, who petted him.

Jane looked so beautiful and peaceful as she read and petted the Lab that Matt started snapping pictures of her. Her legs were long and slim and curvy. When she raised her T-shirt a little, he saw she was wearing a pink polka-dot bikini bottom.

Her butt was tight and round, just great. He took a few more pictures and then stopped when she slowly got up and went over to where the hose was. She lifted it. Splashing her face first, she then began to sip.

Then Mindy got up and snuck up behind her. Playfully grabbing the hose, Mindy sprayed her. Jane yelled and the girls began fighting over the hose, drenching each other.

The wet T-shirt revealed Jane's huge breasts, which she always took such pains to hide at school.

"Hot damn," Jerry Keith said. "Her nipples are as big as chocolate Oreos. Zoom in on 'em."

Matt was cold and hot and hard at the same time. When Jerry Keith grabbed his camera, he got so mad he nearly yelled.

Grizzly was the next to get sprayed.

"I'll be damned," Jerry Keith said, taking more pictures as Matt lunged for the camera. When the girls dropped the hose and looked over, Matt had it in his hand. Her cheeks reddening, Jane tried to cover herself with her hands. Grizzly started barking. Teeth bared, the animal lived up to its name and raced toward them.

The boys scrambled up the nearest oak tree.

Matt wasn't concentrating on driving, when Jane screamed.

"Watch where you're going!"

Instantly he came back to the present.

"Red light!" she cried. "Stop! Or you'll kill us in this thing!"

He slammed on his brakes and the Porsche skidded to a halt as they hit the last red light before leaving town.

She drew a deep, relieved breath but said nothing. He did the same.

His feelings were overpowering him the way they always did when she was too close. Maybe it was her perfume that had him so crazy. What was it—roses? Or jasmine?

Craving fresh air, while she continued her pout or whatever it was, he lowered his window. But the warm cedar-scented breeze just made him hotter.

He'd tried to be nice. He'd paid for his sins in high school. Boy had he paid. He'd even asked her on a date. He hated rejection and he always had to win. Hell, he was out on a limb here. Nobody but Jane Snow ever made him feel this crazy.

And then it happened.

She'd glanced out her window again, so she didn't see it coming. Thus, she didn't flinch or pull away when he leaned closer, cupped her chin and crushed her lips to his.

The second his mouth claimed hers, the same magic that had knocked him senseless under the mistletoe zapped him again, only harder. Must've zapped her, too, because her fingers came around his neck and threaded themselves into his hair. As she began kissing him back, he felt her breasts quiver and go soft against his chest. He pressed her closer into his hard body.

"What's happening?" she whispered, pulling back a little. Her blue eyes were soft and crushed and vulnerable.

"This is what you're so scared of, isn't it?" he murmured. "You want me, too."

"This can't be happening."

His big hands worked through her hair. Before she could cry out, pins showered onto her seat. Next came tangles of platinum-blond hair falling onto her shoulders. Out of the corner of his eye, he noted that the light changed but he was afraid to drive for fear he'd lose her.

"Fire and ice. That's what you are," he whispered as he began kissing her again.

He didn't want to stop kissing her. Not ever. This was better than last Christmas. He'd never felt such mindless lust or need for anyone. Whatever it was, it lit an unquenchable fire in his being.

The guy behind him sat on his horn.

Somehow Matt managed to let her go. Breathing hard, he stepped on the gas and drove carefully, but the first chance he got, he pulled off onto the shoulder—to resume kissing or whatever it was they were doing.

"Work," she said. "We've got to get to work."

"Later," he muttered, grabbing her again. "Kissing the enemy is way more fun."

"This is downright embarrassing," she whispered on a raspy shudder.

"Yeah, it damn sure is. You're a witch, and I'm helpless in your spell."

"Don't tease me."

"Can't help myself, darlin'. Do you have a better explanation?"

"I'm the one girl in town you haven't slept with yet. You want to add another notch onto your gun belt, so you're pouring on the sexual charm mighty strong."

"If you really think that, my reputation as a lover damn sure exceeds the reality. But don't tell anybody."

He smiled down at her and for the first time, maybe ever, she smiled back. He caught his breath. His heart beat wildly. He wanted her to like him. He wanted it more than anything.

He kissed her neck, and then the hollow of her throat. Barely conscious of what he was doing, he began unbuttoning her blouse, kissing the tops of her huge breasts until his mouth came to a lacy pink-and-black bra.

"I never figured you for the sexy-underwear type," he murmured. "Nice."

"Type. I'm not a type."

"Of course not," he agreed, his mouth nuzzling a nipple. He'd spent years dreaming about her breasts. Years. "I've been waiting for somebody like you all my life."

"Somebody like me?"

"Shut up and kiss me."

For once she obeyed him. Their mouths came together again, her tongue mating with his.

"Let's call in sick and go to bed," he whispered.

Before he could stop her, she slipped out from under him faster than if she'd slicked herself with butter. Opening her door, she flung herself out of his car just as Ol' Bill Sinclair drove by on his way to the *Gazette*. When she began buttoning her blouse, the old coot tooted.

"God, now everybody in town will know," she wailed, turning red.

"Get back in the car before anybody else sees you."

"Only…only if you promise not to touch me."

"Hell." When he jumped out of the car too, she started to run back to town. "Okay. Okay." He held up his hands. "I promise. No touching."

She turned and ran toward him just as he recognized Helen Geary's giant beehive hairdo as she whizzed by in her brand-new red Caddy, her eyes out on stems. Helen, being Helen, honked at them too, of course.

"I can't believe this," Jane moaned. "She'll tell everybody."

"What the hell was that all about?" Matt asked once they were both in his Porsche again. He stared at her while she groped on the floor for her hairpins.

"You tell me. You started it, Harper."

He turned the key in the ignition. "That takes me back to Red Rock Public School. That's what you said after you tossed my cowboy hat back at me after you'd sat on it and squashed it flatter than a Frisbee."

"You started that one too, Harper. You shouldn't have pulled the ribbons out of my pigtails."

"Did you know I still have one of those red ribbons?"

"Just like you probably still have the negatives of those pictures."

He growled. "I don't have them. I told you that already."

"Liar."

"There's no use talking to some people," he grumbled.

Aware that she was warier than ever of him, he drove the rest of the way to Fortune TX in a tense, electric silence. He did nothing more to try to break the wall of ice between them. The traffic on the interstate was thick and fast, so he shifted and downshifted, paying attention to his driving instead of her.

When he pulled into his space at the parking garage, she said in the frosty voice he was all too accustomed to, "Let's not go in together."

"Right," he said, his tone as clipped as hers. "Business as usual."

She'd disappeared by the time he had his shirt buttoned, his tie with the flamingos back on and his hair combed. He was about to get out himself when he noticed the corner of a manila folder under her seat. It must've fallen out of her briefcase. After picking it up, he couldn't resist thumbing through it.

It was mainly boring lists that had to do with that after-school care fund-raiser she was chairing.

He read through it and laughed out loud.

She was good, but so was he.

Bake sale. Down-home cooking.

Silent auction at the baseball game in Red Rock.

Then he came to the last item.

She was planning to auction her "down-home" cooking services to the highest bidder.

In a flash he saw a way to turn the tables on her both in work and play.

She wouldn't like it.

Or would she? She'd damn sure kissed him back. Still, it was risky. No matter what, he intended to play his hand for all it was worth. Unlike her, he was a gambler.

Happy birthday, darlin'.

He was whistling "The Yellow Rose of Texas" when he got out of the car.

Chapter 4

How could she have been so stupid? What had she done?

Jane stood in front of the glass doors of Fortune TX and slapped her forehead with her open hand. Harper wanted to be director of market research. He didn't want her. His little seduction routine was just his own perverse version of a game of hardball!

Last week he'd impressed Andrea, Jane's supervisor, and all their bosses in that meeting when he'd demonstrated how the company could best use the Internet to defend brand assets. He'd been creative. She couldn't let herself ever forget that he'd do anything to win. Anything.

Harper was part of the good-old-boy network. That was one of the reasons he was so successful. He didn't work as hard as she did because he didn't have to. He schmoozed. He drove a jazzed-up car to impress people. He was into image rather than substance.

He would probably tell every man at the water-cooler first thing how easy and hot for him she was. He'd get a few laughs, and the male executives would start snickering behind her back. They might even ask her out to get more of the same. If any of them even winked at her, she'd never be able to face anybody again.

Fool that she was, she still felt turned on by the darkly handsome jerk with the talented mouth and hands. She'd even liked the way he'd touched her breasts.

The sun was getting hotter, or was it just thinking about him that made her feel the heat? There was nothing for it but to go inside and face the music.

When she reached her floor, Jane still felt hot and wet and trembly as she skittered past the receptionists, mumbling her hellos so fast neither woman could start a real conversation. Not that they didn't try.

"You look great," Stephanie said.

"Different," Melanie agreed. "What's with the looser hairstyle and those top buttons undone? New look?"

"New man," Stephanie whispered.

"Gotta go," Jane said, not meeting their eyes. She couldn't even manage a smile in her mad desire to escape to her own office where she could close her door, be alone and try to regroup.

"Have you seen that cute green dress in the shop downstairs? It'd be perfect for the new you," Melanie said.

"There is no new me," Jane muttered, horrified that she felt faintly tempted to take a look at the dress.

Even before she got to her office and saw the huge bouquet of daisies, roses, irises and lilies, she didn't have an inkling about how to proceed with her day. She hated teasing or sexual innuendo, even talks about sex and boyfriends between women. She hated sex on television. Love scenes in books made her skim pages until she got past them. That's why Matt's sexy pictures of her had undone her.

Just why sex scared her so deeply was a mystery. Maybe her mother had been too open and flamboyant. Maybe it had to do with the whole town laughing because she'd been born in the pool hall. To Jane, sex was not something to be viewed through keyholes or to be flaunted the way Matt had flaunted those pictures of her.

Jane was at her file cabinet, with her back to the huge vase of lilies and roses and daisies on her desk, when Stephanie popped her head inside the door.

"We're all dying to know. What's the special occasion?"

Jane turned and gasped when she saw the flowers Stephanie was looking at. Moving toward them, Jane said, "Oh, I didn't realize you followed me."

"Couldn't resist."

"I guess… It's my birthday," Jane mumbled.

"Looks like somebody remembered big-time. Who?"

"I—I haven't a clue. My mom maybe."

"So, read the card."

With trembling fingers Jane plucked the small envelope from the flowers. Leaning over them, she couldn't help but inhale their sweet fragrance. "Mmmmmmmm."

Oh my, she did love flowers.

"Name withheld upon request," she read aloud. Then she flipped the card over. "That's all."

When she looked up, Stephanie was still hovering expectantly. "Well?"

"I'm sure you've got work to do," Jane said hastily.

Ducking her head, Stephanie scurried away.

Jane set her briefcase down and began to search for her folder with the information on the fund-raiser. She needed to get approval from her boss, Andrea, for the booth at the baseball game Wednesday night.

But the fund-raiser folder wasn't there.

"Damn."

Frowning, she was shaking the contents of her briefcase out onto her desk when Matt ambled into her office. A mischievous smile lit his dark face, and his hands were behind his back.

"Hi," he said in a low tone.

She glanced down at the contents of her briefcase, hoping he'd go, but he stayed, lounging in the doorway, his long legs planted widely apart.

"You're the last man on earth I really want to see," she said.

"At least I'm in a class by myself."

Something electric in his deep voice made her look up.

His smile widened, and she felt herself soften. She was mush when she sank in a heap into her chair. How could he do this to her with just a smile? He looked male and arrogant and yet charmingly boyish all at the same time and friendlier than a puppy wagging his tail too fast. He appeared to genuinely like her.

He's not to be trusted.

"Aren't you thirsty? Shouldn't you be hanging out at the watercooler or something?" she snapped. "Saying impressive things about that car."

"Later." He smiled again. "Flowers." He strode closer and put his dark, handsome face into the blossoms and inhaled deeply. "Mmmmmmmmmm. Secret admirer?"

For no reason at all she thought of Ol' Bill's anonymous letter in the *Gazette.*

I know we belong together and I'm sorry I haven't told you what's in my heart.

"You tell me," she whispered, teasing him, in spite of herself.

Oh, why couldn't she stop looking at his lips? Or his sparkling green eyes? His eyes were wooing her, sucking her into their depths again, stealing her soul, so she cast her gaze down quickly.

"Read the card," he said softly.

"Been there. Done that. *He* didn't sign his name."

Matt was so close she could smell his tangy aftershave. For a long delicious moment she even forgot to breathe.

"So you think it's a man?"

The intimacy in his gorgeous eyes made her shiver.

"Any guesses as to who?" he persisted.

The warm flush running through her body was terrifyingly pleasurable. He was leading her, teasing her. Why?

Suddenly a lightbulb went on in her brain.

Had he sent them? Just like he'd written that letter? Was he as shy about intimacy as she was about sex? Was it possible he was afraid to tell her? Was it possible that he couldn't put himself out like that, not when she'd rejected him for so many years? What if he really felt bad about those wet T-shirt pictures? If so, the whole thing, the letter, the flowers, was sweet in a way.

Don't be a fool. He's the enemy. He's after your job.

"Are you here to take credit for the flowers?" she whispered, challenging him.

"I'll take any credit I can get," he said smoothly. "Lord knows where you're concerned I damn sure need it."

"You're not afraid," she said shyly.

"Why the hell should I be?"

"What does the card say then?" she asked, testing him.

"Ah, a test."

She stared at him in shock, realizing that she was enjoying this exchange way too much.

"Love, Matt." He blushed when he said it. He actually blushed. His quick smile was unpretentious and sweet.

She felt her own face growing hot beneath his steady gaze. "P-please—don't tease me about this." With fingers that trembled, she placed the card in his. "You know what you wrote…and it wasn't *Love, Matt.*"

"Name withheld upon request," he read aloud in his deep baritone, watching her. "This guy is good. As good as me."

"I wonder why?" Those green eyes of his were still on her. She felt him reading her mind, her heart. Strangely she didn't mind as much as she usually did. "If you really sent them, write the words you didn't say," she said, stealing the sentiment from his anonymous love letter in the *Gazette*.

He took the card and laid it on her desk. With a flourish of black ink, he wrote, "Love, Matt," and then placed the card in her palm. "There. Satisfied?"

Their fingertips touched and again she sizzled.

At her gasp when she pulled her hand free, he gave her another startled look. "Happy Birthday then, darlin'."

"It's been quite a birthday," she said. "Full of surprises."

"For me, too. It's not even 9:00 a.m. yet. Your smiles are getting friendlier. Does this mean you'll go to the Spring Fling with me?"

"I don't think so."

"Don't say no yet. I'll forgive you for high school if you'll forgive me."

"What?"

"After your father talked to the superintendent, I got expelled, remember?"

"It's just too sudden," she said.

"Okay," he murmured. "I guess we'd both better get to work. Happy birthday, beautiful."

"I'm not beautiful. My sister, Mindy, is beautiful. Your Carol is beautiful."

"You've always been way too hard on yourself."

"I can't believe you know that about me."

"I pay attention—when I'm interested. And you *are* beautiful," he repeated. "Furthermore, just to set the record straight, she's not *my* Carol anymore. In fact, she never was. We went out a few times. People in Red Rock thought it meant more than it did."

"Carol thought so, too."

"So you're tuned into the twenty-four-hour grapevine."

"Isn't everybody?"

"I'm a free man, darlin', unless some pretty lady takes pity on me and decides to love and reform me."

"You could definitely use some reforming."

"I'd prefer the lovin' part, but more on that later." He was grinning as he strode out of her office, pulling the door shut behind him.

Alone with his sweet-smelling flowers, she plucked

a daisy out of the bunch, went to the window and twirled it against her nose. She was so wrapped up in her conflicting thoughts and feelings about Matt that she had no idea how long she'd stood there when voices outside in the hall snapped her out of her reverie. Quickly she jabbed the daisy back into the vase and went back to her desk to search for the fund-raiser folder.

Much to her surprise, it lay on her desk on top of the clutter she'd shaken out of her briefcase.

Crossing her arms, she shook her head in confusion. Then she opened the file to make sure all the papers were inside it, and even though they were, she felt vague little prickles of alarm.

She could have sworn it hadn't been there before Matthew Harper had come in to see her.

The River Walk was idyllic. The brown serpentine river sparkled, and sunlight shone through the cypress trees. Jane and Mindy were sitting in a shady spot under a red-and-white umbrella beside the water. There were enough tourists on the old limestone walkways so that Jane and Mindy had people to watch, but their riverside French restaurant wasn't too crowded. Not like a happening Saturday night when all the restaurants, shops and clubs were jammed.

"I hate to cut this short, but I really do have to get back to the office," Jane said. "I have an important presentation."

"First we have to light your candles on your chocolate birthday cake so you can make a wish."

For a birthday that had started off all wrong and had been filled with unsettling surprises, Jane couldn't remember when she'd had more fun. Why was that? she wondered.

As Mindy struck a match to light her candles, Jane closed her eyes.

"Think of something you truly truly want, and your wish will come true," Mindy said softly.

Jane tried to concentrate on the position of director of market research but drew a blank. Instead she conjured a broad-shouldered hunky giant with a sculpted mouth and black-lashed, green eyes, who was wearing a red tie with even hotter pink flamingos flapping all over it.

She squeezed her eyes tighter and tried to focus on the job she wanted. Matt's image was as stubborn as the man himself and refused to budge.

"Are you thinking of something you really want yet?" Mindy quizzed hopefully.

"No!" she snapped and mentally stuck out her tongue at the vision of Matt.

"Mind if I sit down?" murmured a deep, familiar baritone.

Her eyes flew open, and there *he* was—as if she'd truly conjured him. *Mom would love this.*

"I certainly do mind. I was trying to make a wish before my candles go out."

He sat down anyway and closed his eyes. A look of fiendish bliss transformed his dark, rugged features. His eyes opened. He leaned forward and blew out her candles.

"What do you think you're doing?"

"I made a wish for you on your birthday." He began plucking candles out of the cake and licking chocolate icing off their bottoms.

"You can't do that."

"In case you haven't noticed, it's a done deal, darlin'." He licked another candle. "Besides, you were blocked and I was feeling creative. When are you going to realize we're a team?"

"No, we're not."

"We could be—if you'd let it happen."

"What did you wish for?" she asked him, to change the subject.

"I can't say, or it won't come true."

"Don't be ridiculous. You can't make my wish."

"I think it's sweet," Mindy said, watching them both far too intently.

"How did you find us?" Jane asked. "No—don't tell me. Mother?"

He grinned. "She called me again."

"What if I don't want your wish to come true?"

"Then it won't." He signaled the waiter and ordered a piece of cake just like hers.

The cake was thick rich chocolate and sinfully delicious. Being a cook, she was wondering about the exact ingredients as she ate it, while he simply savored his. He began taking a bite of his cake every time she took a nibble from hers. He watched her, and she watched him. Soon she forgot all about cooking. When she ran her tongue across her upper lip, he did the same. There was a rhythm to it. The river flowed by, tourists laughed and chattered, and the chocolate melted on her tongue just as his ripe kisses had.

"Dark, oozy chocolate's my favorite flavor," he said.

"Mine too," she whispered.

"At least there's something we enjoy together." He moved his face nearer hers so that he could whisper. "Besides kissing."

When she felt his warm breath against her cheek, she jumped away from him. Still, it had been a long time since she'd enjoyed anything more than eating chocolate cake while staring into his sparkling green eyes.

"You're dangerous," she said, patting her mouth with her napkin.

"I certainly hope so," he replied.

Chapter 5

"Mother—please!"

The fragrance of Matt's flowers were cloyingly sweet. Jane wished she could ignore them. If only she had windows she could open.

If only her mother hadn't called.

"Mother, I can't deal with this!" Jane closed her eyes and rubbed her temples. "I've got a meeting with my boss in two minutes, so listen to me! Please, quit calling him!"

"If she offers you the job, refuse it. Tell her Matt would be better."

"This kind of help I don't need."

"A smart woman is smart enough to let her man win—at least until she's got him hooked."

"Do you ever read anything that's been written this century? Your ideas are medieval."

"No, your generation is impossible. There aren't going to be any grandbabies. We're going to be extinct."

"Mother!"

"But the cards explicitly recommended—"

"Mother!"

"I really do see him in your future!"

"Mother!" Each *Mother* was louder than the last.

"Stop shouting. It's not good for me, you know."

Her mother took a breath. Jane glanced at her watch.

"Okay. All right. But, Jane, if you were half as smart as you think you are, you'd wear those contact lenses I bought you and play more. But go ahead and keep messing up your own life. Just don't come crying to me when he gets himself snapped up by some floozy, and you realize you're in love with him when it's too late."

"What?"

"You've been in love with him for years."

"Thanks for the vote of confidence."

"I remember the way you trailed around after him on the playground, always pestering him until he pulled your ponytail or something. Remember the time you sat on his cowboy hat?"

"What I remember is having to leave home and go to a private, big city high school because he humiliated me. I didn't get to graduate with my friends."

"Lighten up. Not in this lifetime will I forget that kiss last Christmas. You could barely stand."

"He probably spiked the punch."

"Nobody else was reeling. You can lie to yourself, but you can't lie to your mother. Do you need me to pick you up this afternoon or not?"

"No," she replied wearily, glad her mother had finally changed the subject. "Mindy said she'd do it."

"You could get off your stubborn high horse and ride home with him in that dream machine."

"He nearly killed me in it this morning."

"Helen Geary's version is way different than yours."

When they hung up, Jane got up and ran, shaking, down the hall to Andrea's office.

Jane had left her report and fund-raiser material with Andrea earlier, but now she didn't feel up to the meeting. She felt like yelling and tearing her hair. Talking to her mother frequently did that to her. When she finally reached Andrea's door, she took a deep breath and counted to ten. Then she counted to ten again before knocking.

"Come in," Andrea called from inside.

When Jane opened the door, Andrea, who was tall, black-haired and slim, rose to greet her. The woman looked stunning in a navy suit with gold at her throat.

"I can't wait to talk to you," she said. "I have some very exciting news."

Jane's heart was already thumping madly as she sank

into the chair opposite Andrea's desk and crossed her
long legs.

"You're doing a wonderful job. Management loves
your ideas."

Jane nodded. Then she bit her lips, hoping against
hope that she'd been chosen as director of market research. At least then she could quit worrying about
Matt's motives.

Andrea lifted a folder from her desk. When Jane recognized her own handwriting on the manila cover, she
began to tremble.

"Your ideas for the fund-raiser are fabulous."

"The fund-raiser?"

"They're both passionate and personal. I want to hear
more about your plans for the bake-sale auction
Wednesday at the game."

"I have some friends who are cooking for free, to
raise money for the event. And then—"

The door behind them opened.

"Sorry I'm late," Matt said as he strode inside and sat
down beside Jane.

Andrea picked up another folder with lots of messy
inky-black swirls and leafed through it. "I hope you
don't mind taking on a partner in your fund-raiser project this late."

"I—prefer—"

"A very talented partner," Andrea said quickly,

glancing at Harper. "Matt approached me on this…this morning."

"Oh, really?"

He was smiling with boyish mischief. Only, the charming smile that could make her heart do flips caused a very different reaction under these circumstances. If he'd been wearing his favorite Stetson, she would have snatched it and sat on it.

"I don't need a partner." Jane's voice was calm, but she knotted her hands in her lap so she wouldn't be tempted to lean forward and pound Andrea's desk, or better, his head.

"His ideas for the fund-raiser are almost exactly like yours."

"How absolutely amazing," Jane said, smiling tightly as she remembered her folder that had gone missing.

"You and he both live in the same town. I've decided to put you on the same committee to raise this money. Matt says he's totally free the night before and the night of the fund-raiser."

Why am I not surprised?

"So, he'll be helping you Wednesday night."

Suddenly the temperature in the room plummeted to sub-zero.

"Nice view," Matt said far too pleasantly.

"Isn't it?" Andrea shot him her most dazzling smile, and Jane remembered what her mother had said about some floozy nailing him. Andrea wasn't exactly the kind of woman her mother had warned her about, but maybe good ol' Mom had a slight, annoying point. Not that it mattered. Jane didn't want him. She wanted to kick him or flatten one of his fancy tires. Or maybe strangle him with his loud tie.

It was all she could do to keep her face blank. Somehow she forced a smile, but she couldn't quite control her eyes. No doubt, they were shooting sparks.

Not that Andrea, who was beaming at Matt, seemed to notice. Not that Jane blamed her boss for smiling at the handsome rat. Despite the chill in the room, the man radiated sex appeal.

"This is great," Andrea said. "The two of you on top of this—together."

"Teammates," Matt supplied silkily, winking at Jane. "Hey, I don't know if now's the time, but I've come up with several new ideas. What about a chicken flying contest and maybe some armadillo races?"

Jane began to cough.

"Why, that's brilliant," Andrea said. "The male viewpoint is so refreshingly original. This is so…so Texas. Don't you agree, Jane?"

Jane swallowed. "My thoughts exactly," she said, clasping her knotted hands even more tightly because she itched to strangle them both.

Chicken flying contests—my you know what!

Jane's reaction to being blindsided and put on the spot while in Andrea's office was predictable. What she did about it wasn't. Normally she would have kept her cool and worked behind closed doors to resolve the problem. Today she stormed down the hall, threw open the door to Matt's office and went inside without even knocking.

He was at his desk, on the phone.

Making a date with some floozy, no doubt. At the thought she saw green.

His playful, sparkling green eyes rose to hers innocently when she hurled herself inside his office. Instantly he said a polite goodbye in his low, husky voice, and was off the phone before Jane could blink. He got up and shut the door.

Carefully she stepped across papers, reports, corporate manuals and stacks of files.

"Your office is a mess!"

"I'm phobic about file cabinets," he said.

"You should be ashamed."

He grinned. "Something from my dysfunctional childhood. Haven't told the shrink about it yet."

She didn't laugh as she removed several files from a chair and slapped them on his desk before sitting down.

"Coffee?" he offered as he sank into his leather chair on the other side of his massive desk, which was also overflowing with clutter.

She shook her head so hard several pins flew out of her hair toward him. "This won't take long."

Smiling amiably, he picked up a pin and began to play with it.

She cleared her throat. "You stole my folder on the fund-raiser out of my briefcase."

"Wrong. You left it. I returned it."

"And you stole my ideas!"

"I think our working together could be fun."

"You have absolutely no interest in the children's after-school day-care education fund."

"Maybe I want to become…passionate about the same things you are."

"All you want is to be director of market research."

"Sounds like the pot calling the kettle black to me, darlin'?"

"I've worked hard for everything I've ever gotten. But you…you just get by on your contacts, money, your fancy car, good looks and good-old-boy network. Schmoozing around the ol' watercooler. Telling dirty jokes."

"Last time I looked, Andrea isn't a good old boy. She seems to think highly of me."

"Because she's got a crush on you."

"If she does, is that my fault?"

"You're using it."

"Relax. Spending more time together on this project could be fun…if you'd let it be."

"This is my career. I work hard. All you do is joke."

"I appreciate all you do. I admire you. That's why I'm so interested in getting to know you better," he insisted.

"Sorry, I don't trust your motives. And if you dare joke about me or what happened in your car this morning to your watercooler pals… If they start coming on to me…" She choked at the awful thought and was unable to go on. His handsome face blurred. Oh, God, in another second she would be crying.

She got up to run, but he was faster. He grabbed her and pushed her up against the wall. She twisted her face away from his.

His grip eased. "Hey, I don't want to hurt you." His deep voice was soft. So soft, her knees went weak. "And I damn sure don't want other men coming on to you."

Very gently he cupped her chin and forced her to look at him just as she felt a single mortifying tear slide down her cheek. She wiped it away with the back of her fist and took a deep breath and glared at him.

A muscle tightened in his jawline. Then he drew a deep breath of his own, and he swallowed.

"Let me go," she said.

"All right. But it's not going to be that easy."

When his hands fell away, she opened the door and ran.

The day got worse. During her PowerPoint presentation about corporate branding, the computer she was using went down. When she couldn't get it to work, she grew flustered. Naturally, Matt seized the day. After he jimmied a couple of wires, the computer hummed to life. By the time she was able to start over, she felt shy and unsure because she was running out of time. She talked too fast, lost her focus and forgot to make her most important points. If only Matt hadn't been there, leaning forward, listening to her every word as if he was spellbound. The jerk even complimented her speech and asked several intelligent questions that made her look great afterward.

Then it was his turn. A natural when it came to sports or performances of any kind, he got up and blew everybody away with his smooth presentation. He stared at her the whole time, smiling after every point he made. When everybody clapped and congratulated him, Jane sat in her corner and chewed moodily on her pencil until the lead snapped and she tossed it down.

When their colleagues filed out of the conference room, Matt came over to her. No doubt to gloat because he was sure she'd lost and he'd landed the director of market research position.

"You didn't say anything. Well?"

"Well what?"

"What'd you think of my presentation?"

She jabbed her pencil into the knot of hair at her nape. "You've been a natural-born ham ever since elementary school."

"Surely you don't still hold my clumsy efforts in the school talent shows against me."

"You blew everybody away even back then, and you know it."

"Even you?" he asked.

She felt her face heat. She was sure she was blushing, which was even better for his ego than actually telling him he'd been terrific.

"Did anybody ever tell you, you're way too conceited, Harper?"

"Just you."

She got up and began gathering her books and reports noisily.

"Darlin', are you going to hate me forever?"

"I—I don't hate you."

"Well, that's a start."

"Just leave me alone. Okay?"

"What if it's not okay?"

"Don't be too sure you've got the promotion, Harper. Not until it's announced."

When she walked toward the door, he stepped in front of her. "Is that all you care about? This morning I thought that maybe…" When he swallowed, she thought he looked human, too human; hurt even, and it bothered her. A lot.

She swallowed, too. "Don't think about this morning. And don't brag to anybody about that kiss either."

"Kisses. Plural. And I think we need a repeat."

"Don't even think about it, Harper."

He grabbed her. "What if I can't stop thinking about it, darlin', any more than you can?"

Slowly he removed her glasses. When his mouth touched hers, she melted into his big body. Then it was all over but the kissing—long passionate, drowning kisses, which didn't stop until she was wet and feverish, and he was shaking violently.

When he finally let her come up for air, her legs were wobbly, and she was reeling. Somehow she managed to say in a chilly tone, "This has got to stop, Harper."

"You could have fooled me."

He calmly picked up her glasses and handed them to her.

She shoved them onto the bridge of her nose. Then she grabbed her purse and briefcase and walked toward the door. She didn't look back.

She didn't dare look back.

Chapter 6

Wednesday evening

Jane seethed as she swallowed a nervous breath against the panic that threatened to overpower her. She tilted her chin upward, fighting not to glance at Matt, who was surrounded by kids and their mothers, all wanting to buy tickets to his armadillo races and chicken-flying contests.

Harper was good. What was the use of even trying to compete with him? He could beat her with both his hands tied behind his back. Once again he'd proved that her hard work and discipline and careful planning were nothing against his gut instinct, common touch and savvy charisma. While he was too busy to believe manning his armadillo races and chicken-flying contests, she'd hardly sold a pie. Anytime he had a free second, he strode up and down among the throng hawking his wares.

She clicked her nails against the counter and tried not to feel bored or depressed at her failures or resent the excellent job Matt and his brother, Jerry Keith, had done building booths for her under the bleachers of the baseball stadium. They'd worked cheerfully until nearly 2:00 a.m. last night. Even though Matt had been exhausted, he'd insisted on following her home, which was out of his way.

"Just to make sure you get there safely," he'd said.

"Like you really think there might be a criminal lurking behind every mesquite tree and cactus bush," she'd replied.

"Is it a major crime I want to protect you?" His handsome face had been touchingly earnest as she'd slid behind the wheel.

She was fighting to be a good sport about his popularity. After all, he was outdoing himself for a good cause. *Her* cause. The nagging question was—why? To help her? For the cause? Or to improve his position as contender for director of market research?

She was afraid she knew the answer.

While stragglers trickled by her booth to buy cakes or pies or bicker about her prices, Matt patiently answered his young fans' nonstop questions in between armadillo races. For the most part, Jerry Keith was manning the chicken-flying booth, which was almost as popular. Feathers were flying, chickens were squawking and kids were running wildly about inside the screened booth, screaming in delight.

Upon the rare occasions when Jane sold a cake or pie, she couldn't help glancing at Matt, hoping he'd see she wasn't a total loser. He always smiled back at her.

"Are armadillos really really fast, Mr. Harper?" squealed cute little ten-year-old Susanna Hays, who was jumping back and forth, causing her red pigtails to bounce.

Matt knelt so that he was at eye level with the excited little girl. "When they think you're tracking 'em down to carve out their insides so you can sell 'em on the side of the road as baskets, they can skitter away over the rocks mighty dern fast."

Susanna stilled. "Do bad people really do that?"

"Mostly they're slow though," said Beaver Jackson, pushing his rumpled black Stetson back. His tone was authoritative because he was in the sixth grade. "I got one. Wumpus I call him. He's my pet."

"I've got one too," Matt said, looking up and winking at Jane.

Oh, why didn't somebody, anybody, come up and buy a pie?

"I got a scorpion for a pet," another little boy said. "In a bottle with holes in the cap."

"Well, don't let him out in the house," Matt warned, patting him on the head.

Pretty Annie Grant, the bank teller, and Greg Flynn, a local cop, were ambling among the tables side by side, pretending not to be too interested in each other as they eyed the items to be sold in the silent auction. Annie wrote her name down beneath several items, including the card to buy Jane's cooking services.

Matt watched Annie and then nodded at Jane.

Good. She was glad he'd noticed that at least somebody appreciated her cooking skills. She said a quick prayer that somebody would buy more of her pies so she could sell out and leave. Just being around Matt made her hot and edgy.

"Got any ideas about who wrote that love letter?" cracked a voice to her right as he slapped a ten-dollar bill down. "Two strawberry pies, please."

Jane turned. Ol' Bill Sinclair's weather-beaten face looked like a human road map, but his bright blue eyes twinkled at her with more mischief than most youngsters. *Obviously he knew Matt wrote it.*

"I have an idea or two," she said, not looking at him as she rung up the sale.

"A lot of people do," he said, glancing toward Matt. "You two did a mighty good job together on these booths."

"Matt and his brother did most of it."

"Matt damn sure has a way with kids."

No sooner had Ol' Bill Sinclair paid for his stacks of pies than Matt left his own booth and fans. He stalked straight to the display that described her cooking services, which were to be auctioned.

Feelings of triumph turned to horror when he leaned over and studied the paper with an air of intense interest. A lock of inky hair fell across his dark eyebrow when he lifted the paper and took out a pen.

No! No! Don't you dare!

Bending lower, he scribbled something on the paper, glanced her way and smiled wickedly before returning to his cheering horde. Soon afterward a crowd began to gather around her display. She sucked in air.

What had *he* done?

Soon, she was so curious and terrified to know, she was wringing her hands when Ol' Bill patted her shoulder and said, "Don't you fret. I'll go check it out."

Was she so obvious?

Ol' Bill was back at her booth before she could blink twice. Not that she much liked the mischievous glint in his blue eyes.

"Looks like your Harper's done gone and bought himself the prettiest little cook in town."

"He's not my Harper."

"Well, maybe you're his then. He bid five thousand dollars for your cooking services."

Her cheeks flamed. Her heart raced. She'd kill Harper for this. She would!

"With conditions," Ol' Bill amended softly.

"With conditions?" she parroted.

"Girl, I knew you was a cook, but he must want your services mighty bad. Ain't nobody but a fool with money to burn gonna top that bid. You and he go back a long way, don't cha?".

She could feel her cheeks heating now. "We don't go back at all. And don't you dare print a word about this in the *Gazette*. And don't you dare tell my mother about this either."

Ol' Bill chuckled. "She's psychic, remember. She predicted you'd be born in a special way, just didn't see how."

"Don't you dare go into the particulars of *that* event either."

"What I'm trying to say is everybody in town already knows about you and Matt."

"Did he write that love letter?"

Ol' Bill winked at her. "He's never been one to declare himself. But don't you worry none. It'll all come out in the wash, sweetheart."

He had written it.

Well, that didn't give him rights over her!

"It certainly will come out in the wash," she said as she lifted the wooden door to her booth, slammed it down so hard the whole booth shook and strode over to the display that offered her cooking services. Sure enough, Matt's name was a sloppy swirling scrawl of livid black ink ten times bigger than the other neatly written names. In addition, he'd penned, "Five thousand dollars. With conditions."

As she read the enormous black letters and reread that incredible figure, the home team struck a home run, and the crowd in the bleachers began to stomp and roar again. The sound was so deafening, she covered her ears.

Suddenly Matt was beside her. When he put his arms protectively around her, she began to quiver even as she pushed him away.

"How could you bid five thousand dollars for a few meals? Just what do you think you're doing?"

"Going after what I want." He slid his checkbook out of his hip pocket and uncapped his pen. "After all, it's for a cause we both believe in." His bold gaze drifted from her mouth to her neck.

She gasped, afraid they'd drift lower to her breasts. They didn't. Instead he leaned over the table and wrote her a check for five thousand dollars.

After a moment or two she caught her breath.

He handed her the crisp blue check, which was indeed made out for five thousand dollars.

"Don't play games, Harper. What do you mean by…er…conditions?"

"I want breakfast in bed every morning up until the Spring Fling. I'm not picky when it comes to food. Just geography, which is you serving me breakfast in my bed."

"What?"

"Don't look so shocked. Villains like me always prefer to lure the damsels they want to their den to seduce them."

She pushed her glasses higher up the bridge of her nose. "I will not sleep with you! Or kiss you! Or…or…"

"Oh, and wear your hair down, darlin', and lose the glasses. You're much prettier without them—as I'm sure you know."

"I'm blind as a bat without my glasses."

"Your mother bought you contacts years ago."

"You have no right to know that."

"Everybody in Red Rock knows everything, darlin'. It's part of the town's charm. Lose the glasses."

She was wondering what to do when her friend Annie, who happened to work at the bank Matt's check had been drawn on, walked by again.

"Oh, Annie!" she cried, afraid to be alone with Matt for another second.

Annie turned and smiled. She was pretty and tall. Her lush red hair was down tonight, and her brown eyes were warm and friendly as she made her way toward them.

"I heard you two were working together on this," she said, looking pleased. "You did a great job. Everybody's so happy you finally made up."

"We have not made up," Jane said.

"Oh. I thought—"

"Yes, we have," Matt said.

Jane handed her the check. "Is this good or not?"

Annie looked up at Matt, her sweet face uncertain now. He nodded.

"As good as gold," Annie replied sweetly.

"I guess that settles it then," Matt said. With the swiftness of a swooping hawk, he grabbed her hand. "You're mine, darlin'." His green eyes darkened possessively as he pulled her closer.

Usually she applauded people who were clear about their goals, but he was too much, and she was drowning.

"Starting tomorrow," he persisted, "I want breakfast in bed every day until the Spring Fling."

She yanked her hand free. Speechless and quivering from too many overwrought emotions, she turned to walk away.

"And, oh, Jane—"

She whirled. "What else?" she demanded in a contemptuous breath.

His fathomless eyes were boring holes into her. "I can't wait," he purred, "until tomorrow morning."

Her nerves leaped. Her heart beat faster. She was slow to answer, but when she did, her mouth curved seductively and she could see she'd surprised him.

"Neither can I," she whispered. "You're in for quite a surprise."

"Good. It's about time you decided you have a right to have some fun. We'd be good together."

Chapter 7

Jane got to Matt's ancient, blue trailer about 7:00 a.m. It had rained during the night, but the sun was up and bathing the trees and his horrendously ostentatious, three-story mansion with a magical sparkling peach light.

For a moment she stared at the tasteless house that was obviously being built to impress. The man was too much. There were gaudy turrets and too many rooflines, but doves were cooing around an enormous birdbath. A gray cat lurked underneath a bush nearby. Jane liked the trees and the quiet, and the way the woodsy, warm air smelled sweetly of cedar. She liked the fact that he had a cat, too.

What was she thinking, coming here? Well, there was nothing for it but to deal with Mr. Harper as fast as possible so she could check him off her to-do list and get herself safely to work.

Quickly she got out of her Honda. With an apprehensive smile, she picked up the breakfast tray stacked with covered plates she'd prepared and picked her way across the rocky ground to his trailer.

Scared as she was at facing the devil in his lair, she couldn't help noting that except for the trailer and the house, it really was pretty out here. Dewdrops sparkled on the leaves and turned a spiderweb into a carelessly tossed diamond necklace clinging to the branches of the live oak that shaded his trailer.

Curious, the gray cat followed her and leaped onto a large cardboard box with a picture of a window air-conditioning unit on it. The big box looked too wide to go through the door. Maybe that's why it had been shoved to the side of a rickety set of stairs.

When she placed her foot onto his first flimsy step, the wood sagged, and her heart began to beat with alarm. The trailer was dark and silent and uninviting. Hesitantly, she lifted her hand to the door, but before she could knock, a deep, sleep-slurred voice that made her nerves vibrate said, "Come on in, darlin'."

The cat dashed expectantly up to the door and meowed. For a second or two Jane lingered, studying the fat black spider resting in the center of its web. The spider had several victims already. One was a pretty, blue butterfly still struggling to get loose.

Jane swallowed. She'd dressed carefully in a high-collared white blouse, long blue skirt that brushed her ankles, and white cowboy boots. The better to stomp into his trailer and kick him if he got fresh, she'd thought. She'd worn her glasses, and her hair was snug against her nape and secured with even more pins than ever. Some vain, rebellious part of her regretted that the hairdo, glasses and understated makeup had succeeded in making her look so severe and icy.

Cautiously she stuck her head inside his door while the cat scurried past her. The shadowy trailer was hot, but the coast appeared to be clear to the sink and stove, so she was inside before she realized he'd been asleep on the couch, which meant he was right beside her and close enough to grab her.

When he sprang to a sitting position, white sheets fell to his waist. Even in the semidarkness she could see that he was lean and nut brown—everywhere. Which meant he wasn't wearing much. *If anything.*

His broad shoulders, wide chest and powerful arms were made of sculpted muscle. His drowsy green eyes, and his heavy, tousled black hair made him look so adorable she had to fight for her next breath. With an effort, she pretended to ignore the funny little darts of excitement zinging through her stomach. She knew she should glance away, but then he looked up at her and blushed shyly, and his gaze seemed full of longing. Was the blush a trick? Did he feel shy and vulnerable around her too? It was strange to think such a thing, that he might not always be as sure and cocky as she assumed he was.

Whatever he felt, he was not to be trusted.

Suddenly, maybe because he was so near and looked so male and dear, the trailer felt stifling, and she was burning up. The longer she looked at his wide shoulders and dark chest while she imagined those other more exciting male parts of him under the sheet, the hotter and damper she got.

"You'd better not be naked!" she squeaked when his cat jumped onto the couch and began to purr.

"You're welcome to rip the sheet off and see."

"A dirty trick like that from the likes of you wouldn't surprise me. Well, I'm not afraid of you."

"I don't want you to be." His white smile charmed her.

Shaking a little, she went over to the couch and carefully laid the tray in his lap.

"It wasn't a dirty trick. It was just awful hot last night, darlin', and you're a little early this morning…like always. You had me so busy building those booths for you and then taking them down, plus working for your fund-raiser, that I was too tired to install my blasted window unit last night."

The cat walked over to inspect the tray she'd brought.

"Get down, Julie Baby." Gently he pushed the cat off the couch and lifted the cover from the first plate. Several slices of wet, blackened pieces of toast lay on the plate. She'd cooked them last night and left them out in the rain. When he removed the cover from a second plate, his black eyebrows arched warily at the smell of fermentation.

"Creative. Resourceful. Where'd you find the rotten apples on such short notice?"

"In my compost heap."

"And you accuse me of dirty tricks. Looks like we're made for each other, darlin'." His quick grin as he shoved the tray aside was disarming. "But, hey, no time like now to find out, is there?"

Before she could run, he grabbed her wrist and pulled her down onto his lap.

He was definitely naked. She could feel him under the thin folds of the sheet.

"Our deal didn't include anything but breakfast," she said primly, struggling to free herself until she realized the slightest movements of her hips against his only heightened his arousal.

"You didn't fulfill your part of the bargain, darlin'," he whispered, nuzzling her neck while yanking pins out of her hair. "I bid five thousand dollars for services you have yet to render. Now you have to pay."

Her hair cascaded to her shoulders in skeins of shimmering silk.

"Much better," he said. "And now off with the glasses."

"What do you want?" she asked weakly as he removed them.

"The same thing you do," he replied huskily.

"The position of director of market research?"

"Among other things." He used both hands to pull her snug against his body, which made her achingly aware of how hard and muscular his thighs were against hers.

"Let me go."

"This is way more fun than breakfast." He lifted her hair and lowered his head. With his tongue, he explored her nape. Somehow the gesture was so sweet and sexy and loverly, she could barely breathe.

"Do you know what you do to me, darlin'? Do you know how delicious you are?"

"Do you say such things to everybody?"

"No, you're very special." He buried his hands in her hair, wrapping heavy coils around his fist so he could tilt her head back and pull her face closer to his.

"I don't believe you."

His insistent lips nibbling her flesh were sending wild tremors along the nerves of her jawline.

"Believe me."

"What about Carol?"

"Forget Carol."

"But you two *just* broke up."

"Which is a wonderful thing when you think about it, because her leaving made space in my life for the right person."

A swimming giddiness spun her round and round. She had to get up. She had to get out of here, but he was like a magnet, drawing her, compelling her. She'd never ever felt like this, all hot and hollow and wild.

"You'll say anything," she whispered.

"You're wrong about me, darlin'."

Feeling jealous of Carol, she wanted to snap out something cruel and clever and hurtful, but for some reason she couldn't think of a single insult. Maybe because she desperately wanted to believe she was wrong about him. Maybe because she didn't want him to stop kissing her neck or holding her close and making her feel all warm and sexy.

Had Carol seen him completely naked? Had he held her like this? Kissed her until she was so dizzy she was breathless? Made love to her? On this very couch?

A little moan escaped Jane's lips.

Don't come crying to me when he gets himself snapped up by some floozy, and you realize you're in love with him.

Jane hated it when her mother got inside her brain and said crazy, stupid things that scared her.

When Jane stopped struggling and turned into him, his lips left her neck. Then he leaned closer, bringing his mouth tantalizingly near her own, so close she could almost taste him. Thinking he was going to kiss her, she licked her lips and closed her eyes. She felt strangely excited and he hadn't even kissed her mouth yet.

He was solid and strong, yet she felt his powerful body shaking as he drew each ragged breath. She had the feeling that if she stuck one little toe into this burning tide, she would be swept away. Her head fell back against the couch in an attitude of utter surrender.

He went very still for a long moment. Then much to her surprise, he abruptly let her go and slid to his end of the couch.

She opened her eyes in hot confusion.

He was staring at her as if he felt as lost and disoriented as she did.

She was in the mood to be ravaged, but he looked vulnerable and unsure.

"You'd better go," he said softly.

Not for the world was she about to admit that what she felt was the oddest pang of bittersweet loss and aching disappointment that he'd stopped. Was she nothing more than a game to him?

"You'd better git, darlin', while the gittin's good," he repeated calmly.

"What?"

"I'm afraid you won't be able to resist me if I start kissing you, darlin'. A lot of women can't, you know."

Her eyebrows flew together.

"You're one love-starved woman, darlin'." He chuckled.

She pulled away. "Are you laughing at me? Comparing me to—"

"Looks like I've gotta get up, get my own breakfast," he replied, still in that infuriatingly calm tone. "And since I'm stark naked, you'd better go, unless you want to see more of me than you bargained on."

Her eyes grew huge. Gone was the sweet vulnerable Matt of moments before. Once again he was the old mocking Matt she remembered from grade school.

"You can stay, of course. If you intend to deliver. You know me—I love an audience when I show off, and my favorite audience is an admiring woman."

"I don't admire you." Somehow she managed to stand up even though her legs were trembling. "I don't admire one thing about you."

"Then you'd better leave, before I change your mind. I could, you know—easily."

When he stood, too, and his sheet began to tumble toward the floor, she whirled away from him and fled out the door. But she turned at the last moment and got an eyeful of Matt Harper.

The devil was built like some dark pagan god of love.

"Oh my God… You did it."

"Told you you'd admire me. Wanna stay?"

He laughed when she kept staring at him openmouthed.

"Well, make up your mind before it's too late for us to call in sick."

"I'm thrilled with the money you two raised," Andrea said to Jane and Matt from behind her desk. Her low-key voice, smooth and professional as she thumbed through the pages of Jane's report on the fund-raiser. "I knew you two would work well together."

"Jane can be difficult," Matt said. "She's a little up-tight. Quite the perfectionist."

"I was perfectly happy working alone," Jane muttered through her teeth. She'd been a bundle of nerves ever since he'd lowered his sheet and she'd fled his trailer this morning. His teasing remark was too much. It was all she could do to contain herself.

"Not me, Mr. King of Schmooze. I can get along with anybody."

Jane clenched her fists. With an effort she relaxed her hands and forced a weak smile. If she made a scene, that would only make him look better, which he would use against her.

Matt was beautifully dressed in a navy suit and pristine-white shirt this morning. Even his tie was dark and subdued.

"Your bid was exceedingly generous," Andrea said, smiling at him.

"It's a good cause. Dear to my heart, the company's and Jane's."

He's good, Jane thought bitterly. *Playing it to the hilt.*

"Hey, and Jane's an…er…inspired cook. Breakfast this morning was…er…" He winked at Jane. "A unique experience."

Since Andrea couldn't possibly see their legs, Jane gave him a swift, sharp kick in the shin.

"Ouc-ch…er…and…unforgettable," he said, suppressing a yelp as he leaned down to rub his shin.

"Well, I just wanted to take a moment to thank both of you. And thanks as well for getting your report to me so fast, Jane. I can't wait to show it to the board. I'm sure we raised more money than any other company in the building this year—again. Thanks to both of you!"

Jane smiled at Andrea and stood up to go.

"I'd love to work with you on another project," Matt said to Jane.

"Good day, Harper," Jane said, frowning when he got up and limped out the door.

"Something wrong with your leg, Matt?" Andrea asked so sweetly Jane did a slow burn.

Not that she stayed to hear his answer. On her way out of the building to drive home late that afternoon, she noticed a huge bouquet of flowers on Stephanie's desk, from the same florist Matt had used.

She stopped to admire them. "Very pretty. Who sent them?" Jane asked.

"Carl," Stephanie said dreamily.

Carl was a lawyer for Fortune TX.

"At first he wouldn't admit it. He was so cute about it, teasing me about having a secret admirer."

Thinking of Matt, Jane backed away quickly.

Love was definitely in the air. The last thing she needed was more exposure to that dreaded disease.

Chapter 8

Matt was in the shower when he heard his trailer door slam. Despite the icy water blasting over his hot body, knowing it was her made him even harder, so hard he hurt.

He had it bad. Every time he even looked at Jane, he wanted her all to himself and wondered if other guys felt the same way. Hell, yes, they did. They always had, even before those pictures.

She had those breasts and was built like a centerfold, but that wasn't the only reason why he couldn't stop thinking of her. He remembered the way the guys had joked about her in high school even before Jerry Keith—he was almost sure it was J.K.—had put those pictures of her up for the whole damn world to see. It had been a lot for a girl to take, especially a quiet, shy girl like her. He'd done his share of the joking before he'd asked her to the Spring Fling back in high school. Later he'd hated himself for it.

Matt had dreamed about her last night. She'd crawled on top of him wearing nothing except a wet T-shirt and a pink bikini bottom. Slowly she'd stripped off the T-shirt. Only, in his dream, Jane hadn't minded that he saw her, and she'd taken him into her mouth. He'd awakened sweating and trembling like a hard-run stallion. When he'd glanced at his watch, he'd realized she'd be here any minute, so he'd run to his shower to cool off, hell, to get a grip.

"Matt," came her honeyed voice. When he didn't answer, she began to knock lightly on the bathroom door.

Slowly he turned off the water.

"I'm here," she said.

He sagged against the shower wall, his heart thudding violently.

"I—I didn't want you to come out…and not know."

It was harder than hell not to push the door open and just grab her while he was naked and wet. What would she do if he did that?

Run or melt?

"Thanks for the warning," he muttered as he ripped the curtain aside and yanked a towel off the rack. Whipping it around his waist, he stepped out of the shower and opened the door. He was sure one look at his large, brown dripping body would send her flying back to the kitchen.

To his surprise and delight, she stood her ground. Her shining platinum hair fell to her shoulders. She hadn't lost her glasses or put on much makeup. Still, she was lovely. Too lovely for words. She smelled of jasmine and roses, and he wanted to pull her close so bad he ached. What was she doing, standing there? Did she want to tempt him? Didn't she know she had him half-crazed?

"What's for breakfast?" he managed to say.

She flushed prettily. "Come see. It's ready."

"Give me a minute." He went to the bedroom and dressed fast. As he zipped up his slacks and leaned over the nightstand, he remembered he'd emptied his pockets on the kitchen counter last night. Then he remembered what was in them.

Hell.

He stalked out of the bedroom to the living and dining area and saw that she'd set a single place for him at the table. She'd used white china with a yellow-and-blue pattern on it, a pink place mat and a yellow napkin. Two boiled eggs sat in cute white egg cups that matched the china. He smelled hazelnut-flavored coffee brewing, and the toast was thick and brown instead of black. Looked good. Maybe she was thawing. She'd even opened a jar of homemade marmalade.

Suddenly all he could see were the plastic-wrapped

condoms on top of a pile of wrinkled dollar bills and his keys beside the sink where he'd emptied his pockets last night. When he edged closer to the sink, he grabbed everything, but one of the condoms fell on the floor.

Red-faced, she scooted away from him toward the door. "I—I'd better go."

"Sorry about that," he muttered, picking up the foil packet and jamming it into his pocket before he sat down.

"It's okay."

"Won't you join me?" he asked in a quiet, deep tone.

"I—I...don't think so."

"It's hell always eating breakfast alone."

When she nodded shyly, he poured her a cup of coffee. "Cream or sugar?" he asked, pushing the cup toward her.

"Black."

"That kinda figures."

She laughed—she actually laughed—at something he'd said. The sweet sound lit him up inside.

He broke the egg onto a piece of toast. When the slimy mess oozed all over his plate, he laughed. "I should've known."

He broke the second one, and more slime soaked his toast.

"Raw eggs," he said, glancing up at her. "The deal was cooking services."

She got up to go again.

"More tricks," he said, leaping up and blocking the door. "Again you've failed to render the services I've paid good money for."

She stared straight ahead instead of at him. Her breaths were shallow and choppy, and she stood frozen like a frightened deer.

"Look at me," he whispered gently. Instead of anger, ardor flared inside him.

She gave him a long steady look. "If you'll let me go."

"Okay." He held up his hands and backed away from the door. "Hey, you know something. Maybe I don't blame you for the burnt toast or the raw eggs. I played plenty of tricks on you when we were kids. I should never have snuck up on you with that camera. It was my fault those pictures—"

"I don't want to talk about it."

"Well, maybe I do."

She turned her back on him and pushed the door open. Julie Baby ran inside, meowing.

He stared at Jane's slender back. "There was no excuse for that except that I was an eighteen-year-old moron," he said. "But I want you to know that I, that later…that I've always felt bad about it."

To his surprise, she turned around. Her pretty face was brightly flushed. "You apologized back then."

"Not really. You know as well as I did that my parents forced me to go over to your house and say what I said. The whole thing was a farce. You were upset, and for various reasons, I resented the hell out of you. I thought you were a prissy little tattletale."

"Maybe I—I was."

"For what it's worth, I want you to know I didn't really take those pictures or blow them up, post them in the locker room. I got expelled for it, but I didn't do it."

"It was your camera. I saw you...."

"You saw me grab it back from Jerry Keith after he took the pictures. He must've stolen it back. But if he did it, he's been too smart to ever confess. Probably 'cause he thinks I'd kill him. And maybe I would."

She drew a long breath. "Is that really the truth?"

He stared into her eyes. "Yes and I felt bad about it," he continued. "Not just because I got expelled but because I realized how bad you felt. But I couldn't admit it. Not to you. Not to anybody. Not when they kicked me out of school because of you. Not when I didn't do it and had a major persecution complex. I liked you. I really liked you. I was too stunned to take those pictures. You were just so damn beautiful. The prettiest thing I'd ever seen. But after there was such a stink, I didn't want anybody to know how much I really liked you or how sorry I was, least of all you. Back then I had to be a tough guy. So, since I took the rap and nobody would listen to me anyway, I let everybody think I put them up. Truth was, I wanted to kill whoever did it. But I said you were a snitch and acted like I despised you. Some tough guy. I was a jerk."

He felt his heart thudding in his throat. For a long time she couldn't seem to meet his eyes. She was staring at his chest instead.

"Okay," she finally said. "Thanks for that. Maybe I was an easy mark because I was always way too sensitive."

"I should have made it up to you back then. Do you suppose…it's too late for me to make it up to you now?"

"I don't know what you mean."

"I mean I'd like to start by us being friends."

"How?"

"You could start by going to the Spring Fling with me?"

"Everybody would talk."

"So? Does it matter so much what other people say?"

"It always has in the past."

"How about now? Despite the raw eggs and the toast, I like the way it feels seeing you first thing in the morning. It's nice. All of a sudden it stinks being alone out here so much. People would get used to us sooner than you think."

"You don't seem like the lonely sort," she said.

"People aren't always what they seem, are they? Take yourself. You act all prim and proper, but you definitely have a streak, darlin'. Same as I do."

"A streak?"

"A wild streak."

He was surprised when she smiled.

"So, you get lonely out here, huh?" she said. "Lonely and wild?"

He didn't want to talk about that. "What if we just started by becoming friends? What if people thought we liked each other? Would that be so bad?"

"Depends on how it turned out, and we don't have a crystal ball. So, I can't say."

Filled with hope, he grinned at her.

"It's late. I'd better go, Harper."

He held the door for her and then followed her to her Honda.

"Pretty day," she said.

Spring was in the air. The birds were singing and twittering and chasing each other in the trees. An armadillo was rooting around among the garbage cans.

"What do you think of my house?"

She glanced toward the monstrosity and tried to control her face. "Well, it's certainly—big."

He laughed.

She blushed.

"I didn't build it just for me," he said.

"Wild parties?"

"Maybe one or two. Mainly it's for the future. I want to fall in love, get married, have kids."

She blushed again.

"Like I said, it gets lonely as hell out here."

Her blue eyes burned deep inside him. "Tomorrow I'll cook you a real breakfast," she said as she started the Honda. "It was generous of you to donate all that money to the after-school program. I—I've been a bad sport about it, and I'm really sorry."

"Apology accepted. I'd forgive you for sure if you had the guts to go to the Spring Fling with me."

"We've got a lot to live down, you and I." She blew him a kiss and drove off.

Jane had her cell phone pressed against her ear as she sped down the grocery aisles. Her eyes were stinging a little from her contact lenses.

"You're in love with him!" Mindy accused.

Mindy had a bad habit of ringing her up whenever she was driving around town bored. Jane never got to talk to any of her family long before they began to meddle.

Jane stopped her basket abruptly in front of a row of ice-cream freezers. "Shut up," she whispered. Then she removed her cell from her ear and counted to ten before putting it back.

"You're never mean to anybody except him," Mindy said matter-of-factly. "It's a sure sign you're in love."

"You've obviously been talking to Mother."

"She just hung up. For some reason Helen Geary is giving her fits about that love letter Matt wrote."

"Like how?"

"Mom wouldn't say." Mindy sighed. "You wouldn't hate him so much and be so mean to him if there wasn't a solid bedrock of true love."

"That is the craziest thing I've ever heard."

"Hold on!" Mindy cried.

Jane frowned when she heard sirens in the background. Since Mindy didn't come back on immediately, she began to worry. Her sister could drive her crazy, but she loved Mindy more than anything.

"Sorry about that," Mindy said brightly. "Some cops were chasing some guy. Probably a doper."

"Thank God you're okay."

"Where was I? Oh, yes." She hesitated. "It's true. Everybody in the whole family can see it 'cept you. You've always had a stubborn streak. Especially about him."

"I want to marry a solid citizen...somebody nice and reliable. Not some hell-raising, flirty, picture-snapping, skirt-chasing braggart who ruined my reputation in high school and drives a flashy car."

"The only skirt he's been chasing lately is yours."

"And it had better stay that way."

"See—you *do* love him!"

"I didn't mean that. He was the worst boy I ever knew."

"Which was why he was adorable. He was such a daredevil. Everybody loved him. I even had a crush on him once. But who cares about back then now? He's thirty-five. All grown up. Besides, he's rich and successful. Snow women go for rich and successful in their men."

"He's not *my* man." *Then why are you wearing contacts that are stinging your eyeballs?*

"He could be, if you'd let him be."

"I'm not in love with him. I'm not." Jane opened the freezer and grabbed a carton of ice cream and held it to her forehead. When Mindy laughed at her, Jane moved it down her neck.

"Mother said Carol's back in town for the weekend. She thinks Carol regrets being so stupid for giving him that ultimatum, and she's here to try to get him back."

"And we know this, how?"

"Her mother told our mother. Our mother told me. And now I'm telling you. I think Carol called our mother to warn you off her daughter's property."

"And you just had to call me and tell me first thing?"

"What's a sister for?"

"Sometimes I wonder."

Jane was hard at work at her computer, checking out the most relevant, current and credible marketing research available on Fortune's various products, when Andrea slipped silently into her office and shut the door.

"I just stopped by to say hi," Andrea said as she sat down and crossed her legs.

Jane felt too shy to ask about the promotion. "Would you like coffee?"

"I can't stay. Just wanted to let you know that the board is very, *very* impressed with you."

Jane felt herself glowing as she smiled. She pushed her glasses higher. "I love my job here."

"I thought I should tell you that we're very close to

reaching a decision about the position of director of market research. You're looking good."

"Oh?"

"I'm thrilled for you."

When Andrea was gone, and Jane could breathe again, she sank back in her chair and blew on her fingertips.

"Am I good? Or am I good?" She was so happy she laughed.

Then she glanced at the towering bouquet of yellow roses, daisies, irises and lilies Matt had sent her, and her joy dimmed a little. The roses were open, and they filled the room with their heady fragrance. She wanted to run to him and tell him, so she could share her happiness with him. But this was something she couldn't share with him. Suddenly thinking about how disappointed he'd be in himself, she squeezed her eyes shut. Her joy in her own achievement faded, and she sank back in her chair and stayed like that a long time.

"But we can't both win, can we?" she whispered hopelessly to the roses and daisies when she opened her eyes again.

"This is what I want! More than anything!" The second sentence was louder than the first, as if to convince herself.

The rest of the day she was especially nice to him, at least until she saw him disappear into Andrea's office. When the big oak door stayed shut for nearly an hour—except for the times Stephanie brought in little silver trays with coffee steaming above china cups and plates piled high with chocolate brownies—Jane frowned.

When the handsome rat finally emerged, he slunk past Jane's office, avoiding her gaze instead of seeking it as he usually did.

Which meant—oh my God—the snake felt guilty! Which meant he thought *he'd* won!

He *had* been in there with Andrea forever.

What was going on?

Chapter 9

Friday

Jane rushed into the ladies' room at Fortune TX and locked herself in a stall. She closed her eyes and simply stood there.

Minutes passed. Swallowing deep breaths, she fought to calm herself. Finally, she came out, went to the sink and began splashing cold water on her face. When she raised her eyes to the mirror, she froze at the sorry sight that greeted her.

Who is that ridiculous, pathetic frump in the Coke-bottle–thick glasses and that awful, gray suit, who's having a panic attack over a stupid promotion?

"You, baby," the girl in the mirror taunted. "You're the uptight nerd with the old-lady bun." Jane's frown deepened as she leaned closer so that her ragged breaths misted the glass.

"You're not in high school anymore. What are you so afraid of?" she whispered. "You're thirty-two. Live a little. If you don't, Carol or Andrea or some real floozy will get Matt."

Jane went numb. The tube of lipstick fell from her shaking fingers to the tile floor and rolled, making little, clicking sounds on the tiles before it banged into the metal trash can. Not that she bothered to pick it up. She was too busy curling her hands into tight fists.

Maybe you look smart, reliable and levelheaded. Maybe you look perfect for the responsible position of director of market research. But who really cares?

"I'm tired of being me!" she yelled, shaking her fists at the nerd in the mirror.

Who cares if your mother delivered you on a pool table and people think that was funny? So what if you have big breasts?

Get over it.

Or do something really wild…like…like…

Flaunt them! screamed a voice inside her head.

Resisting the impulse to strip naked, Jane ripped off the baggy jacket and tossed it into the trash. Next, she yanked the pins out of her hair and tossed them on top of the jacket. She tore open the top two buttons of her blouse, not caring that one button hung loose, dangling from a single thread.

Anger consumed her.

She'd wasted years. Years and years because her free-spirited mother had embarrassed her. Because free-spirited Matt Harper and his kid brother had embarrassed her. Years because she'd been so afraid she'd be laughed at again if she ever flirted or acted sexy again, she'd shut down.

No more!

A few minutes later when she stormed out of the ladies' room, and Matt came out of his office, he stopped abruptly, rocking back on his heels, a look of genuine concern darkening his handsome features when he saw her.

"Out of my way, buster," she whispered.

"Whoa!" he said softly. "What cat bit your tail?"

"This has nothing to do with you!"

Slinging her purse higher over her shoulder, tilting her chin up, she sailed past him and Stephanie without saying another word. Jane had never left early before without clearing it first with Andrea. To hell with Andrea. To hell with the promotion. To hell with Matt Harper.

For once Jane knew exactly where she was going. She practically ran all the way to that swanky little dress shop downstairs to look at that soft, figure-fitting green dress Melanie had said would look good on her.

Once inside the store, she didn't stop with one dress.

Not when she'd deprived herself for years. Not when the talented saleswoman pointed out sparkly green beads, earrings and bracelets—not to mention the sexiest, strappy sandals she'd ever seen. If she was on fire, she'd set her credit card on fire. As the saying goes, she shopped until she dropped. When she drove home, the back seat and trunk of the Honda brimmed with pink boxes and bags.

Saturday morning Jane was up early, washing her hair and perfuming her body with lotions and cologne. She put on her soft contacts and shook her clean hair loose so that it fell in glistening curls about her shoulders. She shimmied into her dress and put on her bangles. Today she wanted flash.

When she finally knocked on Matt's trailer in the soft green dress that clung to her breasts and slim waist, enhancing her generous curves rather than hiding them, her pulse was hammering so loudly, she was afraid he'd hear it.

"Just a minute, darlin'," came his sexy, deep voice.

Balancing the breakfast tray pertly in one hand as she stood on the top step, she smoothed her skirt unnecessarily while she waited for him a little breathlessly. The windows of the trailer gleamed. The grass had been freshly mown. A newly installed window unit hummed.

When Matt finally opened the door, he looked so good in his tight faded jeans and crisp white shirt, her legs turned to jelly and her heart really started knocking double time. Then her mind went so blank, all she could do was stare at him like a mute goose.

"Wow," he murmured, smiling shyly at her as a gust of cool air hit her.

"Wow back," she managed to say, and then her mind fogged over completely. Oh, she was hopeless when she got anywhere near him. Always had been. It was a flaw, and the emotions he aroused in her a mystery.

When he took the breakfast tray from her to carry it to the kitchen counter, their fingertips touched briefly and even that made her sizzle. She followed him meekly, walking very slowly on the shag carpet because her strappy, sling sandals were high-heeled. She wasn't used to such feminine, sexy shoes and didn't want to trip. She'd bought the shoes because the saleswoman had told her they made her legs look longer and sexier and because she really *really* wanted to wow him.

When he set the tray on the counter, he picked up a tattered newspaper clipping and shoved it quickly into his pocket, but not before she'd seen and realized what it was.

He'd cut out the unsigned love letter. He'd kept it.

He *had* written it, but he couldn't tell her. At least not yet.

"You look incredible," she whispered to him.

He turned around, his secretive expression confirming her suspicions. "Hey, so do you."

His voice was so thick and strange, she didn't trust

herself to look at him after that. She felt like Cinderella under a spell in her ball gown.

He'd written that love letter because he couldn't tell her what he felt. Maybe now he wished he hadn't written it. Maybe he'd never admit it.

"Your trailer looks great, too," she added quickly. "You picked all your stuff up. And you got your air conditioner…"

"I vacuumed, too."

"Special occasion?"

"Very—*you.*"

She felt his eyes on her mouth and blushed even before his gaze moved lower to admire how she filled out the green dress.

"Now don't go shy on me, darlin', now that you're here," he whispered. "Pretty dress."

Shy? She was burning up. "I can't believe the trailer looks so great." *Shut up about the trailer.*

"Hey, I wouldn't go that far."

Swiftly she set the table and spread out the homemade biscuits, jam and butter. She took the cover off the frittata.

"Looks good." But he wasn't looking at the food as he moved closer.

She dropped the foil cover and backed swiftly toward the door, her courage deserting her. "Well, I just came by to leave your breakfast," she said. "So, there it is. I—I hope you like it."

"Why don't you stay and eat with me?"

"Errands."

"What are you up to? You got a crush on somebody?"

No, I'm in love with you.

I'm in love?

She couldn't very well say that, so she stared at the floor and said something really stupid. "I hear Carol's back in town."

"I know. She called, and I told her I'd found someone else."

"You did?"

He nodded. For a minute more he was silent.

"Stephanie found your jacket and those pins in the trash yesterday. I just want to know one thing. Did you dress like that this morning for me or some other guy?"

Her feelings were too powerful to admit. She felt as giddily thrilled as she had after he'd asked her to the Spring Fling all those years ago. If only he hadn't snuck up on her and J.K. hadn't taken those pictures and plastered them all over the locker room walls. What if they'd gone to the Spring Fling and had had fun together? What if they'd fallen in love? But they hadn't.

Suddenly, Matt, their history, and the power of her feelings for him now were all too much for her. But before she could run out the door, he spanned the distance and slipped a hand around her waist. His fingers seemed to burn her skin. For a long moment all either one of them could do was breathe.

She told herself she should fight him. When she didn't, he eased her closer.

"I've really gotta go," she whispered, in a panic now.

"No, you don't."

He tilted her face up to his and stared at her a long time before he finally kissed her lips. When he felt her fire, he gripped her tighter. "Don't go. Not when you… Not when I want you more than I've ever wanted anyone." His voice went lower. "I want to hold you and kiss you…and make love to you."

"Now?"

"Now. And all the time."

"We can't do it now."

"Who told you that, darlin'? Mornings are the best time." He brushed her soft mouth with his, coaxing her lips open so that his tongue could enter, kissing her with the intensity of a man who had no intention of stopping.

Not that she wanted him to any more than she wanted to stop the progression of his tanned hands that were gently caressing her breasts and kneading her nipples into hard little berries. When she moaned, he pushed his tongue deeper inside her mouth and snugged her closer against his rock-solid body.

Many kisses later, her breasts ached and she was damp between her legs as he led her silently toward the couch. He kissed her again, and then his hands slipped behind her back. She was shuddering as he began slowly unzipping her dress.

Then her hands were fumbling with his belt buckle, when suddenly she heard the sounds of trucks roaring up on the road outside.

"Damn," he muttered, letting her go.

Big tires crunched, spitting gravel against the metal sides of the trailer. When more rocks pinged as another truck pulled up, Matt looked out the window.

"I don't believe this! Jerry Keith won't ever work on my house, and here he and the guys are—on Saturday."

"Just my luck," she whispered. "Whatever you do, don't let him near your camera."

Matt turned back to her, and she looked into his eyes and saw desire and frustration, yes, truly maybe something far more profound and lasting.

She went soft, feeling in that moment that she was completely his. Again he pulled her closer. Cradling her face, he kissed her tenderly. "Come back tonight, darlin'. After they're gone. I'll cook dinner. Something special for just the two of us."

The feel of his body so hot and strong and hard against hers as he gripped her and stared into her eyes was as intoxicating as the strongest drug. But that wasn't why she wanted to say yes even though she knew she shouldn't.

"Take a chance on me," he pleaded. "I swear I won't let you down." His mouth clung to hers for a breathless moment.

"All right," she finally said. "And I'll bring dessert. What's your favorite?"

"Same as yours. Something sinfully rich and chocolate."

He hugged her tightly for a long time.

Something heavy fell off a truck, and Jerry Keith started cussing.

"Hey, Big Bubba. You gonna sleep all day? We could damn sure use a hand out here!"

Matt drew a deep breath and said, "You'd better go."

"They'll know," she whispered as he zipped her dress for her. "Soon as Jerry Keith sees me he'll think—"

"I don't care," he said, his voice rough and intense with need. "Trust me. This time J.K. isn't going to say one damn word about you and me."

A big fist banged on the door. "Hey, Bubba, anybody home?"

Matt got up and opened the door. When Jane stepped up, Jerry Keith grinned and said, "Well, I'll be damned." Then he caught Matt's eye and said, "Morning, ma'am."

She nodded curtly. Then Matt took her hand and led her to her car. The last thing he said was, "Wear that dress again tonight, darlin'."

"You like it?"

"I like you in it. I like the thought of getting you out of it."

Chapter 10

Matt and Jane were sitting outside on a blanket he'd thrown down on two flat rocks he used as his patio, licking the last of their chocolate mousse from their fingers. The smoke-scented air felt so light and balmy, Jane lay down and stretched. Constellations winked at her through the branches of the live-oak trees. The heat from the golden coals in the chimenea warmed her bare arms and legs.

"The steaks were delicious," she said, turning toward him.

"Your chocolate mousse was definitely the high point."

"I ate too much of everything," she whispered, sitting up again, because lying down beside him suddenly felt too intimate.

Matt leaned closer to her. "As I once heard a guy say in Italy, we've eaten. We've drunk." He reached out and took her hand. Slowly he traced her palm with his callused fingertips. "And now it's time for love."

His words made her shiver. "Out here? On these rocks?" She giggled tipsily as she sipped more champagne. Never had she had so much fun with anyone.

"On these big flat red rocks. Why not? This night was made for it...."

She met his eyes and was momentarily at a loss for words. He didn't push it. His grip tightened a little on her hand, but he waited, as if leaving the momentous decision up to her.

A minute stretched into two. This would not be a light affair for her. The urge to get up and run was all-powerful. Quickly, before she lost her nerve, she put her hands on either side of his face and kissed him. It wasn't a perfect kiss. Her mouth didn't meet his at quite the right place or angle. Their noses bumped. She laughed shyly and he went still, as if still waiting.

She wanted more than an awkward kiss, and her hands slipped around his neck. The second kiss was better. And the third was really something.

"Hey, you're getting good," he whispered as he began combing his hands through her hair.

The wind gusted through the trees and cooled her

perspiring body. And yet she didn't want to cool off. What she craved was heat. When she moaned, he kissed her even harder, stealing her breath away.

"Are you sure this is what you want?" he muttered fiercely, lying down on the large, flat rocks and pulling her on top of him.

"Yes."

"I won't hurt you this time. I swear it."

"I believe you." She didn't quite. But she was tired of playing it safe. She hadn't felt so alive or ever had this much fun. It felt good to let herself go for once. Good to take a chance. Even on wild, lonely Matt Harper.

She was sure he'd written that letter in the *Gazette,* and he'd sent her those flowers. And he was still afraid to tell her he'd written the letter. Which meant she wasn't the only one in this relationship who was afraid. She was tired of letting her fears stop her. Wasn't that what life was all about—taking chances? Could one really ever count on anything? Like the next breath? Love?

She wanted this moment, right now, with him, no matter what it cost her. Slowly she sat up and unzipped her green dress so that it fell to her shoulders. His eyes burned her skin.

"Wow. A black lace bra. For once we're on the same page."

She licked her lips. "Your turn."

"What is this—strip poker?"

"Only without the poker."

He sat up, too, and unbuttoned his shirt. She leaned closer and slid it off his shoulders. After folding it neatly she placed it on the blanket.

"Your turn," he said huskily.

Her hands shook as she unhooked her bra.

"I'll take it from here," he said, removing it for her. Bringing it to his nose, he inhaled her scent.

Before he pulled her against his bare chest, she heard the wind in the trees again and remembered that time he'd snuck up on her with that camera, but as his lips plundered hers, she forgot the past. Gradually she was aware only of the exquisitely sensual things his hands and lips were doing to her now. There was the rasp of zippers, the rustle of more clothing being removed and tossed aside, carelessly now. Soon their hot bodies were entwined.

At first she felt shy and strange and scared, but he was patient and slow and infinitely gentle. She grew accustomed to him. He told her again and again that he thought about her all the time, that he even dreamed about her at night.

"I never knew," she murmured, "that I was anything to you. "Until—" She stopped herself.

"Until?"

"Nothing." Now wasn't the time to discuss the love letter.

"Since those pictures in the locker room, I never thought I had a chance."

"But then you kissed me under the mistletoe," she said.

"It happened before I knew it was going to. Since then I've tried to put it out of my mind."

"Me too."

He kissed her again, and this time he didn't stop. After a while she was no longer aware of being separate from him at all. It was as if they were one. He touched her and kissed her, and she was filled with delicious, warm feelings, and she wanted to feel like this always, to never be a separate being again.

He knew just how to stroke her with his lips and his hands, and how to use his body to give her the most pleasure so that her feelings for him built and built into a roaring flame. He sucked and licked and teased and taught her to do the same until they were both incredibly feverish, and she was aching for even more from him. He carried her to explosive heights of delirious passion.

He crushed her to him, his arms wrapping her tightly, his breathing growing fast and harsh as he whispered tender love words into her hair. Freely, she abandoned herself to him, returning his kisses wantonly, running her hands all over him, urging him, wanting him. When she began to weep, he finally shuddered, and she came too, knowing a fulfilling rapture that until that moment she hadn't imagined.

Afterward they lay together beneath the stars. Her eyes stung with unshed tears as he held her close and slid his fingers into her hair, curling long strands of it around his hand. At last her eyes opened and she stared into his, feeling a powerful, soul-deep connection.

She thought of Carol and was tortured by self-doubt and passionate jealousy. Suddenly Jane felt restless, wanting him again, even now when his breaths were still harsh, wanting him like a cat in heat, wanting him more than before.

"I don't think I can get enough of you," she said, aware that she felt shattered and not quite herself after what they'd shared. More than anything she wanted him to say she was special. "At least not any time soon."

She felt vulnerable, different. If her mother hadn't gotten sick, she would never have come home, never have gone to work for Fortune TX. She would never have made love to Matt.

Jane stroked his dark hair as if he was very precious to her. It was probably ridiculous, but she felt that every moment in her life had been charged with some profound purpose leading her to being with Matt like this on this big, flat rock. Maybe she would have told him that more than anything she wanted to belong to him forever, maybe she would have even asked him how he felt. But just as the words began to form in her mind, she saw lights in the trees, and she screamed at him to get up instead.

"Someone's coming!"

"Damn it." Swiftly Matt pulled her against him and

wrapped them both up in the blanket. "Calm down," he growled, even though he didn't sound the least bit calm himself.

By the time his brother's big truck roared up to the trailer, and Jerry Keith hopped out of it, yelling for his big brother, Matt and she were covered by the blanket.

When he saw them, Jerry Keith grinned. Then he laughed. "What the hell?"

Matt swore. "Get out of here!"

Jerry Keith's insolent smirk vanished. He didn't say another word. He stumbled over a rock as he ran toward and jumped back into his truck. Gravel spun when he backed out of the driveway.

No sooner was he gone than Jane threw off the blanket and began to dress hurriedly.

"You told him I'd be here again, didn't you?" she muttered. "You couldn't resist."

"No. Hey, sit down. Calm down."

"And wait for him to bring the whole town back?"

"You don't have to go, you know," Matt said, but he yanked on his jeans.

She cringed away from him when he tried to touch her.

"We could drink coffee, talk," he muttered.

"Talk? About what?" She felt painfully humiliated. "Your brother is probably on his cell blabbing to everybody he knows right now!"

"Look, I'm sorry he came here," Matt said.

"It'll be just like it was back in high school. You're

the stud, and I'm...I'm...the... What am I?" She couldn't go on.

"Is that really what you think?"

"Did you know he was coming?"

"Hey. Hey. Listen to me. I didn't know. Of course I didn't know. I'm very sorry he showed up and embarrassed you. I'm so mad I could kill him."

She hooked her bra and pulled on her dress. "Where's my other shoe?" she begged desperately. "Where is it?"

He sat down wearily and watched her dig through the high grasses beside the rocks. "I'm not the bad guy this time," he said. Even though he was bare-chested, he didn't reach for his shirt. "Why did you make love to me, Jane?"

"What difference does that make now?"

"Was this just part of some game plan to get the director of market research job? I know you're very meticulous."

She grabbed her shoe and shoved it on her foot. "What? How can you even ask such a question when you and your brother set me up?"

"Is that why you wrote that letter in the *Gazette* that got me going?"

"Me? I didn't write *that* letter. You wrote it! If anybody set anybody up, you set me up!"

"Me?" He stared at her. "Sorry, darlin', but your mother called me up and told me you wrote it."

"What? She told me the same thing—but about you, or rather she told Mindy and Mindy told me. And I believed it was all true after you sent me those flowers."

He lowered his black head. "I didn't really send them," he said even more gloomily. "Carl sent them to Stephanie. They were delivered to you by mistake. When you liked them so much, I paid him back the other day at the watercooler and told him not to tell you."

"And you took credit for them? You let me believe—"

"Like a dope, I thought *you'd* written the letter. I thought maybe *you* liked me…at least a little. I wished I'd sent them. I never expected you to believe me. But you did." His voice was stiff and low. "Now I see you've been playing me for a fool the whole time. You've been leading me on just to throw me off course with sex because you want to be the director of market research more than anything." He paused. "Don't you?" When she didn't answer him, he repeated the question. "Don't you?" Beneath his anger, his deep voice sounded bleak and hurt.

"That's right," she whispered, too embarrassed and furious herself to think clearly. "Believe whatever you want."

"I want the truth—plain and simple," he said.

"No! You want the job—just like I do."

"Blond ambition in action. You're good, darlin'. Real good. You damn sure had me fooled. I thought you were sweet. I thought this was the real thing."

His words cut into her heart as viciously as a blade.

"You Snow women are all alike," he muttered. "Not to be trusted."

"Don't you dare talk about my family. And if it's any consolation, you've got the job. You'll win—like you always do. J.K. will blab, and everybody in town will know that big-breasted Jane Snow was out here making a fool of herself by lying with you naked on these flat red rocks. Oh! I—I can't believe I was so stupid."

"Neither the hell can I," he yelled, his voice even louder than hers.

"Were…were you making fun of me even when you said you sent those flowers?" she whispered. "Did you think I was that pathetic?"

He placed his dark head in his hands. "I never thought you were pathetic. Let's just quit talking. This whole thing is out of hand. Fighting isn't getting us anywhere. Go home. I'll try to track down Jerry Keith. We'll figure it all out later."

"Jerry Keith? You're calling him first thing?" She laughed a little hysterically. "To make sure he gets all the details straight?"

"Shh," he whispered.

Tears ran down her cheeks as she stumbled over the rocks and grasses through the cedar brush country to her car. Matt followed her, but he was barefoot. When he stepped into a patch of sticker burrs and began to hop up and down on one foot, yelping her name, she drove off, leaving him in whorls of dust.

"Hell!"

* * *

"Get your lousy ass back here," Matt roared into the phone as he opened a beer bottle and took a long pull. Fortunately it had been fairly easy to track down Jerry Keith once he remembered where he'd written the kid's new cell-phone number.

"Your girlfriend must be long gone," J.K. chortled.

"If you say one word about her to anybody, I'll kill you—"

"Is your date with her for the Spring Fling on or off or what?"

"One word!"

"Gotcha."

"If you so much as hint to anybody—"

"Gotcha." Jerry's voice shook convincingly.

They fell silent for a tense spell. "I feel like hell," Matt finally admitted. "I've never felt this bad."

He drank the rest of the bottle.

"You've got it bad this time." Jerry Keith laughed out loud.

"What the hell are you talking and laughing about? If you tell—"

"You're in love, Big Bubba. You're finally in love."

"Well, she damn sure isn't! She used me. All she wants is a promotion."

"You sure about that? She's chased you her whole damn life. The whole town knows it. That's what this fight is all about. She's tired of being humiliated by putting herself out there for you. Then I show up and catch her without her clothes on. If you're really in love, you've gotta go the whole way, Big Bubba. You've gotta go down on bended knee and promise her your heart and soul. Get her a big ring. You can't pull your tough, macho, silent routine. You've got to throw yourself on her mercy. Women love that."

"I can't believe I'm listening to you—*you,* of all people!" Matt slammed the phone down and opened another beer.

Jerry Keith called him right back. "You still want me to come over?"

"Hell no! I intend to drink until I pass out."

"I'll be right over! I can't ever resist a party!"

"Don't you dare come—"

Chapter 11

Jane couldn't stop crying when she got home that night. All day Sunday she cried for all the lonely, wasted years. She cried because she'd lost Matt forever. She cried because everybody would know and laugh at her. She cried because he was horrible. She cried because he was adorable. She cried because it was spring and there were wildflowers and all the birds outside were making love. But most of all she cried because the sex had been so beautiful, and Matt had made her feel so special.

Matt. Oh, Matt. Matt. Matt.

Monday when she went to work, her face was very pale. She wore her thick glasses so nobody, especially Matt, would see how red her eyes were. When she passed him in the hall, and he said hello, her idiotic heart leaped with sheer joy. Just the sight of him in his dark suit and that awful, too-bright yellow tie thrilled her *that* much. Not that she showed it. Without smiling or looking up from the beige carpet, she mumbled a terse greeting and skittered to her office where she collapsed at her desk and put her head in her hands.

How she longed for him. How she longed for his hands and his mouth and his body. For him—period! She'd lain awake all last night aching for him physically. Which was insane. He was a louse, a jerk. He always had been. He always would be. J.K. and he had set her up again.

You don't know that for sure, said the voice of reason, which she wasn't about to listen to.

"Jane."

Matt stood at her door. His deep voice wrapped her and made some vital part of her come alive.

"Go away," she snapped even as her heart began to ache and race at the same time. "Leave me alone."

"Look at me," he murmured. "Can't you even look at me?"

"No! I can't! I'm too miserable for words. Okay?"

"Not okay." His voice was soft. "I'm miserable, too."

When he wouldn't leave, Jane finally glanced up into his eyes, which were gentle and mournful and filled with some other powerful emotion she was afraid to believe in. He looked exhausted. There were circles under his gorgeous eyes. She wanted to rush into his arms, to comfort him.

"I'm sorry about Saturday night," he said. "About what I said…to you afterward. I was angry."

"So was—"

"Hello, you two!" Andrea said in a lilting tone as she burst past Matt. "Gorgeous day." As always, she looked slim, energetic and incredibly smart in a simple red suit and a black blouse accessorized by trendy, gold jewelry. "It's great to catch you two together. I needed to let you know that the board is meeting in an hour with their decision. We want *both* of you present."

A beat passed. Jane felt her collar, which she had buttoned all the way to the top, tighten painfully. She felt so faint she was sure all the blood had drained out of her brain.

"All right," Jane said at last, trying to keep her voice steady.

Andrea's smile flashed at Matt. "And, Matt, I have a few things I need to discuss with you before the meeting."

"Sure." Although his gaze clung to Jane's for a few seconds longer than necessary, he nodded.

"Well, then, I'll see you later," he said to Jane as he turned and dutifully followed Andrea down the hall.

When they were gone, Jane got up and shut her door and then leaned against it. She felt her control slipping. Her eyes felt hot, her joints achy.

He'd won!

What shocked her were her feelings about it. She closed her eyes in self-disgust.

She didn't care if he'd won. She didn't care. In fact, she couldn't have borne to see him lose. All she wanted to know was what he would have said if only Andrea hadn't chosen that exact moment to interrupt them. The job didn't matter nearly as much as Matt did.

But it was too late.

"Jane Snow."

Dumbfounded when she heard the CEO call her name instead of Matt's, Jane stood up slowly only to remain frozen in front of her seat, unable to move forward and shake the CEO's outstretched hand. Her mouth fell open in shock.

"Way to go," Matt said. He stood and began to clap loudly for her.

He was grinning from ear to ear. His dark face appeared incredibly happy and dear. He looked pleased— *for her*—sincerely overjoyed *for her.* Was he crazy?

"I—I don't deserve it," she whispered, turning to him. "You do."

"Sure you do," Matt said.

She whirled wildly to Andrea. "You have to give it to him. He would be brilliant."

"We know," she said, looking pleased and smug. "We were just getting ready to call his name, too. You two will make a wonderful team."

Matt took Jane in his arms and hugged her.

"Don't you dare kiss me," she whispered against his ear before they drew apart and tried to act like two grown-up professionals. "Or I won't be able to stop."

"Well, that's good news. The best I've heard in a while."

He let her go, threw back his head and laughed. Soon everybody in the room was laughing with them.

"How about we go to lunch and celebrate, and discuss our plans for the future about the…job?" he said.

She smiled.

Jane was in her office, dictating a letter before dashing off to lunch with Matt, when Stephanie buzzed her and said her mother was on the phone.

"Mom, I've got a lunch date. I can't talk now—unless it's urgent."

"Urgent? It's a nightmare! But it'll only take a minute of your valuable time, I swear!"

Jane sighed.

"You were right and I was wrong," her mother said. "Sweetheart, I won't ever meddle in your life or Mindy's again. I shouldn't have let you think Matt wrote that letter."

"Or led Matt to believe I wrote it."

"So, he told you?"

There was a long silence.

"I just wanted you to be happy, sweetheart," her mother whispered.

"Can we talk about it tonight?"

As usual her mother was too full of herself to listen. "Bad as I was, you'll never guess what Helen Geary has gone and done and set the town in an uproar about—and all because of that same letter."

Jane pressed her temples. She knew better than to even try to guess.

"When Helen called me that morning about the secret admirer love letter and got me all excited because I thought Matt wrote it, which Matt's mother more or less confirmed…and then when I teased him about maybe you writing it and I could tell he was intrigued—"

"Mom, I really do—"

"Okay, I'll get straight to the point."

Finally.

"Helen called me that morning because the letter made her so furious she wanted to brain poor Jim." Jim was Helen's long-suffering husband. "She says there were things in that letter that sounded just like Jim. She told me she's been sure he's gaga over their next-door neighbor, Myrtle, for quite a while. Two days ago she caught him talking to Myrtle in the square. But instead of confronting them, Helen wrote a vicious letter to the editor about the author of the love letter. She accused her husband of cheating on her with their next-door neighbor, and Helen didn't sign her letter either. She very deliberately put references in the letter Jim would recognize.

Well, Ol' Bill printed it, and now the whole town's

in an uproar. Jim's up and left Helen and Red Rock, and
Helen's home crying her eyes out. Lots of people have
been calling Ol' Bill, furious about that original letter,
and each one of them thinks he knows for sure who
wrote it, and it wasn't Jim. Several other husbands have
left town too, and their wives are crying as well."

"Spring Fling mischief and mayhem. Ol' Bill ought
to be happy. Goodbye, Mother."

"But, there's more—"

"I'll drop by tonight. Promise. Oh, and I've got some
great news."

Mariachi music was playing as Jane and Matt walked
hand in hand along the River Walk. The sunshine was
golden in the trees, and the tourists were thick on the
old stone bridges above the river. Not that Jane was
aware of the hustle and bustle or the river traffic as
barges motored past them.

"You know what my wish was on your birthday when
we were here the last time?" he murmured, lifting her
hand to his lips.

She shook her head, aware only of the sizzle of his
mouth on her fingertips.

"That we'd end up like this." He stopped and drew
her into his arms. Slowly he lowered his mouth to hers.

"Don't start. You know I can't—"

He laughed. "I wished that we'd end up like this. Together." He kissed the tip of her nose and even that made her feel a little faint with desire. "Forever."

"Is that what this is?" she whispered. "Forever?"

"Do I have to go down on bended knee, darlin'?"

"Definitely. On two bended knees."

"Here? In front of everybody? This is a very expensive suit."

"I have a better idea," she said, grabbing the end of his yellow tie and tugging him playfully toward the stone stairs to the bridge that led to the street level.

After a short walk in the brilliant Texas sunshine, they stood before the Alamo.

"Here," she said. "In front of the most sacred shrine in the heart of all true-born Texas cowboys. Or at least in the hearts of guys who want to grow up to be cowboys."

A tour bus pulled up and parked beside them, spewing diesel fumes.

"Not to mention ten thousand tourists," he murmured as he ripped off his tie, threw it on the ground as a pad for his knees.

He knelt. "Forever?" he said as he handed her a tiny black box.

She opened it and sank to her knees too. "Forever," she agreed, smiling radiantly at him.

He removed the sparkling diamond solitaire and slid it onto her finger.

She threw her arms around him and kissed him on the mouth.

"Does this mean we have a date for the Spring Fling?"

She nodded happily. "We may be the only couple there."

"Let's get a room at the best hotel on the river and make love all afternoon," he suggested huskily.

He didn't have to ask her twice.

"I love you," Matt said as he lifted her into his arms and twirled her round and round in the breathtaking hotel room fifteen stories above the sparkling river and cypress trees.

"Tell me again," she whispered.

"I love you."

"Now kiss me again."

"Not before you tell me."

"I love you. I always have. And I always will," she said.

When he pulled her closer and began kissing her again, his mouth was teasingly gentle. Even so, she was soon too dizzy to stand.

"I have to lie down," she murmured.

"Great idea." He carried her to the bed, and they went into each other's arms again, petting, fondling, touching, undressing.

Soon they were naked, and he lay beside her, stroking her, his eyes reveling in her voluptuous beauty. When his hands cupped her heavy breasts, and his fingertips circled her dark areolas and nipples, she began to feel pleased with her generous endowments, even proud of them. His tongue laved each breast. Then his mouth went lower, plumbing the delicate nub of flesh with an expertise that made her gasp shyly and then clutch his head closer when she began to throb with desire.

He brought her to the edge before he took her lustfully. He made love to her again and again with a fevered passion that left them weak and spent.

They napped and woke up in each other's arms.

He kissed her mouth lightly.

"I love you," she said.

"Me too." He ran a fingertip down her belly. "Forever," he added. "When you were six and I pulled that ribbon out of your hair and you stuck your tongue out at me, did you realize where it would lead?"

"I don't think I thought much past squashing your cowboy hat.

"Oh, dear." She laughed. "What if our cats don't like each other?"

"Darlin', this is a done deal." He kissed her again.

And, of course, they couldn't stop.

Dear Reader,

What's a self-motivated, big-hearted and independent young woman to do when she finds herself in love with her best friend? How can she make him see that there's more going on between them than friendship? How can she get him to realize that she's through playing "little sister" to his overprotective "big brother"?

It's a tough one. Especially if the best friend and substitute "big brother" in question has painful and deep-seated reasons of his own for not letting himself love his "little sister" as the woman she is.

Luckily, Annie Grant is no quitter. One way or another, she will find the true love she yearns for—whether Greg Flynn will finally open his eyes and see her as a grown woman ready for real love, or not.

And getting Greg to see her as a woman isn't Annie's only problem. There's also her secret admirer, crazed video-store clerk, Dirk Jenkins.

Annie loves Greg and Greg can't deal with it—and in the meantime, Dirk, gone seriously postal, is determined to save Annie from her own "nowhere" life—if he has to shoot someone to do it!

Buckle up, folks—and I do hope you enjoy *Hidden Hearts*.

Best always,

Christine Rimmer

HIDDEN HEARTS

Christine Rimmer

For the boys—Steve, Matt, Jess, Ed and Tom

Chapter 1

Annie Grant regretted two things as she stared down the barrel of the big, black gun.

One: That she never told Greg Flynn she loved him.

Two: That she'd told Dirk Jenkins she *didn't* love *him.*

Dirk was the one on the other end of the gun. His hand shook—and so did the gun. Sweat beaded at his temples and his left eye twitched. "It's all right, Annie," he said in a ragged whisper, sneaking furtive glances right and left. "I know you didn't mean what you said."

It's all right? What was he *thinking?* When a person points a gun in your face, it's *not* all right. Annie cleared her clutching throat and opened her suddenly dust-dry mouth—to say what? Something along the lines of *Dirk, put the gun down, please.*

But before she could get a word out, Dirk commanded, "Don't talk. And come out from behind that counter. Now."

The counter in question was Annie's teller station at Red Rock Commerce Bank. Annie shot a quick look around. The other tellers went about their business, handling late-afternoon transactions. Out on the main floor, customers stood at the high circular counter, filling out deposit tickets and updating checkbook registers, or waited in the comfortable central seating area to speak to a loan officer. No one else seemed to notice Dirk and his gun. It was business as usual—for everyone but Annie.

This couldn't really be happening, could it? Annie gaped at the sweating, shaking Dirk. Keeping her gaze locked on his, she slid her hand beneath the counter and gave the silent-alarm button a push.

There. She'd done it. The Red Rock Police Department had been notified.

Greg Flynn was an officer with the Red Rock PD Annie prayed that he'd answer the call....

But no. On second thought, let someone else come and save the day. She didn't want Greg anywhere near here. Dirk might just shoot *him*....

"Get your hands up where I can see them," Dirk ordered in that scary, raspy whisper. Sweat had begun to trickle from under his spiky straw-colored hair and drip down his sharp-boned, too-pale cheeks.

The good news—the extremely excellent news— was that he didn't seem to have noticed she'd sounded the alarm. Annie sent a little prayer of abject gratitude winging heavenward as carefully, *slowww-ly,* she put her hands up in the air.

That was when Myrna Plotz, the teller in the station next to Annie's, glanced over and saw what was happening.

"Ohmigod!" Myrna let out a shriek piercing enough to shatter glass. "A gun! My God, he's got a gun!"

Big mistake on Myrna's part. Dirk swung the gun her way. "Shut up or you're dead."

Beneath the heavy coat of blusher Myrna always wore, her cheeks went sickly gray. "Omigod! Okay, okay. Whatever you say!" She subsided into pitiful whimpers.

Myrna's shriek had alerted everyone else. They all froze in place. Pens hung poised above check registers. More than one mouth gaped open. Every saucer-wide eye was focused on Dirk.

Lowering the gun a little, Dirk glanced over his shoulder and saw all those terrified faces. "Yeah. That's right. Nobody move," he commanded, and turned back to point the gun, once again, straight at Annie. His dishwater eyes were narrowed to slits. "You, either, babe. Stay right where you are till I say different."

In the tiny part of her brain that *wasn't* expecting any second to be shot in the face, Annie registered that Dirk sounded a little like James Cagney in *Public Enemy.* A movie buff, Dirk worked at the local video store. He'd often tried to amuse Annie with his bad imitations of old-time movie stars.

And look at him now. Playing Cagney again—this time for real. "All a youse behind the counter, get out here where I can keep an eye on ya. Do it now, or one a youse gets it right between the eyes. You too, Annie."

Youse? Annie thought. *Youse.* Oh, God. To be shot in cold blood by a crazed video-store clerk doing a bad Cagney imitation. Did it get any worse? She pondered that question as she and Myrna and the other tellers filed out onto the main floor of the bank.

Dirk turned and shouted at the two bank officers staring wide-eyed from their glassed-in office areas. "You get out here, too, both a youse!" The women rose from their desks and came out into the main room.

"Okay, now," growled Dirk once everyone was assembled. "Everybody flat on the floor, facedown." He waved the gun at Annie. "'Cept you, Annie. You get over here, by me."

Though she'd rather have stuck her hand in a basket of rattlesnakes, Annie moved to Dirk's side. All around the room, folks dropped to their knees and then stretched out, faces to the floor.

"Put yer hands behind yer heads and lace yer fingers, elbows out."

They all obeyed.

"Good. Now, none a youse make another move," Dirk warned out of the corner of his mouth, laying on the Cagney. "Or I'll blow yer brains to smithereens."

"Put that weapon on the floor, young man." It was Mr. Apoupopolis, the bank's security guard. His .45

drawn and pointed at Dirk, the guard emerged from behind a potted ficus tree in the corner.

Bless you, dear, sweet old Mr. Apoupopolis, Annie thought.

But then, in a lightning-quick move, Dirk hooked an arm around her neck and hauled her right up against him. The barrel of that big, black gun dug into her temple. "Drop it. Or Annie's dead."

Oh, great idea. Kill the one you say you love....

Absolutely, positively. This could not be happening. Annie's heart was beating so hard she feared it would punch a hole in her chest. Her knees shook. Her hands and feet felt numb.

"Drop it, I said," Dirk growled. "Now."

Mr. Apoupopolis did as he was told.

"Now kick it over there, against the far wall."

The gun went spinning—away from all the stretched-out customers and bank employees.

"Now get the hell over here and get down on the floor with yer hands behind yer head."

Mr. Apoupopolis moved closer to the others and then dropped down to join them.

Dirk gave Myrna a shove with the tip of his high-topped tennis shoe. "You. Get up." Quivering, making weak mewing sounds, Myrna scrambled to her feet. "Annie." Dirk's hot breath touched her ear. "There's a cloth bag stuck in the back of my belt. Take it out." Annie reached a shaking hand behind him and found the bag. "Give it to Myrna." She passed it to the other teller.

Dirk took the gun away from Annie's head for a moment to wave it at Myrna. "Now, get back behind that counter." Myrna scuttled to do his bidding as he guided Annie around so they faced the teller area again. "Empty those drawers into the bag—and do it fast. No funny stuff."

As Myrna went from station to station filling the bag, Dirk put his gun to Annie's side and pressed his sweaty cheek to hers. "I'm getting us outta here, Annie," he muttered. "You and me. Outta this town. You won't be livin' at your folks' house any longer, working here at the bank, taking lessons in flower arranging. Uh-uh. You'll be with *me*. We'll be outlaws, babe. It's gonna be one wild and crazy ride."

Annie's stomach rolled. She felt her lunch rise toward her throat and had to gulp it back down. Oh, God. Dirk had always been totally harmless—until now. What had gone wrong? Could what she'd said to him yesterday actually have driven him round the bend?

She dared to speak. "Dirk. Please. I told you I didn't—"

"Shut up." He jabbed the gun into her side—hard. "I know you love me, whatever you say." He scowled at Myrna. "Get a move on." Myrna emptied the final drawer and scurried back around the end of the counter holding the bag full of cash. "Here. Give it here."

Myrna whimpered and shoved the bag toward Dirk.

"Annie. Take it." Dirk drilled the gun into her ribs again to emphasize the order. She'd be black and blue there tomorrow—if she lived that long.

She tried, one more time, to get through to him.

"Dirk. Listen, I—" He jabbed her with the gun again. "Ow!"

"You want to draw your next breath, then do like I say."

Annie took the bag.

"Drop," Dirk said to Myrna, who instantly assumed the proper position on the floor. "Okay, babe." Dirk planted a sweaty kiss on Annie's cheek and raised the gun to her temple again. "Let's get the hell outta this dump." He scanned the floor and all the terrified people spread out there. "None a youse move if you want to keep on breathing." Each word dripped with fake-Cagney menace. "Come on," he said to Annie, and hauled her around to face the door.

He was dragging her toward it when a police officer came in through the main vestibule, duty pistol drawn and ready.

It was Greg!

Annie's pounding heart stopped dead in her chest—and then lurched to pounding life again. *How can this be happening?* Annie asked herself desperately for about the tenth time. *This just can't be real....*

Greg had his gun trained on Dirk. "Let her go, Jenkins."

Dirk only tightened his stranglehold on Annie—and turned *his* gun on Greg. "Annie's with *me* now, Flynn. Get down on the floor."

Slowly, Greg shook his head.

"What are you, crazy? I'll kill you, just watch me."

Still, Greg refused to drop. Instead, to Annie's abject

horror, he holstered his pistol and began to stride slowly and deliberately toward her and Dirk.

"Back," Dirk growled, shaking and sweating worse than ever. "Not one more step."

Annie couldn't keep silent. "Greg," she pleaded. "Don't…"

But Greg only kept coming. He looked from the gun Dirk had pointed at his broad chest, into Dirk's eyes and back to the gun again. The strangest half smile curved the mouth that Annie had only last Friday so thoroughly kissed. "Jenkins." He actually shook his head and softly advised, "Give it up."

"Yer dead," Dirk muttered—and fired.

Myrna screamed as a thin jet of water erupted from the barrel of Dirk's gun and wet the front of Greg's khaki uniform.

Chapter 2

"A squirt gun," Myrna marveled, checking her hair and makeup in the magnifying mirror she always kept close at hand. "Dirk Jenkins just held up the bank with a squirt gun!"

By then, two other officers of Red Rock's small police department had arrived on the scene and led Dirk away—to get him the psychological help he so clearly needed, they said.

Greg stayed behind to get the facts as to what had occurred before he arrived. He conducted interviews with Myrna, most of the other employees and several customers.

Mr. Apoupopolis took off his uniform hat and shook

his silver head. "Don't I feel like a damn fool? But that pistol looked like the real thing to me."

A murmur of agreement went up. "Yeah, I would have sworn it was."

"Scared ten years off my life…"

"I thought it was real, and I knew by the look in those shifty eyes that he meant to use it."

"And he did!"

That brought a laugh. Not from Annie, though. She was looking at Greg and he was looking back at her…. She wanted more than anything to run to him, to fling herself into his strong arms. But she didn't. She stayed right where she was. Somehow, now that she knew she wasn't going to die, she was finding it as impossible as ever to show him how she really felt.

He spoke to her, two words: "You okay?"

"Fine," she lied.

And that was it. He looked away and Annie glanced down at her hands. They were shaking. That gun had looked so real! She'd honestly believed for about half a second there that Dirk had killed Greg.

Myrna looked up from her magnifying mirror, lip-stick poised. "So, Greg…" Myrna had gone to Red Rock High and graduated the same year as Greg. She'd always flirted with him every chance she got. Right then, she was shamelessly batting her thickly mascaraed eyelashes in his direction. "How in the world did you know it was only a squirt gun?"

Greg shrugged. "My nephew, Leon, has one just like it."

"Amazing," Myrna simpered, and let out a big fat sigh. Annie tried not to glare at her. Really, she couldn't blame Myrna for going gaga over Greg. The guy was a total hunk—six foot four, shoulders for days, and boy, did he fill out his uniform pants. Females of all ages had always drooled over him and probably always would.

After the interviews, Greg hung around. He drank the bank's free coffee and chatted with Annie's supervisor and with Mr. Apoupopolis. Annie went about her business, acutely aware of his presence the whole time—and also kind of stunned that she was back at her station, handling deposits and withdrawals, everything more or less normal again, when she'd been certain twenty minutes before that by now she'd either be dead or hauled off to Lord-knew-where in Dirk's ancient Chevy Luv pickup.

Annie's workday ended at six. She closed out, grabbed her purse and headed for the door to a chorus of see-you-tomorrows and a quick thank-you from her boss, Aleta Andrews, for having the presence of mind to hit the silent-alarm button at the crucial moment.

Greg fell in beside her. He slipped an arm around to push the vestibule door open for her, then moved ahead to get the outer door, too. "You walk over?" He knew she always did, weather permitting.

She gulped and managed to answer, "Yeah," a heated thrill shooting through her just to be at his side. They emerged into the bright May sunshine and she slanted him a glance. He was looking straight ahead.

Was he avoiding her eyes? Her heart sunk at the

thought. But no. He *was* here. Beside her. He was taking her home. And they *would* talk. She'd tell him…everything.

What was in her heart. What she longed for. What she'd dreamed of practically all her life.

They reached the Blazer with the Red Rock Police Department logo on the side panel. He opened the door for her, as he had done when they came out of the bank. She looked at his strong, tanned hand gripping the door handle, at the golden hairs shining on the back of it….

And memories of Friday night washed over her in a warm, arousing wave. He had touched her everywhere, that same brown hand cupping her breast and then moving lower, causing her to moan and cry out in delight.

She felt the pressure of tears scalding the back of her throat. After all these years, finally, they'd shared a beautiful, unforgettable night.

But then, Saturday morning, everything went wrong.

"Get in," he said.

Annie gulped down the tears and jumped up to the seat. Greg shut the door.

As he'd been doing all weekend and that whole never-ending Monday, Greg Flynn cursed himself for a rotten dirty dog.

He'd taken advantage of Annie in the worst way possible: he'd taken her to bed.

He'd also loved every minute of it.

Couldn't stop thinking about it…

Saturday, he'd tried to apologize, but it hadn't gone so well.

Mentally, Greg called himself twenty kinds of low-down, stinking, sorry-assed skunk. Damn it to hell, he felt so bad, he could hardly even bring himself to meet those big brown eyes of hers—and she didn't seem to want to look at him, either. She stared out her side window. They drove the short distance to her place in a silence so total, it echoed in his ears like a siren's wail.

Annie's mother, Naomi, came flying out of the rambling, ranch-style main house, a dish towel trailing from one hand, when Greg pulled the Blazer into the driveway. Annie barely got her feet on the ground before Naomi was grabbing her and wrapping her in anxious arms.

"Are you okay? Oh, baby. I just got off the phone with Patty." Patty Flynn, who lived two houses down, was Greg's mother—and Naomi's best friend for the past three decades or so. "Patty said that Lou Lynn Brakefield said that Taffy Miers said that Sherrilee Anderson was at the bank today when that strange Jenkins boy came in and—"

"Mom." Annie managed to wriggle free of Naomi's embrace. "Mom. It's okay. Everything worked out all right." She stood back, held her arms wide and looked down at herself. "See? I'm fine."

"Oh, thank the Lord." Naomi shot an adoring glance at Greg. Somehow, to have Naomi look at him like that made him feel like more of a scum-sucking creep than ever. "And Greg, thank God you got over there. Even if that gun wasn't the real thing, everybody thought it was. That crazy boy could have whisked Annie off to heaven knows where. Anything might have happened if you hadn't—"

Greg waved a hand. "Like Annie said. It all turned out fine. Nobody got hurt and nothing was stolen."

Naomi sniffled. "You just get over here," she commanded.

Dutifully, he went to Annie's mother and let her give him a hug. Naomi was a small woman, about five foot one, several inches shorter than her daughter. She wrapped her arms around his waist and squeezed hard. He looked down at her red head—same color as Annie's, but curlier and threaded now with gray. "Thank you," she whispered.

He took her gently by her kid-size shoulders. "It was no big deal."

She gazed up at him as if he'd brought the moon down from the sky and laid it in her little hands. "Thank you," she said again, stepping back, tipping that chin that was so like Annie's to an insistent angle. She swept her dish towel toward the front door. "Y'all come on in. Have some cold tea."

Annie answered for both of them. "Mama, not right now. Greg and I have to talk."

"About the incident at the bank," Greg added too quickly. That drew a startled look from Annie. He slid his gaze away from hers and focused on Naomi. "Strictly routine. But I still have a report to fill out."

"Oh, well, then. Drop by later if you've a mind."

"Thanks," Greg said, keeping it noncommittal. He wasn't in any kind of mood to be coddled by Naomi—let alone having to face Annie's dad, Ted Grant, who trusted him and counted on him to look after his baby girl.

Naomi caught her daughter's hand. "You're sure you're all right, hon?"

"Positive." Annie squeezed Naomi's fingers and then gently pulled free.

"All right, then. All right…" Naomi headed for the door, dish towel fluttering in the warm May breeze. Greg and Annie stood there in the driveway, watching her go to keep from looking at each other.

When she disappeared inside, Annie turned to him. "Come on, then." She sounded pretty grim—not that he blamed her. "Let's go to my apartment."

Annie's place was over the Grant's three-car garage. Ted Grant had built it for Annie's older brother, Hank, the year Hank turned eighteen, so that he could live at home but still have his freedom. Hank had lived there until the accident, seven years ago. And now it was Annie's.

An outside stairway led up to a wide covered landing furnished with wicker chairs, plump cushions and lots of potted plants, all feminine and pretty. All Annie. When Hank had the place, the chairs had been molded plastic, not a potted plant in sight.

Annie led Greg inside.

The moment the door closed behind him, he wanted to spin on his heel, yank it back open and get the hell

out of there. Everywhere he looked reminded him of
Friday- night—the cream-colored sofa where he had
first kissed her, the jut of counter that marked off the
kitchen. He'd backed her up against that counter and…

Don't go there. Get it out of your head.

Annie asked kind of hesitantly, "You want a beer or
something?"

He did. He wanted a river of beer, enough beer to
wash away the too-sweet memories, enough to get himself falling-down, blackout drunk, enough to make him
forget what he'd done—and what he was damn well
never going to do again.

"No, thanks. Not on duty."

"On *duty?*" Her face flushed an angry red. Even the
cute dusting of freckles across her nose looked mad.
She said his name—his whole name. "Gregory Stephen
Flynn. What are you saying to me?"

Defensiveness tightened his gut. "Well, just what I
said to your mom. That I have to talk to you about Dirk
Jenkins and the attempted robbery and kidnapping."

Those brown eyes gleamed with anger. "Excuse me.
You needed to be *alone* with me to talk to me about poor
Dirk and his squirt gun? What makes me so special?
You interviewed everyone else right there in the bank."

Damned if she didn't have a point. But the thought
of questioning her with half the town looking on, and
all those Friday-night memories bouncing around in
his brain… He just couldn't do it. He baldly lied, "I
thought you'd be more comfortable if we talked in private."

"Comfortable." She was looking at him as if he'd just poisoned her old cat, Muffy, who right then came strolling in from the bedroom, thick gray tail held high. Annie scooped the cat up and scratched her behind the ear. Muffy purred in ecstasy, the only one in the room who looked the least bit happy. "You thought wrong," Annie added flatly. She set Muffy down and turned for the kitchen area.

He watched her walking away from him, her slim shoulders back and her head held high, that long, silky red hair swaying with each step.

Greg loved her hair. Always had. Friday night, he'd had his hands in it, buried his face in it, breathed in the clean, warm, sunshiny smell of it. It had poured through his fingers, trickled over his arm, tickled his chest when she—

Stop thinking about Friday night. "Listen. If you'd rather come down to the station—"

She halted at the refrigerator and sent him a frosty look. "You're here now. Let me feed Muffy and we can get it over with."

Dead silence, except for the popping sound as she pulled the ring off the cat-food can, the plop as she dropped the contents into Muffy's bowl, the clunk as she put the bowl on the floor and the tiny meow of glee from Muffy. Annie rinsed the can, tossed it in the bin under the sink, slammed the cabinet door a little harder than necessary and then marched around the jut of counter toward him again.

She flung out a hand in the direction of the couch,

the glass coffee table and the two matching armchairs grouped together near the front window. "Sit down."

He trudged over and dropped into one of the chairs.

Once he was seated, she moved to the end of the couch and perched on the edge. "All right," she said, back ramrod straight, hands folded tight in her lap. "Interview me."

He waded in. "I just need you to tell me what happened. From the beginning."

"There's nothing to tell that you don't already know. Dirk walked into the bank, came straight to my window and stuck a gun in my face. A squirt gun, as it turned out. But I wasn't aware of that at the time."

"What did he say?"

"'Don't move, don't talk'…something like that. He told me to come out from behind the counter. But I didn't, not right away. I managed to push the alarm without him noticing. *Then* he told me to put my hands up. I did. Myrna looked over and saw he had the gun. She screamed—and I think, the rest, you know."

"That's all? Jenkins told you not to move, then he told you to come out from behind the counter—and then to put your hands up?"

She glared at him good and hard before admitting, "There was also something about how he knew I didn't mean what I said."

"'What you said,' when?"

With obvious reluctance, she explained, "After that anonymous love letter came out in the *Gazette,* I started kind of worrying that it might be from Dirk."

Greg blinked. "You never told me that."

"Well, Greg. You know, I don't have to tell you *everything*."

The letter had appeared a week ago Monday and the town of Red Rock was abuzz over it, over who might have written it and who it was meant for. The letter spoke of undying devotion, of a man who wanted one last chance to work things out, a chance to get past misunderstandings.

Greg tamped down his frustration with her. If she'd been worried about Dirk, damn it, she should have *told* him. He prompted, "Go on."

Annie let out a big sigh. "Oh, I don't know. It was only, with the way Dirk looks at me lately, I got this creepy feeling that he'd written that letter to me. And, if you don't mind, could you not get your jaw all knotted up like that? So I've been nice to Dirk, so I've tried to be friendly. Is that some kind of crime?"

At that moment, Greg was too busy wanting to snap Dirk Jenkins's scrawny neck in two to answer.

Annie continued, "He showed up here Sunday…."

Greg could hardly believe his ears. "You invited him *here?*" It came out sounding like an accusation, and hell, maybe it was.

She sent him a huffy look and flipped a swatch of that satiny hair back over her shoulder. "No, I did not *invite* him. He came here all on his own. I sat him down and told him right out that I was sorry if he'd gotten the wrong idea about him and me, but I'd never meant to be anything more than his friend, that I—"

"Hold on." Greg was still back with the part about how Dirk had been right here, at Annie's place. "You let him in?"

"No." She said the word on a rising inflection. "I talked to him out on the landing." She laid on the sarcasm. "Okay with you?"

It was far from okay, but he managed, somehow, to nod. "Go on."

"That's all, basically. I told him yesterday that he had to understand I wasn't ever going to get involved with him in any girl-and-guy kind of way. He left. I thought that was the end of it. I'm kind of thinking, now, though, after what happened today, well…it could be that what I said to him kind of sent him over the edge."

Greg wanted to shake her. "Damn it, Annie. You never should have encouraged that wacko." He probably shouldn't have said that, he realized—after the words were already out.

She scowled so hard, the soft skin around her mouth turned white. "Thank you so much for your input. And I *didn't* encourage him. And what does it matter, anyway, unless maybe you're getting around to blaming me for what happened?"

He sat back. "What the hell? No way."

"Well, you sure do sound like it."

"I'm just trying to get to the bottom of this, that's all."

"Yeah," she said. "Sure." She folded her arms tight under those soft breasts he wanted to touch again—but never would.

Don't look at her breasts, a desperate voice in his

mind commanded. He cleared his throat. "You're saying Dirk claimed he wrote the love letter to the *Gazette*?"

"No. I said I *thought* he did. But he said he didn't. He said he wished he had, though. He said he wished he could—" she closed her eyes, sucked in a long breath "—sweep me up and get me away from here, off somewhere that I wouldn't be living over my parents' garage and working at the bank and…taking flower-arranging lessons over at the Posy Peddler. Dirk seemed to think my life was pretty pitiful." She looked off toward the front window and muttered, "Right at this moment, I kind of agree with him."

What was that supposed to mean? *Keep to the interview,* he thought. "So that was it, then? Today, at the bank, Dirk Jenkins tried to rescue you—from your own life?"

She turned her head his way again and gave him a tight little nod. "The holdup, followed by his taking me and the money on the run with him, was evidently his solution to the problem. I guess." She shifted on the sofa. "Are we done?"

"Just about. I want you to be aware that you would be completely within your rights to press charges."

She let out a scoffing sound. "Against poor Dirk? Oh, please. I just want someone to make sure he gets counseling."

"That'll happen, I promise you."

"Thanks. And now, *Officer* Flynn. You can go."

He knew he ought to do just that. But he didn't.

"Annie, look. I think you're going to have to face the fact that you shouldn't have—"

She put up a hand, palm out. "Stop. I know what's coming. I can see it in your eyes and I don't want to hear it."

He said it anyway. "You know I warned you when you started encouraging that guy. I told you he might get the wrong idea about things."

Her face flushed an angry red. "Uh-uh. I refuse to feel guilty for paying attention to a lonely guy who could use a friend. And I'm sorry, but Dirk's unstable mental condition is just not my fault."

"Annie, if you would only…" He realized he hadn't a clue how to go on.

She asked too quietly, "What, Greg? If I would only *what?*"

He had no answer. No answer at all.

Annie started talking again. And what she said didn't have a damn thing to do with Dirk Jenkins or the incident at the bank. "You know, you do treat me like a kid. You pretty much always have. Until Friday night. And now—ever since Saturday—you act like Friday night was some big mistake."

He looked away. "Annie…" He didn't know what else to say. The silence stretched out.

Annie broke it. "You know what? Thinking I was about to get shot in the head has made a few things crystal clear to me." She paused. After a moment, she said low and intently, "I'm not talking to a man who won't even look at me." So he forced himself to face her.

And she said, "For your information—just in case you somehow managed to forget, I'm twenty-four years old. Yeah, I live over my parents' garage, but I do pay rent. I pay my way, period. I run my own life. I do all this because I am what is known as an adult—and you, of all people, ought to realize that, considering what happened Friday night."

Friday night, Friday night, Friday night. The damn words seemed to echo in his brain. He wished, desperately, that she'd stop talking about it. His wish was not granted. Not by a long shot.

"Get used to it," she said. "It happened. It happened at last. You and me…in my bed together. *I* thought it was wonderful."

"Annie, could we just not—"

She shook her head and kept on talking. "I know you've always told yourself I'm like a little sister to you. You've certainly told *me* that often enough. I know that Hank asked you to…look out for me."

Hank. There. She'd done it. Mentioned Hank.

He didn't want to talk about Hank, not now. He wished he was a thousand miles away from there.

"You *have* looked after me," she said. "You've always been there, whenever I needed you. But I'm *not* your little sister. And it's about time you accepted that." Now there was a tightness in her voice. She seemed to have trouble making herself continue. But she managed it. "If you don't want to…go any further with me, that's your choice. I'll learn to live with it. But you should see yourself. You can hardly look me in the eye.

You're acting like a guilty man, and that's really dumb. There's no reason for you to feel guilty."

So why did he feel like a belly-crawling snake?

"How many times do I have to tell you?" She was pleading with him now, those big brown eyes begging him to understand. "I'm all grown up. I'm a woman and I know what I want. I…well, I want *you,* Greg. But if I can't have you, one way or another, with you or without you, I'm going to find a grown woman's love and happiness."

He spoke around the log that seemed to have gotten itself stuck in his throat. "You think I don't want that for you—love and happiness?"

She made a low sound in her throat. "Sometimes I wonder. Sometimes I think you'd like me better if I'd never had the bad taste to grow up."

"That's not true."

"Isn't it? Then why won't you admit to yourself that I'm a woman now? Why is it you've always acted so strange every time I have a date—and don't shake your head at me. Ever since my first date with Jim Ridley, when I was fifteen and a half, you've treated the guys I went out with like they were borderline child molesters or something."

"I did not. I never did that."

She pinned him with a burning look. "And, you know, I've always wanted to ask, but somehow I never dared. Nobody dares. Nobody ever even mentions it. They know just by looking at you that they'd better not."

"What in hell are you babbling about now?"

"Your Harley, Greg. Tell me, what's with your Harley, anyway?"

He was getting damn tired of this. "I don't have a clue what you're talking about."

"Oh yes you do. You know very well. That bike was your pride and joy."

Why was she doing this? "The damn bike doesn't matter."

"That's where you're wrong. I think it does matter. A lot. And I want to know why, ever since the accident, you keep that bike under cover. You have it all shined up and ready to go. But you never ride it. You haven't in seven whole years. What's the deal with that? Where's the sense in that? A bike should be ridden. But you never ride yours. You keep it tucked away in a dark garage—just like you think *I* should stay tucked away forever, your 'little sister,' seventeen and untouched."

Greg shot to his feet. "That's enough, damn it."

She said very softly, "No. No, it's not. It's not nearly enough."

He couldn't take any more. "I've gotta go."

She wasn't listening. "Things are changing around here, Greg, whether you want them to or not."

"I've gotta go," he said again—in case she hadn't heard the first time—and he turned on his heel and got the hell out of there.

Annie waited until he shut the door behind him to get up and engage the lock. Once that was done, she went back to the couch, sank to the cushions and burst into hopeless tears.

Chapter 3

"Visine," Myrna advised the next day when Annie showed up for work with puffy eyes from crying all night long. "Really gets the red out." She dug around in her huge purse and produced a small plastic bottle. "Be my guest."

Annie muttered, "Thanks. I'm okay," and went back to setting up her drawer.

"Well, I'll tell you this," Myrna said out of the side of her mouth. "I wish he looked at me the way he looks at you."

Annie almost smiled. "Why do I get the feeling we're not talking about Dirk?" Myrna chuckled. Annie added, "You have your moments, Myrna, you know that?"

"You need a shoulder to cry on, sweetie?"

Annie almost said yes. But then she reminded herself that Myrna was constitutionally incapable of keeping a confidence. "I'm okay."

"You keep saying that."

"And eventually, I'll start believing it."

Myrna let out another laugh—a laugh that stopped abruptly as Ryan Fortune himself entered the bank. "Whoa," she whispered, "look who's here."

The Fortunes were the most important family for miles around. They owned a piece of just about everything in Red Rock. Ryan Fortune lived with his third wife, Lily, at the huge family ranch, the Double Crown. In his late fifties, Ryan was still a fine-looking man, broad-shouldered and strong from years of ranch work.

He was also the president of Red Rock Commerce Bank—*and* the CEO of Fortune TX, Ltd.

He strode right up to Annie. "Annie Grant, isn't it?"

Oh, God, she thought, what now? Had she done something wrong? Annie drew her shoulders back and pasted on a cordial smile. "Uh. Yes. Hello, Mr. Fortune. How may I help you?"

He held out his big, sun-browned hand. She stared at it, kind of stunned for a moment—and then she realized he wanted her to take it. So she did.

He gave her a firm shake and, as he released her fingers, a regal nod. "I wanted to personally commend you, Annie, on your quick thinking Monday when that poor kid tried to hold the place up with a water gun."

A *commendation*. Annie forgot her misery over Greg

for a moment and blushed in pleasure. "Oh. Yes. I…well, thank you, Mr. Fortune."

"Call me Ryan."

"Okay, Mr., er, Ryan."

"I understand you're a good worker, always pleasant, always on time. And you had the presence of mind under pressure to get your finger on that alarm and do what needed doing. Damn fine work, and that's a fact. Expect a bonus in your next paycheck."

She stammered out a couple more thank-yous. Ryan Fortune gave her another of those kingly nods and went off to find Aleta.

"Those Fortunes have their moments," Myrna whispered after he was gone. Annie, still feeling the glow of being singled out for a Fortune's praise, thought so too.

When Annie's lunch break came, Myrna handed her a business card embossed with an image of a well-manicured hand wielding a pair of golden scissors.

"Shear Indulgence," Annie read. "That's over on Travis Avenue, right?"

Myrna nodded. "Best salon in town, bar none. Ask for Trixie. She'll do you right. And my advice, whether you want it or not? Use that bonus you're getting to treat yourself to the works. Hair, makeup consultation, manicure, pedicure…"

"Myrna, are you telling me I need a makeover?"

"Honey, take it from an expert. Nothing lifts a girl's spirits like a little pampering and a few new grooming products. When I'm down, I get a do-over. Perks me up every time."

* * *

Greg went on duty at noon that day. He left his house at eleven-thirty through the kitchen door to the attached garage, and found himself pausing on his way out, one foot on the step, one on the concrete floor.

The Harley crouched in the shadows, a low, muscular shape beneath a gray tarp. His killer 1990 Fat Boy. He'd spent every cent he owned to buy that machine, used, way back when.

And then kept on spending as he customized it himself.

Hank had had a bike, too, also used. Extremely used. A '51 Indian Chief. Every free minute they had, it would be the two of them, out in the Grants' big garage, ragging on each other as they rebuilt those machines. Hank said he'd never own anything but his Chief and Greg swore the only real bike was a Harley.

"Best damn time of my life…"

Greg winced as he realized he'd said the words aloud to the empty garage. Things were getting pretty bad when a man started talking to the walls.

He stared at the gray shape in the corner. Annie was right. It was a hell of a machine and deserved to be ridden.

Not by him, though. Even after all these years, the memory of what had happened still ate at him, just kind of gnawed away at his insides. Straddling the Fat Boy, kicking her over, and roaring off down the street… The very thought of that made his stomach churn and his heart pound as if it was about to explode.

Not going to go there. Uh-uh. No, thanks.

Maybe he should sell her....

Something deep inside him rebelled at the thought. But maybe whatever that something was would just have to get over it. She was worth at least thirty thousand. A man could almost buy a new pickup for that. But even as he told himself what he could do with the money, he knew he'd never sell that bike.

Some things you keep, no matter that you'll never use them, no matter that they could net you a nice chunk of change. No matter that every time you saw them, even covered by a tarp, you got a tightness in your chest and a gut-deep ache for a best friend who was gone and never coming back.

Greg pulled the kitchen door closed and pushed the button on the wall beside it. The garage door rattled up, letting in the bright sun and the muggy noontime heat.

He climbed in his old pickup and pulled out into the sunshine, trying not to think of Annie, trying not to wonder if she was ever going to speak to him again.

At first, Annie really didn't plan to take Myrna's suggestion. But then, that night, as she lay in bed, feeling lonely and kind of lost, suffering from the cramps she always got the first day of her period, she remembered what she'd said to Greg when he walked out on her Monday.

Things are changing around here, Greg. Whether you want them to or not.

A different hairstyle and a manicure couldn't exactly be considered a major change. But a girl had to start somewhere.

When she got to the bank the next day, she requested some extra time at lunch. Aleta gave it to her, so she called the number on the card and asked for Trixie.

"Perfect timing," said Trixie as Annie settled into the styling chair. "I had two o'clock free and I just got a couple of cancellations. We've got hours."

Annie laughed at that and caught Trixie's eye in the mirror. "I need that much work, huh?"

"Are you kidding me? You're a cutie."

Annie scrunched up her nose and watched the freckles there kind of fold in on themselves. "Maybe that's my problem. Too cute, not enough sex appeal."

"Sounds like man trouble."

"Please don't ask."

Trixie suddenly looked dead serious. "Honey, I gotta be honest with you. Myrna kind of filled me in." Surprise, surprise. "And I'd already heard about that, er, little incident at the bank the other day."

Annie heaved a sigh. "Yeah, everybody in town's probably heard about Dirk and his squirt gun by now."

"I just hope that Dirk Jenkins gets himself a good shrink."

Annie forced a smile. "The word I got was that Dirk will have all the counseling he needs."

"That's what I like to hear. There's talk he might eventually be released into the custody of his sister. She lives down in Laredo."

"Well, good," Annie said, for lack of anything better.

Trixie braced her fists on her generous hips. "All right, then. Let's get down to it. Makeup, manicure, pedicure…"

"And the hair."

Trixie threaded her fingers up under the heavy strands and lifted them. They sifted down to spread on Annie's shoulders. "It *is* gorgeous."

"You know what? Cut it." A little thrill shot through Annie as she said those words.

"You don't mean…?"

Annie nodded. "Exactly. Short."

Two and a half hours later, Annie left Shear Indulgence feeling pampered as you please. A slight breeze tickled her neck. It was wonderful not to have all that heavy hair weighing her down. And she liked the way it looked, too. Straight and soft and feathery around her face. She thought the style brought out her eyes and accentuated her cheekbones.

Mama would probably have a fit. Annie's mom had short hair herself, but she'd always loved that Annie kept hers long. "You've got the hair for it," Naomi Grant would say. "Stick-straight, thick and so shiny."

Yeah, Mama might be miffed. But she'd get used to it soon enough. Mama was getting better and better about accepting things she couldn't control.

After Hank died, both her mother and dad had become way too protective and interfering. Annie had put up with it for a couple of years.

She'd missed Hank so bad—still did—but she couldn't even imagine what it must have been like for her mom and dad. They say when you lose a child you never really get over it. When you lose a brother, you didn't either; Annie knew that from her own experience.

But Annie still understood that it was even worse for her parents. For a long time, her dad wandered around like a ghost of himself. And her mama would sometimes go whole days without getting out of her bathrobe. So Annie had let them boss her and coddle her because she knew it was something she could stand for a while, something that gave them a tiny bit of comfort in their suffering. Eventually, though, she'd made her stand and gotten it clear to them that they had to let her live her life for herself.

Now, except for the saddest times—Hank's birthday, a little at Christmas, always on the anniversary of the day he died—they were as "over" his death as they were ever going to get.

Greg, though…

In some ways, seven years later, he seemed the least over it of all of them. As if he had doors in his mind and heart now, doors that he always kept shut. And parts of himself that he couldn't even get to.

It—the shutting of those hidden doors—had happened really slowly. At first, after the accident, Greg had seemed the strongest one. They'd made him go to grief counseling and it had seemed as if it had really helped him. Greg and his parents, Patty and Joe, had been the rocks the Grant family had clung to when their lives were one big, terrible shipwreck of unhappiness.

Over time, so gradually you could hardly see the change occurring, things had gotten better. Annie's dad started smiling again now and then. Her mother quit spending the day in her robe with her hair sticking out all over the place.

But Greg…

Well, okay. Maybe he'd had those shut doors inside himself since the accident and Annie just hadn't seen them—maybe she only saw them now because of what had finally happened between them. Or maybe she was totally off base about the whole thing. She wanted Greg and he'd made it painfully clear she wasn't going to have him.

So she was inventing all this stuff about him and the shut doors. If there were shut doors, well, that was something to open, then, wasn't it? Something to break down…

Oh, and why was she even thinking about him anyway?

Today wasn't about Greg. Today was about the beginning of the changes she, Annie Elizabeth Grant, was going to make in her life.

The really cool thing, too, was that Trixie would donate Annie's long hair to be made into wigs for chemotherapy patients. That pleased Annie greatly.

The makeup, though…

It was a little too much, Annie thought as she walked along, a little too sculptured looking. A little too glam.

So she made a quick detour home before returning to the bank. There, in the privacy of her own bathroom, she washed her face and reapplied the blusher, liner, mascara and lipstick Trixie had sold her, but with a lighter hand. She strolled back to the bank feeling pretty good about everything. Definitely the best she'd felt since Saturday morning, no doubt about that.

But then, just as she made it to the parking lot and was heading for the big glass doors, a police-issue Blazer pulled up beside her. Greg leaned across the passenger seat and shoved open the passenger door.

Annie stepped back. "What? Am I getting arrested?"

He looked…she wasn't quite sure. Even behind the dark glasses he wore to cut the bright Texas sun, he still seemed kind of…stricken, maybe. As if he'd just gotten some terrible news. "Get in," he said. "Please. Just for a minute."

She felt her shoulders starting to slump and jerked them back. "Why?"

"Annie," he said, as if that was any kind of answer.

With extreme reluctance, she climbed in and shut the door. "You're blocking traffic." She stared straight ahead. "Better move this thing."

He pulled forward into an empty space, then put the Blazer in park and turned off the engine.

Out of the corner of her eye, she could see his hand draped on the steering wheel. He was turned toward her. But he wasn't saying a word. The black police radio in the dash crackled. A voice gave instructions.

Annie tipped her head toward the sound. "Shouldn't you get that?"

"It's not for me."

Another voice came on. There was a quick exchange and then silence. Annie gave up staring straight ahead and looked at Greg. "So? The minutes are passing and you haven't said anything I needed to hear."

He took off his hat, dropped it on the console between them and shook his golden head. "What the hell did you do to your hair?"

She gaped at him. "You know, that is about the rudest thing I've heard all day. And is that why you're wearing that low-down, brokenhearted expression— because you hate my hair?"

He took off the shades and tossed them on the dash above the steering wheel. "Look. It's just…it's fine. It shocked me, that's all."

"You are such a bad liar."

Those blue eyes shifted away, and then back. "I'm not lying."

"You hate it."

"Hell, Annie…" He was the picture of manly misery. "It's only…did you do that to yourself because of me?"

She'd heard about enough. "Excuse me. I didn't *do* anything to myself. I got a haircut. People get haircuts all the time." She ran her hand over the short, feathery strands. "And you know what? I happen to like it. I think it looks *good* on me."

He kind of squinted at her, and then shook his head. "It's not that it looks bad."

"Gee, thanks."

"It's only…"

She waited for him to finish. He didn't. She reached for the door handle.

"Damn it, Annie. Wait."

"For?"

"Look…"

"Any time you're ready to actually say something, just let me know."

"It's only that I keep thinking…"

"What?"

"Well, why can't we just go back to the way it used to be between us?"

The way it used to be…

Greg, the big-brother figure—Annie the adoring "little" sister. They'd go to movies together, hang out at the lake. Play pool sometimes over at that roadhouse right outside of town. Greg would always win. Sometimes— like last Friday night—they'd rent a movie and watch it at her place, a huge bowl of popcorn on the couch between them, his hand bumping hers when they both reached in the bowl at the same time.

Greg and Annie. The way they used to be. Everything fun and innocent, the only kisses the occasional peck on the cheek.

And then, maybe, as he had two years ago, he'd find someone special, start taking her out. Break Annie's heart all over again. Two years ago, he'd even gotten engaged. Her name was Heather Delmasio. Greg had known her since middle school. She was sweet and pretty, a really good person. But it didn't matter how sweet and good Heather was. Annie had hated her for having Greg as her guy—hated her, and despised herself for feeling that way.

In the end, it hadn't worked out between Greg and Heather. Heather had moved to Corpus. And Annie and Greg had gone back to their just-like-brother-and-sister act.

The way it used to be…

Impossible. And he really ought to know that. "Because it's *not* the way it used to be," Annie said. He looked so lost and sad, she couldn't help softening toward him a little. "That's it?" she asked, gently now. "That's what you wanted to talk to me about? You and me, going back like it was?"

After a moment, he nodded. "Yeah. I miss you, damn it." What was she supposed to say to that? Before she could come up with something constructive, he added, "I feel like the world's biggest jerk, you know."

"Well, my advice on that would be, stop it. As I've already told you about a hundred times, I did what I wanted to do. And now *you're* doing what *you* want to do. Period. Over. End of story."

He kind of leaned toward her. She saw such confusion in those beautiful blue eyes—and also a certain spark that made heat flare down inside her. He sank back to his own seat. "I hate this."

What could she say? "Yeah, well…me, too." She reached for the door handle again. "I'd better go."

Now he was the one looking straight ahead. "Guess so."

"Greg?"

He made a low noise, just to let her know he was listening, though he continued to stare at the adobe facade of the bank as if there was something totally fascinating about it.

She wanted…oh, she didn't know. To ease his misery a little, she supposed. She *loved* him. Even if he couldn't let himself love her back except in a brotherly way, she wanted the very best for him. She told him, keeping her voice gentle and low, "You've always been too hard on yourself about things, you know that? Sometimes you act like everything that ever went wrong in this world is your own personal fault. But it's not. It's just not."

He turned toward her then. What she saw in his eyes melted her midsection and got her heart going in a deep, heavy rhythm. She stared at him and he stared at her and she wondered how he could lie to himself the way he did. How could he even think that they might go back the way they'd been?

He said her name, on a breath. "Annie…" And, so slowly, he leaned her way.

She waited, heart pounding, every nerve burning. Knowing he was going to kiss her. Not quite sure that she would kiss him back—but wanting to.

Longing to…

The scent of him came to her: soap and manliness and a hint of aftershave.

"Greg," she whispered.

And then, without warning, he jerked back into his seat. He swore low. "Sorry. So damn sorry."

"See?" She leaned on the door and it swung open. "You just proved it. You just showed yourself why we can never be the way we were." She swung her feet to the blacktop and got out. "We *aren't* the way we were. And we're never going to be again."

Shoving the door shut, she turned for the bank. She walked fast. And never once did she look back.

Chapter 4

After work, Annie dropped by the main house to deliver the pound of coffee her mom had asked her to pick up on the way home. Her folks were sitting at the kitchen table, eating their evening meal, when she walked in.

At first, there was dead, stunned silence as both of her parents stared at her—specifically, at her hair.

And then her father cleared his throat. "Why, Annie. You look…beautiful. Just beautiful."

Right about then, her mother dropped her fork and burst into tears.

"Naomi? Sweetheart?" Her dad had that look he always got when her mother became emotional—as if he wanted to make it all better but he didn't have the faintest idea how.

Annie set the coffee on the counter, whipped a tissue from the box that waited on an open shelf and rushed to her mother's side. "Here you go, Mama."

Naomi snatched the tissue with a sob. "Oh. Oh, my." She wiped her eyes. "Why am I doing this?" She sobbed some more.

Ted Grant unfolded his long, thin body from his chair. He stood six foot five, even taller than Greg, and towered over his tiny wife. "Ahem. Well. I'll just leave you two ladies alone for a few minutes, I think."

Naomi waved her tissue at him. "Sit right back down, honey. Your food'll get cold." Annie's dad dropped into his chair again and Naomi commanded, "Just eat. Eat."

So Ted Grant dutifully picked up his knife and fork, sawed off a bite of pork chop and stuck it in his mouth.

Annie knelt by her mother's chair. "Better?"

"Oh. Oh, yes. It's only…" She reached out a hesitant hand and touched Annie's hair. "My, my," she said in a kind of wonderment that managed to be both infinitely sad and happy at the same time. "It does suit you."

Annie beamed up at her. "Whew. Had me worried there for a minute."

Naomi waved her soggy tissue again. "Yes, well." She took a moment to blow her nose. "It does kind of make me realize. You're not my little girl anymore."

"Sure I am, Mama. But maybe just not quite so little—and more a woman than a girl."

"Yes. That's so true. And isn't it crazy? But when I looked up and saw you standing there in the doorway,

I remembered that time Hank took you for your first ride on his motorcycle. You had on a helmet, but when he rode off with you, your long hair was streaming out from under it, blowing in the wind."

Annie felt her own eyes filling. "Yeah. That was the first time he got the thing started. He was so proud."

Naomi swallowed a sob. "He was. Oh, he was."

Annie surged up and wrapped her arms around her mother. "It's hard, huh?" she whispered.

Naomi made a tight sound in her throat and hugged Annie back. When they broke apart, they both looked across at Ted. Annie gave her father a big brave smile. "Okay over there, Daddy?"

Her dad put down his fork. "I remember that day, the first day Hank got that old bike going. Not a day goes by I don't…" He paused, swallowed. "You know, you two'll have *me* bawling if you keep this up."

Naomi dabbed her eyes some more and looked up at Annie. "Sit with us. Eat. There's plenty."

Annie hesitated. "I've got my class in half an hour. And I have to go up and feed Muffy."

"Just sit with us then, for a minute or two."

Annie glanced at the clock on the wall over the stove. She did have a few minutes to spare. "I might have some applesauce."

Her mother beamed. "Yes. Good idea."

So Annie washed her hands, got a bowl and a spoon and sat down with her parents. They talked of the big neighborhood barbecue coming up that weekend, and of the Red Rock Spring Fling, the weekend after that.

The annual neighborhood barbecue was always held around the corner in Crockett Park. Annie was doing the tables for that—crepe-paper flowers and checked tablecloths, nice and casual and bright.

When her mother mentioned Spring Fling, Annie couldn't help thinking how she'd always dreamed of someday attending the Fling on Greg's arm. And not as his "little sister," but as his date.

Never going to happen, she reminded herself, and tried not to let herself feel low about it.

Her mom was watching. "Annie, hon, why the long face?"

She smiled wide. "Long face? Not me. And Mama. Daddy…" They both looked at her expectantly. She forged ahead. "I've been thinking of making a move. You know, shaking things up a little. Trying something new. I'm considering San Antonio, or maybe even Dallas."

Later, at the Posy Peddler, as she learned to make really cute, inexpensive mini-arrangements using a champagne glass as a vase, Annie congratulated herself on how well it had gone with her folks.

Her dad had gotten kind of misty-eyed and her mom had required another tissue, but they'd both promised to support her, one hundred percent, in anything she decided to do.

It would be quite a change.

For her whole life up till then, Annie had never considered living anywhere else but Red Rock. She loved her hometown and she'd always pictured herself there—getting married, having kids. But in her dreams, it was Greg she married, Greg who was the father of her babies. In her dreams, she'd never given up hope that the day would come when he'd finally see her as a woman, when he'd ask her out for real and they could get started on the rest of their lives…together, in the truest sense.

Without him, well, life was too short to hang around in her hometown, wishing.

And hoping…

And after what had happened Monday with poor Dirk and the squirt gun, she kept asking herself, what if it had been a *real* gun? What if Dirk had actually shot her?

You just never knew what might happen in life, and if she ended up dying too young the way Hank had, she wanted to go knowing she'd taken a few chances, that she'd gotten out there, seen the big wide world a little. If she couldn't spend her life at Greg's side, she simply wasn't going to waste it hanging around in Red Rock, mooning after him.

And both San Antonio and Dallas had whole schools dedicated to the study of floral design. She could take more classes, get a broader range of expertise. And her dad had said he and her mom would definitely help her when she opened her shop—whether the shop ended up in Dallas, or right there in Red Rock.

So, then. Onward and upward and she wasn't looking back.

That night at home she spent two hours on the Internet, checking out the options for floral-design training in Dallas and San Antonio. And Thursday, at work, she talked to Aleta. The Fortunes had banking connections all over the state. It was just possible that she could have a job set up and ready to walk right into, wherever she decided to go.

Aleta said how she'd hate to lose Annie, but she did understand how Annie might want to broaden her horizons a little. She'd check into what was available statewide and get back to Annie in the next week or so.

Then Aleta held up that morning's *Gazette.* "Did you happen to get a look in the paper today?"

Annie hadn't.

Aleta handed it over. The squirt-gun holdup had made the bottom of the first page. Terrific, Annie thought glumly. Dirk and his squirt gun were getting almost as much attention around town as the ongoing mystery of the unsigned love letter.

"See here?" Aleta rose from her desk and pointed to the third paragraph. "You're mentioned by name. 'Bank teller Annie Grant helped to thwart the would-be felon by pushing the silent alarm that brought Officer Gregory Flynn to save the day.'" Aleta wore a pleased little smile. "Very nice, don't you think?"

Annie stared at Greg's name, right there in black and white, and a wave of sadness washed over her.

But no. Sadness wasn't going to bring her down.

Things were shaping up. They definitely were. And whenever Annie started to get feeling low over Greg, well, now she had a different future to start looking forward to.

It wouldn't be the life she'd always imagined. But

maybe it was time for her to start dreaming a whole new kind of dream.

Dreams.

Greg was having too damn many of those.

Most of them featured Annie doing things with him—and *to* him—that weren't the least bit sisterly. He was waking up running sweat and rock hard three or four times a night.

And when he wasn't dreaming of Annie, he was dreaming of the accident seven years ago, of him and Hank, flying down that farm road, laughing, engines roaring, side by side.

Of that split second that lasted for an eternity, when Hank shot him the high sign and turned back to the road, where a fuzzy little possum had appeared out of nowhere…

Greg would wake sweating from those dreams, too.

Insane. He hadn't dreamed of the accident in years. Why now, all of a sudden? He knew why, of course. Because of Annie. Because of what had happened between them, because of the way everything had gotten so completely messed up.

The dreams—of Annie and of the accident—had to stop. Too bad Greg couldn't figure out a way to make that happen.

By Friday, he was a wreck. He needed a shot of caffeine every couple of hours just to stay alert on the job.

About eleven that morning, he pulled into Karol's Koffee Kup to get himself a much-needed jumbo coffee—lots of sugar, hold the cream. Karol's had a narrow glassed-in entryway where folks were always piling up on each other. Greg pushed through the door, eager to get the caffeine and get back out to his Blazer.

Just inside the entryway, he bumped into Ol' Bill Sinclair. Bill, white-haired and wiry with a perpetual gleam in his eye, helped run the *Gazette*.

"So how's the town hero doing today?" Bill asked.

Greg grunted. He'd seen the article the day before. "If you're referring to what happened at the bank Monday, don't."

"You gotta admit, it's one hell of a story. You took it right in the chest, and saved the day."

"I knew it was a squirt gun, Bill," Greg said wearily.

Bill chuckled and clapped Greg on the shoulder. "Well, from what I hear, it was a hell of a moment. Wish I'd been there."

"And we're blocking traffic," Greg suggested, wanting nothing so much as to move along.

"Got a point there. Catch you later." Bill went on by.

Greg made the mistake of turning to watch the older man go—and plowed right into someone else.

"Excuse me, I—" He reached out to steady the very pregnant woman he'd almost knocked over—and saw who it was. "My God. Heather…"

His ex-fiancée put her hand on her huge stomach and gave him a big smile. "Greg. How've you been?"

An image of Annie's sweet face flashed through his mind. I've been awful, he thought. "Great," he said. "Terrific. You're back in town?"

Heather shook her full head of black curls. "Just a visit. Seeing my mom."

He spotted the ring on her finger. "I heard you got married. And now, here you are, a baby on the way. Good for you."

Heather nodded, her face kind of glowing. "Yeah. Lots of changes—good ones."

"*If* you don't mind," said an impatient voice behind him.

"Uh. Sorry." Greg turned toward the man who'd spoken, tipped his hat and stepped to the side.

Right then, behind him, Heather let out a cry. He whirled back to her. "Heather?"

She was clutching her big belly—and she wasn't smiling anymore.

Greg grabbed her arm again. "Here. Sit down."

Heather only held on tighter to her bulging stomach and cried out again.

"Heather, oh my God!" Heather's mother, Leah Delmasio, emerged from the main part of the restaurant and rushed to her daughter's side.

Heather panted. "I think…oh!" She blinked and looked down over her huge stomach, past the hem of her skirt. Water trickled along the insides of her legs.

With sirens blazing, Greg drove Heather and her mother to San Juan Hospital, a sprawling medical facility on the outskirts of San Antonio. Once they'd checked Heather in, Leah followed after her daughter to see that the nurses made her comfortable. Greg waited a few minutes and then decided there was no reason to hang around.

He was just turning to go when Leah reappeared.

"Thank you, Greg," Leah said solemnly, looking up at him through black eyes very much like Heather's.

"Is she all right?"

Leah actually smiled then. "At the moment, she's not feelin' so hot. But once she's had that baby, she'll be fine."

"Her husband…?"

"I'm going to call him right now."

"Good. Well, then, give her my best. And my congratulations. On her marriage—and on the baby, too."

"I'll do that—and Greg?"

"Yeah?"

"She *is* doing fine, you know? Happy. In love."

"I'm glad for her."

"So when you gonna marry that sweet little Annie Grant?"

Greg blinked and stepped back. "I, uh…"

Leah Delmasio grinned wide. "Don't look so shocked. Heather told me all about it, back when you two split up."

"Told you…?"

"You know. That you were already taken. That she wanted her *own* man."

What Greg wanted was out of there. Fast. "Uh, well. Mrs. Delmasio, I really have to—"

Leah leaned closer and pitched her voice to a volume fit for sharing secrets. "I got a few words of advice for you, Greg Flynn—advice from a woman who's been married forty years, every one of them worth it, with six sons, two daughters, fourteen grandchildren, number fifteen on the way."

"I, uh—"

"Get married. Be happy."

Greg only stared at her.

Leah Delmasio clucked her tongue. "Well. Better make that call. My daughter wants her husband."

"Uh. Yeah. Good idea."

Leah pulled a phone from her purse as Greg shook himself, turned on his heel and headed for the exit—fast.

Chapter 5

"Hot dog?" Greg asked, flipping back the smoker lid and gesturing at the open grills flanking it. "Ribs?"

Naomi considered. "Give me some of that chicken, I think—a drumstick."

Greg forked the chosen piece off the smoker grill and carefully set it on Naomi's plastic plate. "There you go."

"Looks perfect."

Crockett Park was packed with neighbors, friends and family. Annie, the one-woman decorating committee, had done up the borrowed folding tables in red, white and blue and strung little lights from the oaks and cottonwoods, so that later, when it got dark, the party wouldn't have to end. Bernie Bell, who owned the video and music shop where Dirk Jenkins used to work, had provided the sound system. Country music filled the late-afternoon air.

Greg shut the smoker lid and gave Naomi a wink. "My dad's own special sauce."

"Joe's sauce is always the best." Naomi granted him a sly little smile. "Heard you saved the day again yesterday."

He grunted, thinking of Heather groaning in the back of the Blazer behind the safety screen, of Leah's calm voice offering reassurances. "Not a big deal."

"A little girl, I heard—and they named her after Leah."

"Good choice."

"Lucky Leah." Naomi sighed. "So many beautiful grandchildren…"

"Yeah," Greg agreed, his thoughts going straight where they shouldn't: to Leah's unsolicited advice the day before.

So when you gonna marry that sweet little Annie Grant…?

"Annie did a beautiful job on the decorations," Naomi said, and Greg tried not to look startled and guilty at the mention of her name—especially given what he'd just been thinking. "She's a treasure, that daughter of mine." Naomi was staring off in the direction of the park's central natural-rock fountain, where Annie stood with a girlfriend, observing the antics of two of Greg's nephews.

Dougie, Greg's sister's boy, was chasing Leon,

Greg's older brother's son, around the fountain, shooting him with one of those huge, Day-Glo-colored water guns. Leon had the now-famous squirt gun, the one that looked just like Dirk's. He was darting low and turning to shoot, outgunned by his cousin's massive plastic weapon and not seeming to care in the least.

Annie laughed, the sound bright as bells, as Leon's shot found its mark at last and Dougie let out a fake cry of agony and then shot him right back. Greg stared— and not at his nephews. Annie's hair gleamed in the sunshine that speckled down through the sheltering oaks. He still couldn't quite believe she'd gone and cut it. And okay, he supposed the new style looked fine on her.

It was only…

Damn it, she'd always worn it long, trailing down her slim back, straight and shining.

"The new cut looks good, I think," said Naomi, and Greg got the creepy feeling that Annie's mother might be reading his mind or something.

He shot her a look and she smiled sweetly back at him. "Yeah," he said. "It looks real nice."

"Changes." Naomi sighed again. "Guess you can't stop them from happening, huh?"

What could he say? "Guess not."

"And now she's moving away. Of course, I understand. Young people want adventure, to try new things." Naomi leaned closer. "But I'm hoping she'll settle on San Antonio. There, she'd only be a skip and a jump to get back home for visits."

Annie moving? Leaving Red Rock?

He must have looked as stunned as he felt, because Naomi laid her little hand on his arm and asked softly, "You didn't know?"

"Nope."

Naomi chuckled. "And here I thought she told you everything."

She did—until recently.

Naomi added, "Well, if she asks for your opinion on the move, do me a favor and recommend San Antonio."

He hardly heard what Annie's mom was saying. He just couldn't believe it. Annie wouldn't leave home.

"Greg? Did you hear me?"

"Uh. Yeah. Sure. Will do."

Right then, two of his nieces came racing up, clamoring for hot dogs.

"Thanks," Naomi said. She headed for the table a few yards away, where Ted was already tackling a plateful of barbecue.

Greg stared blindly after her, feeling sucker punched. Annie leaving town? No way. Impossible...

"Uncle Greg, come on. Hot dogs, please!" His nieces held up their plates.

Greg served them—and all the friends and neighbors who quickly lined up behind them.

An hour after Naomi dropped the bomb on him about Annie, Greg's brother Joey finally showed up to relieve him at the grills. Greg grabbed a beer and started looking for Annie. He found her at the lemonade stand a couple of neighbor kids had set up under a cotton-

wood in the northwest corner of the park, near the
street.

"This is *so* delicious, Mary Lee," Annie said. She took
a sip from a paper cup. "Mmm. Really hits the spot."

Mary Lee Jurgenson, a budding ten-year-old entre-
preneur, suggested, "Have another one, then. Five cents
off for a refill."

"You know, I believe I will." Annie handed over her
cup.

The other girl, Pansy Farquest, refilled the cup while
Mary Lee took Annie's change and dropped it into a
shoe box painted pink and decorated with glued-on buttons and seashells.

About then, Mary Lee spotted Greg. "Officer Greg.
Get your lemonade. Only twenty-five cents a cup."

Annie turned and saw him and he got that funny
feeling in his stomach—the one he was always getting
when she looked at him lately.

Mary Lee kept pitching. "Best lemonade in the
whole wide world."

Greg realized he was kind of gaping at Annie and
made himself turn to Mary Lee. "Sorry, Mary Lee." He
held up his longneck. "I've already got a beer."

Mary Lee wrinkled her button nose. "What do you
want with an icky old beer when you can have the best
lemonade in the world? Fresh-squeezed, too—ouch!"
Pansy had elbowed Mary Lee in the side. The two girls
whispered together, then Mary Lee confessed, "Okay,
it's not fresh-squeezed. It's from a can. But it *tastes* like
fresh. Just ask Annie."

"Truth in advertising," said Pansy solemnly. Mary Lee gave the other girl a sour look.

Annie spoke up then. "Best lemonade I ever tasted. Bar none." She sent him a glance from under her lashes, kind of teasing and watchful at once.

He wanted to grab her and…

No. Better not go there.

Three pair of feminine eyes were watching him.

"You could drink the lemonade *after* you finish your beer," Mary Lee suggested.

Greg realized he was outflanked, not to mention out-maneuvered. "Yeah," he agreed grudgingly. "Guess I could."

"Better buy it now, though," Mary Lee warned. "It's going awful fast." He imagined it probably was, with Mary Lee strong-arming anyone who walked by. "We might run out by the time you came back over here."

So Greg handed Mary Lee a quarter and Pansy poured him a cup of lemonade.

Mary Lee advised, "If you want more, bring your cup back. Five cents off for a refill."

"I'll keep that in mind," he answered dryly. He turned to Annie—and saw she was walking away. "Hey. Wait up."

Annie paused and turned back. The look in her eyes warned him—of what, he wasn't quite sure. "Yeah?" she said when he caught up with her.

He didn't know where to begin. "You eat yet?"

She shrugged.

He prodded, "Yes or no?"

She answered reluctantly. "No."

"Well, how 'bout we go fill up a couple of plates?"

She looked at him for a long, distinctly uncomfortable moment. It wasn't that hot out but he started to sweat. Finally, she said. "And?"

"Hell," he said. "Eat."

She considered his suggestion as he stood there feeling like a fool, lemonade in one hand, beer in the other. After about a year, she shrugged again. "Sure. Why not?" She turned and headed for the double row of tables near the barbecue grills.

Since he didn't know what else to do, he followed, trying not to spill the lemonade—and also not to let himself stare at her backside. She really filled out the pair of snug white shorts she was wearing.

He realized he'd made a mistake to let her do the leading when she marched right over to the table where her parents and his parents were sitting together. He'd been picturing a private talk. He'd figured he'd get it out of her about the move she was planning, and explain to her that it would be a bad decision. How could he do all that with his mom and dad and Naomi and Ted sitting right there?

"Got room for us?" Annie smiled wide enough to take in the whole table. A murmur of welcome went up from the two sets of parents.

There was a space on either side of the table. Greg scowled. He wouldn't even be sitting beside her. Which was fine. What the hell did it matter if they sat side by side or not?

It didn't. Didn't matter in the least…

They set down their drinks and went over to the grills and the serving tables to load up their plates. When they returned, they slid into their seats and picked up their plastic forks and dug in.

The talk at the table was easy and general. Ted and Joe planned an upcoming weekend fishing trip. Naomi and Patty discussed the burning question of whether or not Naomi should get new curtains for the den. All four of them—Patty, Joe, Ted and Naomi—joked about the upcoming Spring Fling, where every year something inevitably went crazy or wrong. They wondered aloud what scandals and disasters were in store this year.

Annie and Greg were mostly silent.

He noticed she wasn't eating a lot. Annie loved barbecue. As a rule, she could really put it away.

But not that day.

Greg wasn't eating much, either. He finished off his beer and got up to get a second one.

Annie said jokingly, "Hey. What about your lemonade?"

What the hell did she care? He didn't want any damn lemonade, never had wanted it, and she knew he hadn't. He realized he was furious with her. Just hopping mad. And then he realized how out of line that was. He looked in her eyes and that funny, scary feeling tightened his gut again.

What the hell had happened to him? Lately, he couldn't even take a little kidding.

But then, he *knew* what had happened.

That Friday night.

"I'd rather have a beer," he said, careful to keep his voice even. Then he headed for the coolers.

When he came back to the table, Annie was getting up—and taking her mostly full plate along with her.

"Where you goin'?" he demanded.

Annie ignored his question. "See y'all later…" She turned and walked away as a series of sharp looks zipped around the table—Naomi to Ted and Ted to Joe, Joe to Patty and Patty back to Naomi again.

Greg scooped up his own plate and followed behind her. She was moving pretty fast. He had to lengthen his stride to catch up with her.

"Hey. What's the hurry?"

She sent him a peeved sort of look and kept walking.

"Annie. Come on…"

She stopped stock-still, though she didn't look at him. Out of the corner of her mouth, she said, "What do you want?"

He hardly knew where to begin. "Well, I…"

She turned and faced him, dead on, tipping up that soft little chin. "Excuse me. Was that supposed to be an answer?"

He fisted his hands to keep them from grabbing her. "We have to talk."

She let out a laugh. It was not a happy sound. "You're something, you know that? Lately, you're always telling me how we have to talk. And then, when it comes down to it, you've got nothin' to say I haven't heard before—well, except about my hair. That was new and different. And not the least appreciated."

He knew everyone within a twenty-foot radius was watching. And he felt about two inches tall. "Look. In private. Okay?"

Her mouth pursed up tight. "Private?"

"Yeah."

Her narrowed eyes seemed to bore twin holes right through him. "All right. In private." She whirled and started walking again, out of the park, toward the street. Shaking his head, he followed after.

When she passed a trash bin, she tossed her still-full plate and her paper cup into it—hard. He did the same with his plate and the beer. She hit the street and walked even faster. He kept up, a step or two behind, trailing her down around the corner and up the block where she lived.

At the Grant house, Annie tore up the driveway and around to the stairway on the side of the garage. She pounded up those steps as if the devil was on her tail.

I guess that devil would be me, Greg thought bleakly.

She yanked back the screen—he caught it before it could slam in his face—and shoved through the door. Greg went in right after her, but a lot more quietly. Gently, he pushed the door shut.

They faced each other, both of them breathing hard—and really not from exertion.

"Rrrreow?" asked Muffy from her favorite spot on the sofa. The cat purred so loud, Greg could hear it where he stood by the door.

Annie stalked over there and picked Muffy up. She cuddled the cat close and scratched her under the chin. "Okay," she said tightly. "Go ahead. Speak."

Speak. It was something you'd say to your dog. Anger curled through him again, hot and dangerous. He quelled it, raking off his hat and hooking it on the coat-rack by the door. "Your mom tells me you're moving away."

Muffy squirmed. Annie let the cat down. Muffy strutted around the couch and back to the bedroom. Annie watched her go, looking up only when Muffy disappeared from sight. "Yeah." Her eyes gleamed, defiant. "I'm moving. So?"

"Well…"

She plopped down on the couch. "There you go with the 'wells' again. I don't think you've started a single sentence without that word at the beginning of it—not in the past week or so, anyway." She stared off toward the front window, refusing to look at him.

"I just want to know why you've suddenly decided to leave town."

That had her snapping her head around. She glared at him as if he didn't have a brain in his head. "Let me put it this way. I think it's time for a change."

He dared to approach her. She watched him coming, mouth set, eyes stormy. Once he got opposite her, he lowered himself into an armchair, braced his elbows on his spread knees and canted toward her.

He tried to speak quietly. Reasonably. "I'm just not getting it, that's all. You've always said how you love it here in Red Rock. How you'd never live anywhere else but your hometown."

With a hard huff of breath, she looked out the window again, her chin set and her mouth a thin line. She stared at the wide Texas sky and the crown of the front-yard oak as if they were a lot more interesting than he'd ever be. "I changed my mind. People do that sometimes."

"Annie," he said, carefully. "Please…"

She whipped her head around once more, skewered him with another angry look. "Please, what? There's nothing more to say."

"That's not true."

She seemed to think about that. And then her shoulders kind of drooped. "You know, you might be right. Maybe there's a *lot* more to say. Too bad it's nothing you're gonna sit still to hear."

"That's not true." He said those words and then almost wished he hadn't. Yeah, okay. There were a few subjects he'd prefer not to talk about. But, damn it. Whatever it took, he had to get her to see that she was making a huge mistake, to go running off, starting all over again in a strange city, when the life she'd always loved was right here.

Why would she do that? Only one reason. Because of *him*. "It's my fault, isn't it? My fault that you're leaving?"

Something happened in her sweet face—a softening. A gentling. When she spoke, her tone had mellowed. "You've got to stop blaming yourself for every darn thing that happens. Human beings have free will, you know? Unless you tie them up or put a gun to their head, they're generally going to do what they want to do. And whatever that may be, it *won't* be Greg Flynn's own personal fault." She wrapped her arms around herself, tipped her red head to the side. "Like what happened with Hank, like the accident—"

He sat back, abruptly cutting her off. "I'm not here to talk about that."

She shook her head. "No. I guess you're not. But maybe you *should* talk about it. You never do." She shifted on the sofa so she was leaning toward him. "Think about it. You two were racing. Maybe you shouldn't have been. Maybe he'd still be alive if you hadn't—or if that possum hadn't wandered out into the road, if Hank hadn't swerved to miss it." She threw up both hands. "If, if, if. The fact is, you both made a free choice to do what you did. There were consequences, terrible ones. But it's no more your fault than it was Hank's."

He didn't need to hear this—didn't *want* to hear it. "Annie."

"What?"

"Don't…"

She looked at him for a long time, her eyes so sad and soft, her mouth kind of trembling. "Nobody blames you, Greg. Not my parents. Not me. And I know enough about my brother to know he never would blame you, either—if by some miracle, he were still here."

"Don't," he said again, the word betraying him, com-

ing out raw and broken. She only shook her head again
and slowly rose from the sofa. He sat back farther in the
chair, his legs braced apart, his hands gripping the chair
arms. "What are you doing?"

She didn't answer, only stepped around the low glass
table and kept coming. One more step and she was right
there in front of him. Yet another, and she stood between
his spread thighs.

He looked up at her, his heart racing, his mouth dry.
His palms were sweating. Damn. He sucked in a breath,
got a whiff of her fresh, sweet scent. He gripped the
chair arms harder and tried not to stare at her slim bare
legs, not to follow them upward, to the outward curve
of her hips beneath those white shorts, and higher to the
way her bright pink T-shirt clung to her breasts....

She gave the command in a tender voice. "Say it.
Right now. Tell me what Hank told *you*, there, on the
side of the road, before he shut his eyes and never
opened them again."

"Don't..."

She lifted her hands. He jerked back, but there was
nowhere to go. She leaned forward a little farther and
captured his face, cradling it between her soft palms.
"Say it," she whispered.

"I've said it. I've told you. A hundred times."

"So tell me again." She held him prisoner with her
cool, soft hands, with her unwavering gaze.

He opened his mouth and the words came out, the
ones that were burned forever into his brain. "'Look
after my folks. Take care of Annie.'"

A tender smile curved her lips. "'Take care of Annie…' Did it ever occur to you that there's more than one way to take care of me?"

"Don't," he said again. He couldn't say it enough. "Damn you, Annie. Don't."

But she only went on as if she hadn't heard him, brown eyes velvet soft and shining. "Or maybe it's only, if you never really live your own life to the limit—if you never love me like the woman I am, if you never ride your Harley—well, that makes Hank a little less dead to you, that's a way to pay Hank back, because you're here. And he's not."

"No," he said, the word ragged, dredged up from someplace ugly and deep.

She wouldn't stop. "Or maybe, if somehow you could keep me from growing up, if I could always be seventeen, if things could always be the same between us, you my 'big brother,' me your 'little sis,' it would be like…holding time still, wouldn't it? The good times you and Hank had, the friendship you shared, it would seem like all that happened just yesterday. Maybe if you take Hank's place in my life, it makes him seem, I don't know, a little less gone to you, as if he's not really dead."

"No," he said again. But even he wasn't sure he believed his own denials anymore.

"Oh, Greg," she whispered. Her eyes brimmed. Two fat tears escaped and made a pair of gleaming trails down her satiny cheeks. "There are other, better ways to keep Hank alive in our hearts. Can't you see that?"

"Annie. Don't cry."

She shook her head—and she lowered her mouth. Their lips met.

Heat and light exploded inside him. He wanted to grab her, haul her down across his lap. But somehow, he restrained himself. Somehow, he let it be just a soul-searing, mind-blowing kiss and nothing more. He reached up, cupped her face, as she cupped his. He felt the tear tracks, the warmth and the wet beneath his palms, and the feathery ends of her hair brushing the backs of his hands.

He kissed her, a kiss that was not the least bit brotherly, a kiss that was long and wet. And so very deep.

She moaned into his mouth and he speared his tongue in deeper, tasting her, sucking in the sweet scent of her, longing for nothing more than to stay right there, in that chair, Annie bending above him, their mouths pressed together, till the end of time.

She was the one who pulled away—slowly and reluctantly, with a small, sad sigh.

He looked up at her and she gazed down at him.

She said, "When Dirk Jenkins first pointed that squirt gun in my face the other day, when I thought that maybe I was going to die, I wished I'd done two things differently. I wished I'd never had that talk with Dirk the day before. And I wished that I'd told you straight out, at least one time, that I love you."

"Annie—"

She stopped him by sliding a hand against his mouth. "Shh. Let me say this." She held his eyes. "Will you? Will you let me finish?"

He gulped, gave a quick, hard nod.

She took her hand off his mouth, held his face again between her palms. "I love you, Greg Flynn. I've loved you—been *in* love with you since I was maybe, oh, ten years old. I've waited and I've wished—I've prayed even—for the day when you would finally see me as a woman." She sighed. "And you know, for a while there, when I was fifteen, I really thought it was happening, that you were looking at me and seeing more than only Hank's little sister."

When she was fifteen…

Greg shut his eyes against the memory of that.

"Come on," she whispered. "Come on. Look at me." So he did. He opened his eyes and she said, "But something went wrong. I never understood it. For a while, you were coming over all the time, even when Hank wasn't there. I was so happy. And then you just stopped. You avoided me. That hurt so bad…" Her voice trailed off.

After a moment, she continued, "And then, after Hank died, we kind of slipped into friendship. Didn't we?" He only stared up at her. She asked again, "Didn't we?"

"Yeah," he admitted at last.

"And since then, since Hank died, I've been your good buddy, your 'little sister,' your substitute-for-Hank best friend. But always, forever, I've believed that some-day—if I was only patient enough, if I wished and hoped and dreamed hard enough—you would come to me. You'd make love to me. You'd see that it was you and me, together, that mattered, that *we* were always meant to be."

With tender fingers, she brushed at his hair, a touch that burned and soothed at the same time. "It hurt me. It hurt me so deep, when you started in with Heather, when you two got engaged. And then, well, she broke it off with you. You never said why, what had gone wrong between you. But I didn't care why. I dared to hope again. And then, a week ago yesterday, it finally happened. All my dreams came true."

"Annie—"

"Shh. All my dreams came true…for a night. And then it was Saturday, when you told me my dream coming true had been nothing but an awful mistake. And after that, well…" She let her cradling hands drop away and straightened up tall. "After that, I've had to realize that there are just some dreams that are never going to come true. I've had to start making myself a new way of looking at my life. I'm not going to be just another not-quite-so-crazy version of poor Dirk, creating fantasies in my head about someone and telling myself I can make those fantasies come true. Because I do know that it takes two to make love work, it takes two to make it real. And I've begun to understand that since it's not going to be you and me, together, as a man and a woman, I want to try something completely different. I want to get a new start in a new town."

She backed away, out from between his legs. Turning, she went to the window and stared out at the bright afternoon, at the deep green oak branches blowing lazily in the wind. "They have banks and florist shops in other towns, too, Greg." She faced him and gave him her sweetest smile. "Believe me. A new start is what I want now. I'm going to make that new start and I'm going to be fine."

Chapter 6

Sunday, Monday, Tuesday...

For Greg, the days melted by in a fog. Annie was leaving. She *wanted* to go.

He slept the night through undisturbed now. He had no more dreams—of him and Annie, or of the accident. The dreams seemed to have faded away, been banished somehow by the things she had said to him Saturday—and by the stark reality of her going.

Strangely, now the dreams had left him alone, he missed them. Missed the pain and the passion in them. Even missed the way they woke him, shaking and sweating. Now his sleep was deep and dreamless, without meaning, cool and empty as the darkness at the bottom of a well.

He went to work, joked around with the guys at the station, drove his Red Rock PD Blazer up and down the streets of his hometown, responding to the calls when they came, intervening in more than one domestic dispute, handling the occasional drunk-and-disorderly, stopping a convenience-store holdup in progress—and feeling zero satisfaction as he hauled the perp off to the cage at the station.

Everything just felt so…programmed to him now, his life a rote exercise. Get up, eat, work, sleep—and start the whole cycle all over again. All the joy and brightness had somehow kind of leached out of it. As if he was a pale copy of his real self, going through the motions, numb to it all.

It all centered down to Annie, to the damn scary fact that she had told him she loved him—loved him as a woman loves a man.

And now he found himself wondering…

Had he always known? All those years she said she'd been waiting and wishing and dreaming…of him? Had he known, deep down, how she really felt? Had he known and denied her for a decade and a half?

When he thought of that—that he might have done just that—he got an awful feeling deep in his belly. Even through the numbness, he could feel it, his gut twisting as if a pair of cold, hard hands were busy wringing the hell out of it.

And then he'd try to make excuses for himself.

After all, for about half the time she claimed she'd been loving him, she'd only been a kid. Then, it would have been wrong to get anything going with her. He'd learned his lesson the hard way on that one. But later, more recently, at least since she'd turned eighteen, well, from then on, if she'd felt that strongly, there should have been nothing to stop her from telling him, from getting it out there for both of them to deal with.

Nothing to stop her…

Except maybe her own bone-deep awareness that as soon as she told him, as soon as they stepped over the line from friendship to something more, he'd go seriously south on her.

Which was exactly what he'd done.

Friday night—*the* Friday night, when popcorn and a movie at her place had turned into kisses and then passionate lovemaking…that night had been a damn miracle, as it was happening.

The most beautiful, perfect night of his life.

It wasn't until the next morning, in the harsh light of day, that it had started to seem all wrong to him, had started to seem a betrayal, somehow. A betrayal of Hank and the promise Greg had made to him.

"Take care of Annie…"

"I will. You know I will…" His final vow to his dying friend.

Then again, if he wanted to get down to it, down to the things he hardly let himself think about, that vow went back farther than Hank's dying breath.

It went back, as Annie had reminded him Saturday, to the year she turned fifteen.

On Annie's fifteenth birthday, she'd had a party, with ten or twelve girlfriends, at her house. That was before Greg and Hank got their bikes, but still the two of them had been out in the garage during most of the celebration. Hank had paid next to nothing for a junked-out Model A and they were working it over, putting in a new engine, replacing the clutch before they got around to the big challenge of handling the bodywork.

Naomi called them in when it was time for the cake. They washed up a little in the concrete sink outside and trooped on into the house, where the girls were gathered around the table, giggling and whispering to each other. Greg and Hank kind of hung back in their greasy overalls, the way men fresh out of the garage will do in a kitchen full of fluttery females.

Naomi lit the candles and they all sang the birthday song.

Naomi said, "Okay, Annie. Make that wish."

And Annie looked right over the bright heads of her girlfriends and straight at Greg. He'd met her eyes and…

Ka-bam.

Something inside him just broke wide open and he *knew*…

He wanted her. He wanted her bad. His best friend's fifteen-year-old sister. He was twenty and that made her jailbait, but at that moment, he couldn't have cared less.

"Okay," Annie said, still looking right at him. "I've got it. Got my wish." And she blew out every one of those fifteen candles in one big burst of breath.

After that, Greg started finding excuses to be around Annie. He'd come over to see Hank—when he knew Hank wasn't even there. Annie always seemed so excited, so glad, when he'd show up. They'd sit at the table and talk, or go out back and flop down on the lawn.

It was innocent. Nothing ever really happened. But in his mind and heart, he knew what he wanted. He was trying to get around the fact that she was only fifteen, trying to make it right with himself, to make a pass at her, to kiss her…or more.

Then, after weeks of that, Hank and Ted paid him a visit. Greg was living in a cheesy apartment out near the highway, his first place of his own. He answered the knock and there they were: father and son. And they were not happy. They had a long talk, the three of them. Hank was kind of simmering mad that his best friend would even consider putting the moves on his little sister. Ted was more even-handed. He reminded Greg that Annie was too young for him, that it just wasn't right for him to go chasing after her.

Greg looked in both their faces and knew they had him nailed, that he'd been doing exactly what they thought he had: chasing after Annie, warming up to kissing her and touching her and doing things to her that no twenty-year-old guy should be doing with a girl her age.

He'd apologized. And he'd meant it to the depths of

his soul. By the time they left, Hank had cooled off a little.

Ted had clapped him on the shoulder. "You're a good man, Greg. We think the world of you."

And Greg had sworn to himself he'd never let Hank—or Ted—down again.

After that, it went just as Annie said. He avoided her as much as possible. He only talked to her when there were other people around. More than once, he caught her watching him, a sad look on her face, a searching light in her eyes. But they never spoke about it. He made sure there were no opportunities for any heart-to-heart discussions of why he'd chased after her and then suddenly stopped.

He supposed, by the time of the accident, he was used to things the way they were. He'd gotten into the habit of seeing Annie in a certain way.

They lost Hank. And he and Annie grew close. But he'd always kept strictly to the promise he'd made that day when Hank and Ted came to see him.

He'd never again so much as considered putting a move on her.

Until *that* Friday night.

And since then, everything had gone haywire. He was walking around like a shell of himself, going through the motions of his life without really living it. And Annie was leaving town.

Late Tuesday afternoon, when he got off duty, Greg went home to the three-bedroom house on Alamo Court that he'd bought a year and a half before on an FHA loan. Lately, the damn place seemed kind of echoing and empty, though until *that* Friday, he'd been contented as a cat in a creamery there.

He got a beer from the fridge and a Man's Meal dinner from the freezer and turned on the oven. Then he parked himself at the round oak table he and Annie had refinished together. He stared at the salt and pepper shakers as he sipped his beer.

The oven beeped and the doorbell rang at the same time. Greg got up, put the dinner in to heat and went to the door to find Ted Grant standing on the porch.

Ted smiled that low-key, easy smile of his. "Got a minute?"

Greg shrugged, though a sudden uneasiness tightened the muscles between his shoulder blades. "Sure. Come on in."

Greg got Ted a beer and they sat at the table together.

"Place is lookin' good," Ted said.

Greg knocked back a big gulp of brew. "I'm working on it."

Ted leaned a long, skinny arm on the table. "Haven't seen you around much lately."

"Yeah. Sorry. Been busy." Lame, Greg thought. Really lame.

Ted sipped, set the beer down and picked at the label. He glanced up at Greg from under graying brows. "You know, there's nothin' I hate more than meddling parents."

Greg's stomach knotted up the way it was always

doing lately, and the tension between his shoulder blades pulled all the tighter. "Is this about Annie?"

Ted let out a heavy sigh. "Yeah. 'Fraid so."

Greg shoved back his chair. "I think I need another beer."

Ted grunted. "You know what? Get me one, too."

Greg did the honors and then dropped back into his seat. "So, all right. Hit me with it."

Ted took a long drink, and then plunked the beer down. "You in love with my daughter?"

Greg swallowed. Hard. His heart galloped as if it was trying to race itself out of his chest. And then he said it, he confessed it. "Yeah. I guess I am."

"Well, hot damn," said Ted, looking nothing short of relieved. "It's about time."

Greg drank more beer, a big, long guzzle of it—and then almost choked. Somewhere in mid-guzzle, his throat had locked up tight.

Ted added, "Truth is, we been waitin' for years now, your mom and dad, me and Naomi."

Greg managed to speak. "Waiting for…?"

"Why, for you two to come to your senses about each other."

Greg realized his mouth was hanging open. He shut it—and looked away.

Ted must have known what was going through his mind. "Come on, man. That was nine years ago. Annie was too young. When you started coming around to see her, we all got worried. You two could have burned the house down with those looks you were giving each other. I knew I had to step in then, or there'd be trouble on the way. But now..." Ted seemed to run out of words.

Greg prompted, "Now, what?"

"Son, I'm not tellin' you—either of you—what you should do, how you should live. But it seems only right I should at least let you know that I—and Naomi, too— we're completely aware that this ain't nine years ago. And whatever's gone wrong between the two of you, if you work it out and end up together, you'll make Naomi and me about as happy as two old folks are likely to be, and that is no lie."

After Ted left, Greg took his dinner out of the oven. Though it was his favorite—Salisbury steak and cheesy potatoes—he tossed it in the trash. His appetite had vanished. He got another beer out of the fridge, opened it—and then left it on the counter untouched.

He wandered into the living room. For a while he stood at the big front window, looking out at the yard, thinking he really needed to get going on the landscaping he and Annie had talked about. Put in a few bushes, sod the muddy patch of lawn.

When staring out the window got old, he meandered back to the kitchen again—and then out the kitchen door to the garage.

He went straight to the hunk of chrome and steel in the corner and whipped the tarp away. Beneath it, the big, low bike gleamed, silver-metallic paint catching the light and shimmering, the detailing fresh and sharp as new.

He swung a leg over, straddling her, gripping the fat rubber handles. She was, according to just about any source you might name, the most primitive ride on the planet. On the open road, she shook like an overloaded dryer in a cheap Laundromat. But so what?

As Hank used to say, *God didn't make motorcycles for sissies to ride.*

Greg sank back on the seat and his gaze kind of wandered to the shelves on the far wall—to the two dusty black helmets waiting there, side by side. One had been Hank's, the helmet he should have been wearing the day that he died.

Somehow, Greg had ended up with it.

Two helmets, he thought, and for what felt like the first time in a week and a half, Greg Flynn let himself smile.

Chapter 7

Annie stood at the open refrigerator trying to decide what to fix for dinner. Muffy sat on the floor a few feet away, purring in contentment and giving herself a nice bath after polishing off a full bowl of Fancy Feast.

"So, Muffy," Annie said to the cat. "You think chicken? Or hamburger steak?"

Muffy stopped bathing long enough to give Annie a low-eyed contented look, then went back to licking her paw.

"No input from you, huh?" Annie reached for the plastic-wrapped tray of chicken breasts.

And right then she heard it. Coming down the street. That low, rough rumble…

Annie tossed the chicken back into the fridge, shoved

the door shut and ran to the front window as the sound came on louder—deep, hard and mean.

At the window, she paused, eyes tight shut, wishing…

Daring, once again, to dream.

And then she looked down and…

Greg!

On his beautiful silver Harley, right there in the driveway, black helmet gleaming in the fading sunlight. He gunned the engine. The sound rose to a rumbling roar.

Annie pressed her face to the window—and he saw her! She waved as she spotted the other helmet strapped on behind him. He turned in the seat, got it free, held it up.

"Five minutes!" She mouthed the words at him through the glass. Her heart suddenly so light it seemed to lift her right off the ground, she signaled with five fingers spread wide and then whirled from the window, headed for the bedroom to yank on some jeans and her sturdy Acme boots.

Below, Greg watched her vanish from view.

Not ten seconds later, Ted and Naomi emerged from the main house.

"Lookin' good," said Ted.

"Just beautiful." Naomi, trailing her dishcloth, beamed at him.

Greg turned off the rumbling bike, his mind, his heart, his soul, the whole of him filled with Annie. "Takin' Annie for a ride. Five minutes and she'll be down, she said."

And Ted threw back his graying head and laughed. "I were you, I wouldn't want to wait that long."

"Go on." Naomi beamed and waved her dish towel at him. "Get on up there. You know you want to."

It was all the encouragement he needed. Greg jumped off the bike, kicked the stand down and grabbed the key and the extra helmet. With a last, quick wave for Ted and Naomi, he headed for the stairs that led up to the apartment. When he got to the door, he pulled back the screen, raised his hand to knock—and then reconsidered. He tried the doorknob first. It opened. He stepped through, easing the screen gently shut.

Muffy sat on the floor in the kitchen, watching him through wide green eyes. He took off his helmet. "Hey, Muff."

The old cat gave him a soft, welcoming "Reeow."

He set both helmets on the kitchen counter as he strode by, moving fast, toward the bedroom.

He stopped in the doorway.

Annie was right there, facing the far wall, pulling on a pair of jeans over those long, slim bare legs of hers. Her high, round little bottom was pointed right at him. The view was terrific; she wore a purple satin thong.

He cleared his throat.

She jumped about a foot in the air. "Oh! I was just…" Blushing red as her hair, she hobbled around to face him.

He couldn't wait any longer—to touch her, to kiss her, to do all the things he'd denied himself for so damn long. He shoved the door shut.

She let go of the jeans. They dropped around her ankles and she straightened up, eyes wide as headlights, mouth all trembly and soft.

He reached her in three big strides. "Annie…"

She bit her plump, trembling lip. "Oh, Greg…"

He didn't know where to start, didn't know how to tell her. "Annie, everything you said the other day…"

"Yeah?"

"It was dead on."

She blinked. "Yeah?"

He nodded. "Somehow, I've had it all mixed up in my head—you and Hank, the accident. Annie, I gotta tell you true, after all these years…"

"Yeah?"

"When you were fifteen—I *did* want you then. So damn bad."

He'd never seen her look so happy. She sighed. "Oh, I knew it."

"But it was wrong then, you and me."

"I know that, too—oh, not then. I wouldn't face it then. It broke my teenage heart when you turned away from me. But as I've gotten older, as I've grown up, I've come to understand that it wouldn't have been right, not then."

He touched her hair, traced the perfect shape of her ear. "I spent a lot of bad nights dreaming of you then, training my mind not to go there, you know?"

"I do. I think I do."

"And then, when Hank died…I don't know, it all kind of got messed around in my head, just like you said. That I could take his place a little, be like the brother you lost, that if I kept you a kid in my mind, it would be…" His throat clutched up.

She suggested softly, "Like Hank wasn't gone?"

He gulped. "Yeah. Yeah, like that. Though it's crazy and makes no damn sense and I know it, somehow, I did think of it like that. Damn. Annie…"

"Yeah? Say it."

"When Heather broke it off with me?"

"Yeah?"

"She told me, then…"

"Told you…?"

"That she felt like the odd one out whenever you came around, that I ought to face the fact that you were the one I wanted, and not go breaking any other poor girls' hearts trying to convince myself that they could take your place."

"No. Really? Heather said that? She said that two years ago?"

He confessed, "Yeah."

"But you wouldn't listen to her?"

"That's right. I told her she was full of it. That she had it all wrong. But Annie, she had me pegged. And I was damn furious at her for it. It's crazy. Wild. Now, I'm kind of starting to think that everybody in Red Rock knew you and I should be together. Everybody had it figured out."

Her smile was wide and bright as a new day. "Everybody except you."

"Damn," he said. "Annie…" He looked down at her

shining face, at her soft breasts swelling beneath her purple T-shirt, at those beautiful bare legs, at the purple polish on her pretty toes. He looked down—and pure lust slammed through him, heating his blood, tightening his jeans. He muttered, "I was going to take you for a ride."

"But?"

"All I can think about is laying you down on that bed."

She lifted those slim arms and rested them on his shoulders. "Well, how 'bout this?"

"What?"

She surged up on tiptoe. "You take me for a ride, right here and now, on my bed." She gave him a beautiful, very naughty grin. "And then later we'll see about getting out on that bike."

What could he say to that? What did he *need* to say to that?

Not a damn thing.

It was a moment for action.

So he wrapped his arms around her and lowered his mouth to hers. She opened for him instantly, surging up tighter against him. He put his hands on her satiny bare bottom and tucked her up close, grinding himself into her. She moaned his name and he whispered hers as he let go of her mouth and kissed her cheeks, her chin, her sweet, freckled nose.

He took the bottom of her T-shirt and tugged. She raised her arms and off the thing went. Her purple satin bra came next. And then, after she stepped out of those jeans that were trapping her ankles, he took down that sexy little thong. He took all her clothes away, every last stitch.

And when she stood before him, naked at last, pale skin flushed, red hair feathery-soft around her heart-shaped face, breasts high and full and tipped in pink, he could hardly believe his own eyes.

He and Annie, like this…

Again.

At last.

He sank to his knees before her. She put her hands on his shoulders, her eyes met his—and a shudder went through him. He kissed the shining red curls at the place where her creamy thighs met and then he lifted a hand and petted her there. She eased her thighs apart, moaning, and he put his mouth against that soft, secret place.

"Oh," she said. "Greg… Oh, Greg…"

He pulled her body close, his hands cupping her bottom, and she moved against him as he kissed her, a deep, purely sexual kiss. He ran his tongue along that hot, wet groove and he slid his fingers in from behind, stroking.

She clutched his shoulders. She cried out. And then she sighed.

And then she went still, except for the quivering that started where he kissed her and spread out, until her whole body shook and her knees gave way and he caught her as she sank to the floor.

He helped her to stretch out and he moved above her. He kissed her some more, in that secret wet place between her thighs, kissed her until she begged for mercy and the quivering started all over again.

A hundred slow, deep kisses later, they lay on her bed, both of them naked, facing each other.

He held out his hand.

She took the condom from him. Brown eyes shining, she whispered, "I like a man who plans ahead."

He admitted, "I've been a little worried. About last time. We didn't use anything and I—"

She put a finger to his lips. "It's okay. We were lucky."

He kissed the tip of that finger. "No baby on the way?"

She shook her head against the pillow. "No baby…"

"But someday…"

She nodded, eyes shining even brighter. "Yeah. Definitely." She reached down between them. He groaned when she touched him. Slowly, she slid the condom on. "There…" She encircled him with her soft hand.

And he groaned again.

And then she wrapped her top leg around him and guided him home.

Greg threw his head back and pushed into her so deep. The world flew away. There was only him and Annie and the magic between them.

He held on so tight. He didn't think he could bear it, didn't think he could last. And yet somehow, he did. They moved together, slow and deep and so very good.

At the end, when he felt himself going over, he

pushed in hard and high. She clung to him. He felt her slick inner muscles contracting around him.

He let out a cry. She cried in answer.

And the hot, sweet, wet pulsing began.

"About you leaving town," he said sometime later, when he could think again. "If it's something you think you have to do..."

She kissed his chin. "Not now I don't. Oh, no. I'm staying right here—though I am considering driving into San Antonio a couple of times a week. There are some really good floral-design schools there."

"You're sure about staying in town?"

"I am absolutely positive."

He brushed a few strands of flame-red hair out of her eyes. "Did I tell you I like your hair?"

She giggled then. "As a matter of fact, no."

"Well, I do. And I'm sorry I was such a jerk before. I was just used to it long, that's all."

"You were used to a lot of things."

He faked a scowl as he let his hand wander down over her cheek and her obstinate chin, along her satiny throat and lower still. He cupped a beautiful, full white breast and flicked the nipple with his thumb. "I was a damn fool."

She gasped, a tiny, delighted sound. "I'm so glad you got wise."

"Yeah. 'Bout time, huh?" He bent his head, licked that tight pink bud.

She groaned and clutched his head. "Oh, yeah. It sure is."

He let go of that tempting nipple and lifted up to take her mouth. They kissed. And then they kissed again.

Finally, he pulled away and reminded her—reminded them both, really, "We still haven't gone for that ride."

"That's right. We should do that." But she only held on tighter. "In a minute. Oh, it's crazy. But I'm afraid to let you go."

He kissed her neck, whispered, "Don't worry. I'm not going anywhere. I love you, Annie. Guess I always have."

She sighed. And then she cupped his face and told him, "And I love you. Always."

They stared at each other. And then he asked, "Enough to be my date for the Spring Fling this year?"

Her eyes misted over. "Oh, how did you know? It's been one of my fantasies, to go to the Spring Fling with you."

"Is that a yes?"

"You bet it is."

He kissed her nose. "Well, okay then. About that ride…"

The Harley waited in the driveway, silver paint and bright chrome gleaming. Down the street to the west, the sky flamed in swirls of purple and orange as Annie put on her helmet and swung a leg over, settling in behind Greg.

He started her up. She purred, loud and proud.

Annie wrapped her arms around Greg's waist. He guided the bike down the driveway, straightened her out and off they roared toward the setting sun.

Dear Reader,

I truly enjoyed crafting *Dream Marriage*. I married shortly after college graduation and have dabbled at a few careers, all the while juggling family life with work. Because of my own experiences, writing about a married couple came easily for me. In *Dream Marriage*, Gareth and Laura struggle with the meaning of commitment in their lives. As they come to terms with how their careers affect their marriage, they successfully reawaken the love and passion that originally brought them together. Their romance is set against the backdrop of Red Rock, Texas, the town that is home to many members of the Fortune family both old and new!

I was honored to be part of this anthology and I hope you enjoy visiting Red Rock.

All my best,

Karen Rose Smith

DREAM MARRIAGE

Karen Rose Smith

For my husband, Steve.
To thirty-three years and many, many more. Love, Karen

Chapter 1

As Laura Manning stood at the vanity in her mother's upstairs bathroom, she didn't know whether to laugh or cry!

She'd been in so much turmoil over the past six weeks since Gareth had been gone, she hadn't thought her life could get any more topsy-turvy.

She'd been wrong.

Staring down at the stick that had come with the pregnancy test, her eyes filled with tears. Of course, she wanted a child. Of course, she'd love it with every fiber of her being. But for all intents and purposes, when Gareth had left for Tokyo, *she'd* left *him*.

He'd told her he'd be home by May 2. Today was May 2.

How could they find a connection again when he didn't understand the gravity of what was happening to their marriage? How could she tell him she was pregnant when they had problems to solve first?

Laura ran her hand through her dark brown shoulder-length hair, still staring at the stick, reliving her last night with Gareth, as well as their argument. At twenty-seven, she was ready to be a mother, even though her year-old business was now flourishing.

Yet being a single mom and running a business was something else entirely. Could she do it without Gareth?

She'd *have* to do it without Gareth if he couldn't compromise. She wouldn't use a baby to hold their marriage together.

She simply wouldn't.

Gareth Manning opened the gate in the stucco courtyard wall and strode to his front door, expecting it to be open. It was locked.

Setting down his large suitcase and his laptop computer, he found his keys in his pocket and opened the door. He'd expected Laura to be home, making dinner, creating hors d'oeuvres for a party she was going to cater.

But when he stepped into the skylit foyer, there was

complete silence in the thirty-five-hundred-square-foot house.

Nothing had gone as planned—not Laura's reaction to his business trip…not her decision to stay with her mother for a few days…not his fax to the *Red Rock Gazette* that was supposed to tell Laura he wanted their marriage now as much as ever. From the looks of it, someone on the staff had tampered with that letter, omitting names. Now that the town was in an uproar about it, he felt like a fool for writing it.

On top of that, whenever he'd tried to call Laura, he either hadn't gotten an answer here or her mother had told him she just needed time.

Time for what? They were married!

As Gareth stared into the dining room with its coffered ceiling, the empty oak table seemed to send a solemn message. To the right, the living room didn't show a magazine out of place. To the left, the family room with its exposed beams was deserted, too. The house was H-shaped and he'd bought it for them about a year after his management-consultant business had succeeded beyond his wildest dreams. But, now, as he left his suitcase and computer in the foyer and walked through the family room to the spacious kitchen beyond, he felt a dread he'd never experienced before.

There was no sign of Laura.

In the kitchen, he crossed to the pantry. The oversize freezer and extra refrigerator she'd purchased for her catering business hummed. Opening the freezer, he saw it was full of supplies and labeled containers. The refrigerator was the same, and he breathed a sigh of relief. She was obviously cooking here and catering from their kitchen.

But if she was still at her mother's…

The master suite was on the other side of the house opposite the kitchen. Passing the French doors that led to the pool out back, he went through the dining room and down the hall to their bedroom. The brightly colored quilt spread across the bed without a wrinkle. He didn't spot any of Laura's jewelry on the oak dresser or her lotion on the nightstand.

Opening the walk-in closet, a lead weight fell to the bottom of his stomach. The night before he'd left, she'd packed a small suitcase. Now her larger valise was gone also, and so were her summer clothes.

The trip from Tokyo had been wearing, and his beard stubble was heavy. But he had to find out where his wife was.

He had to find out *now*.

Ten minutes later, he parked outside a house on the other side of Red Rock. As he went up the two steps to the front porch, he had only one goal in mind—to bring Laura home.

Laura's mother, Janice Bates, was an exotic-looking woman of Italian descent, with olive-toned skin, dark brown hair and green eyes. She was taller than Laura and about thirty pounds heavier. But her daughter had inherited her beauty, her poise and her tact.

Now, however, she didn't look tactful. She looked worried as she opened the door to him. "Gareth! You're home."

"I told Laura I'd be home by May 2. What I want to know is why she's still here rather than in our house."

"You're going to have to ask *her* that question."

"Is she here?"

Janice glanced nervously over her shoulder. "Yes. She was doing something upstairs. But I don't know if she wants to talk to you—"

"*I* want to talk to her. We haven't seen each other for six weeks." The change in time zones was catching up to him and his voice was clipped with a frustrated edge.

"Come inside," Janice finally invited. "I'll get her."

Laura's background had been very different from his. He'd grown up in a two-bedroom box house in San Antonio with his uncle Isaac. Laura, however, had grown up in this small community not far from San Antonio with every advantage a child should have. Her father was a doctor and doted on all his kids. They'd wanted for nothing. The two-story house with its brick and tan siding was spacious.

When Laura descended the steps into the living room, Gareth experienced the same thrill of attraction he'd felt the first time he'd laid eyes on her. Then she'd been a paralegal working in an all-purpose firm. For one of his first management-consulting contracts, he'd seen an attorney there. His eyes had met Laura's, they'd smiled and the rest had been history.

Now, however, Laura didn't look as if she were remembering their first meeting. There wasn't the welcome he'd expected on her face. There wasn't even a smile.

Her mother discreetly left the room.

"I didn't expect you to be here." He tried to keep his tone even.

"I told you if you left on this trip I wouldn't be in our house when you got home."

"I thought you were overreacting. I thought you'd change your mind. Why wouldn't you take my calls?"

Laura had pulled her dark hair back into a ponytail. The style emphasized the beautiful oval of her face, her wide-set green eyes, her bangs that she brushed aside when she was nervous. She brushed them aside now.

"We've grown apart," she said finally.

Crossing to her, he towered over her. "Laura, don't make a mountain out of a molehill. I've always traveled in my work. When you worked with me, you understood."

After he'd met Laura, she'd become his personal assistant. Once they were married, he'd worked out of a room in their apartment. One of his early contracts had involved analyzing a department's makeup for Ryan Fortune. The magnate had recommended him to other businesses, and Gareth's career had taken off. He'd rented an office in a strip shopping center, and Laura had worked beside him every day until a year ago when she'd decided she wanted to be a caterer and somebody should replace her in his office.

"We worked together, Gareth. But you didn't travel as much then. You dealt with local businesses. You traveled for a few days, came home and did the rest by fax. But this past year, you didn't even notice how much you were away."

"You've been busy, too," he accused. "Some nights when I get home, *you're* not there."

"I'm building my clientele. And why do you think I started doing it in the first place? I was tired of having supper alone."

"You started your catering business because of my trips?" She'd never told him that. Or had she told him and he hadn't listened?

"Not entirely. But I wanted something of my own. I wanted a life."

"We *have* a life!"

"No. You have your work. You have dinner with me when it's convenient for you. For the past three years I've been asking you to spend more time with me, but each time I asked, you brushed it off."

Certainly he hadn't, had he? Yes, he spent a lot of nights working…. He ran his fingers through his short-cropped brown hair. "I was working to make our future secure."

Her voice was incredibly sad. "Our future was secure before I stopped working for you."

That was true, he supposed. He'd made a lot of money in a short amount of time and had invested it well. Still, he wasn't sure what she was suggesting. "What do you want me to do? Sit by the pool all day and drink margaritas?"

She shook her head. "Of course not. But if we're going to have a marriage, something has to change."

Gareth knew he wasn't good at change…for a lot of reasons.

Trying to remain rational and reasonable on very little sleep, he suggested again, "Come home with me. I've traveled halfway around the world and I haven't slept since I left Tokyo. I'll change clothes. We'll go have a nice dinner somewhere and—"

He saw her chin quiver as she blurted out as if she'd been practicing for six weeks, "I think we've grown too far apart. I think we need a separation."

"We've been separated for six weeks!" He couldn't keep the anger from his tone now.

"Whose fault is that?" she asked softly.

Laura had always been more passive than assertive, more peaceful than confrontational. What had gotten into her? Another question was more important. "Are you blaming me for the distance between us?"

She didn't have to answer him. Yet it wasn't only blame he saw in her eyes. The emotion looked like des-

olation, and that unsettled him even more than her re-
fusal to come home with him.

"All right," he gave in, not knowing how to handle
this woman he didn't understand anymore. "You win
for now. I know if I throw you over my shoulder and
carry you home, you'll leave if you don't want to stay
there. But I don't think a separation is the answer. After
I get some sleep and have a shave, I'll be back. We've
been married for five years, Laura, and I'm not about
to throw that away. I won't let *you* do it, either."

Then he left her standing in her mother's living
room. Whatever was broken, he was going to fix. He
loved Laura and he wasn't going to let her go.

"Winning the contract to make desserts for the
Spring Fling is a big deal," Laura's mother mused aloud
as she concocted a beautiful table decoration from
baby's breath, silk daylilies and pink silk roses. "Are
you sure you'll be able to handle making enough?"

Laura was working on another centerpiece for the
serving table, using the same array of flowers as her
mother. "Corrine and I will do fine. I have two weeks
to pull it all together. That's plenty of preparation time.
We can make and freeze most of them before the event."

"It's still an awful lot for two people. The whole
town could show up."

"I'll hire high-school girls to help me serve."

As Laura was growing up, her mother had always

added to her self-doubt, rather than wholeheartedly supporting her. Her older sister, Victoria, on the other hand, had always received praise and backing. But Vickie was very different from Laura, with her sun-streaked brown hair, her high IQ, her perky cheerleader-like attitude, her medical-school degree. She'd always forged ahead with self-confidence and an oldest child's demand for attention.

Positioning another rose just so, Janice prophesied, "If you do a good job with the Spring Fling, your reputation will be made. Some of the Fortunes usually come. If you get into *that* circle you won't have to worry about underbidding your competitor. Take these flowers, for example. You kept your bid down by going to that flower warehouse and doing these yourself. Any other caterer would have included the price for fresh bouquets from the florist."

"Maybe. Maybe not. I like doing flower arrangements. But if you're getting tired, you don't have to help."

"I'm not getting tired. I was just thinking I'd like to be doing one of these for a party for Tony. I can't believe he didn't want me to throw a graduation party for him on Friday night."

Tony was nine years younger than she was, the baby in the family. His graduation on Friday night would be a milestone, only he wanted to celebrate it differently than his parents expected. "Kids now want to celebrate graduation with their friends, not with their families."

"Well, I don't like it. How am I going to know those parties are properly chaperoned?"

"You could get a list from Tony and call the parents." The fact that she was pregnant was making her think about this in a whole different way.

"If I did that, he'd never speak to me again." Her mother's tone was wry.

Laura laughed. "You might be right."

"I promised I'd get him a cell phone. I should do it before Friday night. Then he can call in and let me know where he is and what he's doing."

Laura hid a smile behind the flower arrangement. Her brother would *love* that idea.

"So…" her mother began conversationally. "How did it go with you and Gareth? He didn't stay very long."

Knowing the subject would come up, Laura tried to keep the tremor from her voice. "I told him I think we should separate for a while. He didn't take it well."

"I suppose *not*. Are you sure you know what you're doing? Gareth's a good man. It seems foolish to throw five years away."

"I'm not throwing them away. I need some time to think."

"You've had six weeks. Haven't you thought enough? Sometimes, Laura, I just don't understand you. What do you *want* from your marriage?"

That was the crux of the matter. She knew exactly

what she wanted. She wanted a connection with the man she loved, as well as communication. Once in a while, she wanted to be swept off her feet. At the beginning, she and Gareth had had all of that. But then he'd become consumed by his work, and she'd felt more and more lonely. They didn't have the kind of marriage they should have to bring a child into the world. She wasn't about to tell her mother about her pregnancy. Not yet.

"What did you expect when you married Dad?" Laura asked, instead of answering.

After Janice shoved a stalk of baby's breath into the Styrofoam beside a daylily, she answered, "I didn't expect anything. I mean, I wanted children, and I expected your father to support us. I knew his work as a cardiologist was important, and I would always come second to that."

"I don't want to be second to Gareth's career. And if we have children, I want them to come first for both of us."

"You're not being realistic."

"I think I am. Is it so extraordinary to want to feel special? To want to know I'm valued for who I am?"

"You've been watching too many talk shows."

"I haven't been watching *any* talk shows. I don't have time. But even Dr. Phil would agree a husband should support a wife just as much as a wife should support a husband."

"You always did have your own ideas of the way the

world should be," her mother said with a sigh. "I'm going to take a break and see what Tony wants for supper. If we go to the mall for a cell phone afterward, do you want to come along?"

"No. I have to work on menus on the computer and make a list of supplies I'll need for the next week or so."

"All right. We'll stop at that ice-cream shop you like so much and bring you home some Rocky Road."

Rocky Road used to be her favorite ice cream. Now the idea of it almost made her turn green. "Vanilla would be good."

Her mother looked at her askance. "Vanilla?"

"For a change."

Janice Bates shook her head and left the kitchen.

Other than the missed period, which wasn't all that unusual for her, Laura had used the pregnancy test because she felt nauseous every evening, not in the morning, like most women. She felt particularly sick if she didn't rest in the afternoon. She'd noticed other changes, too. Her breasts had felt fuller. Gareth would appreciate that change—

Tears came to her eyes. She simply didn't know what to do.

When she thought about the past five years, she remembered all the good moments, as well as the lonely ones. But the good moments had become fewer and farther between. She remembered the night a friend of hers, who liked her crab balls, had asked her to make them for a party. She had, and at that party someone had asked her if she took orders. Something had made her say yes. She'd started small, mainly taking jobs when Gareth was away. But as he was away more and more, she'd decided to make Delicacies by Laura a business. A year ago, after Gareth had returned from a week-long business trip, she'd brought up the subject.

"You want to do what?" he'd asked when she'd broached the idea.

"I want to open a catering business. We've got this huge, beautiful kitchen I can work in. And I can buy an oversize freezer and refrigerator and put them in the pantry. It will be perfect."

"You have to get a permit or a license. A health inspector has to inspect the premises. There will be start-up costs. You'll need a refrigerated van. You might even need help. Have you thought about any of that?"

She'd gotten angry then, which was unusual for her. She'd retorted, "Of course I've thought about all of that. I've even made up a business plan and enrolled in food-management courses at the college in San Antonio. I need training to get a permit. I'm not a child, Gareth. I have a brain, and common sense—and a knack for making creative food."

He'd frowned and run his hand through his thick, dark brown hair. "It would be a full-time job. You'll run yourself ragged working for me and doing that, too."

"I won't be doing both."

At that, he'd pinned her with his hazel eyes and asked, "Just what are you suggesting?"

"I'm suggesting you replace me. I'm sure an employment agency could find you the right office manager in a week."

"Are you serious about this?"

"Yes. I'm completely serious. I need to do this, Gareth. I like catering, and I want to do it as more than a pastime. I need something to fill my life when you're gone."

"Maybe we should have a baby," he'd suggested.

"If we had a baby, would you not travel as much?" Hope had blossomed in her heart at the thought.

"I'm a consultant. I go to companies who need me. That's not going to change."

So be it, she'd decided that night. Then something in her life had had to change. She'd ordered the freezer and the refrigerator that week and had started looking for a van. Gareth had separated himself from that whole process, and a week later began interviewing applicants to replace her as his office manager.

Now the phone rang, breaking the sequence of Laura's thoughts. Knowing her mother was probably involved with Tony in a discussion about the cell phone, Laura placed the floral picks on the table and went to the cordless phone on the counter.

When she picked it up, she said automatically, "Delicacies by Laura."

There was a heartbeat of silence, and then, "It's Gareth."

She knew the sound of his voice as well as she knew her own name. It always had the power to make butterflies dance in her stomach. But she didn't know if she did that to *him*. All the hours he worked…all the trips. Could he be having an affair? Her heart answered, *No. Not Gareth*. She believed her heart.

"I thought you were going to get some sleep." It was the first thing that came to her mind and she didn't analyze it before it came out.

"I couldn't sleep." His voice turned lighter. "Now, if you'd come home and crawl in beside me—"

"Gareth…" Sex between them had always been fiery and passionate and erotic. But in the last few months, even that had become matter-of-fact.

"I thought I'd try," he admitted.

"If you didn't sleep on the plane, you need to sleep now."

"I need to settle things between us more."

Running her finger along the edge of the counter, she murmured, "This has been building for a while. We can't fix it in a day."

"But we *can* fix it?" There was hope in his voice.

"I don't know." She thought about their baby, the love she still felt for him, and her throat closed around a huge lump.

"Laura?"

"Why did you call?" It was hard pushing the words out. She hadn't been ready to see Gareth earlier, but now she didn't want the call to end.

"Uncle Isaac's birthday is tomorrow."

She had it marked on her calendar. "I know. I promised to make him a carrot cake."

"He left a message on the machine here. He wants us to come over to his place. I called him, and apparently there's something he wants to show us. I told him I'd buy steaks and barbecue them on his grill. Are you going to come along?"

Her hesitation was momentary. "Yes, I'll come along. You know how important Uncle Isaac is to me." Gareth's uncle had filled a place in her life that her own father had left empty. When she was growing up and even now, she hardly ever saw her dad. He was always on call and spent nights at the hospital with critical patients. When Laura had met Gareth's uncle, she'd been comforted by his kindness. She loved Uncle Isaac as if he were her own uncle, and she wouldn't miss his birthday.

"I know he's important to you," Gareth said. "I have to go in to the office tomorrow, but I should be home by five o'clock. Will you still be at your mother's?"

She knew he wanted her to say she'd be coming home, but she couldn't. "Yes. I'll just make the carrot cake here. Is there anything else I can make?"

"That won't be necessary. We'll stop on the way to

buy the steaks and anything else we need. I'll pick you up at five-thirty."

It was going to seem odd to have Gareth pick her up at her mother's, but it was silly for her to drive, too.

"Laura, when I was in Tokyo I faxed—" He stopped.

"What did you fax?"

"Never mind. It doesn't matter. I just want you to know this house is empty without you."

"The house was always empty without *you*." She couldn't help saying it because it was the truth.

After a throbbing silence, Gareth's voice lost its warmth. "I'll see you tomorrow at five-thirty."

"I'll be ready."

After she said it, she knew it was a lie. She wouldn't be ready to see him again. She wouldn't be ready to be cooped up in a car with him again. She wouldn't be ready to face her love for Gareth Manning along with her resentment and the knowledge she was carrying his baby, too.

She prayed this birthday party with Gareth's uncle would give her some answers, because she couldn't seem to find them on her own.

When Gareth picked her up on Monday evening, his luxury sedan looked as if it had just gone through a car wash. And *he* looked…

He'd gotten out of the car and was coming up the walk. His white-and-red-striped polo shirt made his shoulders look even broader. His black jeans made his legs look even longer. His precisely trimmed dark hair waved over his forehead, as if he'd taken a comb to it right after a shower. When he came close to her, he smelled of spicy aftershave, and she felt her resistance to the attraction between them melt. She wondered if her decision to stay with her mother had been the right one.

He wasn't smiling, though, and she wondered if he was thinking about their conversation last night and the truth that she'd put again in front of his nose.

"Let me take that." A gift bag dangled from her wrist. His hands went under the cake box to lift it from her arms.

The brush of his arm against hers sent a jolt through her. Her head jerked up, her eyes collided with his and she saw the desire there. She'd missed him so.

He'd said he'd missed her. But had he missed more than the sex between them? For the past few years that's all he'd seemed to want from her. It simply wasn't enough.

Her throat tightened as she took a step back.

"I was going to come in and say hi to Tony. He must be excited about graduating on Friday."

"He's out with friends. I came on out because…"

"Because?" Gareth prompted, holding eye contact.

"Because I knew if you came in, Mom would give us both the third degree."

"I've always held my own with your mother, Laura, and I don't have anything to argue about. I want you back home. Maybe she thinks that's where you should be."

"What my mother thinks, and what I need, are two different things," she responded with spirit.

"I don't think we should be having this conversation out here over a box of carrot cake. Come on. We can talk in the car."

Agreeing with him this time, she followed him to the car. However, once inside, they didn't talk. There was strained silence, as if neither of them had any idea where to start. Before they knew it, twenty minutes had passed, and they were stopping at a grocery store. A short time later, they were pulling up in front of his uncle's house.

It was a small ranch house that was squeezed in between two other ranch houses. Live oaks lined the streets of the old neighborhood, and all the houses were well kept. As they walked up the curved concrete path, she knew Gareth would be pleased to see his uncle. Gareth didn't talk about his childhood much. His mother had died when he was around eight. For some reason his father had left Gareth with Isaac Manning. Gareth wouldn't talk about it. But she did know neither Isaac nor Gareth had heard from him for a couple of years now. The last note they'd received told them he was working on a fishing boat in Alaska.

When his uncle opened the door, he hugged Gareth, grocery bags and all. "Good to see you, boy. It's been forever." Then he leaned back and took a look at Laura. "You're looking mighty beautiful today."

She was wearing a green-flowered blouse and culottes and had to admit she had taken extra care with her appearance. She didn't know if Gareth had even noticed.

After a hug, she leaned back and grinned. "Here's your carrot cake. I think we should refrigerate it until dessert, though."

"No problem there. My refrigerator's empty. Gareth said he was bringing the groceries."

The small house was air-conditioned, and nothing had changed since the last time she'd been here. The tweed tan-and-brown sofa faced the TV. Gareth had bought his uncle one with a larger screen last Christmas. The pine tables, the tan recliner and anything else sitting about was more for convenience and comfort than any attempt to look stylish.

"We can stow these groceries," Uncle Isaac said, "then have supper out on the patio. Laura, why don't you go on out and look at my new rosebush. Tell me if you like the color."

After Laura slipped the cake into the refrigerator, then let herself out onto the patio, Gareth headed for the door. "I'll get the rest of the groceries."

"Wait a minute, boy."

Gareth looked over his shoulder at his uncle. "I know. You want to know about the Tokyo trip."

"Sure, I do. But even more, I want to know what's going on with you and Laura. What's the story, son?"

Chapter 2

"What makes you think something's wrong?" Gareth asked.

"All I have to do is take one look at you," Isaac offered. "Your feet are wide apart, your spine's as straight as a stick, your pride's sittin' on your shoulders as if it's waitin' to pour over."

Purposely, Gareth tried to relax. Did Laura see that same defensiveness in him? Was that another wall between them? "Laura went to stay with her mother when I was away, and now…she thinks we need some time apart." He said it as if he still couldn't believe it. He said it as if he was talking about another couple, not the two of them.

"And just what are you going to do about it?"

His uncle's question rankled because he hadn't figured out the answer yet. "I'm working on it."

"No, I don't think you are. You can't just argue with her about this. You've got to *do* something."

All of his life, Gareth had realized action was the best course. After his father had left him with his brother, Gareth had put all of his energy into making Isaac like him…making Isaac proud of him…making Isaac his friend as well as his guardian. He'd been proactive in his career, too, going after consulting contracts with plum companies. That had paid off, too. So now when his uncle talked about action, Gareth realized he needed a plan. But flowers, a date to a concert in San Antonio…those just didn't seem right. What did Laura want most of all? Day-to-day contact? That might be the place to start.

"We'll get over this bump in the road. Trust me."

His uncle slapped him on the back. "I do. You'll figure out what's right for you and her. But you'd better figure it out fast. The more time she's at her mother's, the worse it's going to get. Now, let's put those steaks on. I'm starved."

While Gareth barbecued the steaks, Laura set the redwood table on the covered patio with thick paper plates. As the meat sizzled, his uncle disappeared into the garage and Laura went inside to fix a salad. A few minutes later she returned.

"Are you hungry?" he asked.

She hesitated a moment and then said brightly, "Sure. I'm going to put the candles on the cake and get it ready for after dinner."

Gareth didn't like the feeling that Laura was trying to elude him. He didn't like the stilted conversation between them. He didn't like the rock in the pit of his stomach that told him he'd better fix this situation fast.

Ten minutes later, he opened the kitchen door and found her still fiddling with the candles. Crossing to her, he dropped his arm around her shoulders. "That looks wonderful. I don't know if he'll have enough air to blow them out."

The contact of his fingers on her bare arm was instantaneously electric. The best thing they'd ever had going for them was the chemistry between them. Now he was going to have to use that to remind her why they'd gotten married.

She tensed, but she didn't pull away. "I'll help him if he runs out of steam," she said lightly.

"Is that the cake with the pineapple in it?" he asked.

"I like that recipe best."

Her body was so close to his that their body heat combined in the kitchen. The temperature kept going up as her perfume filled his nostrils, as the sweet femininity of her tempted him. Now he turned her to him, forgetting about the cake…forgetting the steaks on the table outside…forgetting his uncle was in the garage.

"I'm not sure we even said hello when I got home."

"No, we didn't," she agreed, her eyes going wide.

"There's more than one way to say hello."

As his arms went around her, the look in her eyes told him she wasn't going to resist. It told him she'd missed him, too. That missing had been a palpable ache in his chest that had gotten even worse when she'd said she was staying at her mother's. Now, as he bent his head slowly, he savored every nuance of anticipation.

Her long dark lashes fluttered down on her creamy skin. Her mouth parted ever so slightly for him. Her body swayed to meet his. Everything about Laura had always turned him on, and tonight was no exception. Although he was hungry for her, he wasn't going to rush, or take, or steal. Slowly, he nibbled her upper lip, realizing he wanted to give her so much pleasure she'd want the kiss to last all night. When his lips moved to the corner of her mouth and she gave a soft sigh, he knew he was creating the desired effect. Then he was laving her lower lip with his tongue. Her soft moan was the signal he needed. His teasing, kissing foreplay changed into something serious. When his lips sealed to hers, he took possession. As her arms went around his neck, his tongue seductively slid into her mouth. Her body was tight against his, familiar yet exciting, the same and yet different, arousing as it had been the very first time.

There were always fireworks when they kissed.

That's what kept them coming back for more. He'd missed the fireworks, and her soft seduction, and the sounds she made when he pleased her.

Then, suddenly, Laura's arms slipped from his neck and she was pulling away. "Gareth, we can't do this." Her voice was shaky and her breathing was as uneven as his.

"Why not? We're even married." He tried to keep his voice light, teasing.

"We've always had chemistry. We both know that. But that's just going to confuse everything."

"Maybe it can make everything a lot clearer." He kept his tone even, wondering how she could deny what was so obvious to him—they belonged together.

However, she shook her head and moved to the screen door. "If the steaks are done, they're going to get cold."

"Damn the steaks, Laura! Aren't *we* just as important?"

"Right now, your uncle is the one who's important. It's *his* birthday, and I don't want to spoil it."

Just then his uncle emerged from the garage onto the patio and called into the kitchen, "The steaks look great. I have something to show you two when we're finished. You're going to love it."

Gareth raked his hand through his hair in frustration. Yes, they were going to celebrate his uncle's birthday tonight. But he was also going to figure out how to get Laura back into his arms.

* * *

At dinner, Laura sat next to Gareth on the bench across from Uncle Isaac. Her husband's kiss had shaken her more than she wanted to admit. The passion between them had always been a bonfire, and she'd known from the moment she'd first met him that they could be consumed by it. Tonight that bonfire had to be doused. She couldn't let it interfere with her logic and her feelings, and the direction she knew she and Gareth had to go. She had a baby to consider now and she couldn't be persuaded to overlook their problems because they were good together in bed. However, as they made conversation with Uncle Isaac, catching up on the latest trends in the supercenter where he worked as a department manager, she was aware that Gareth was attempting to remind her of the desire between them any way he could. He reached around her for a napkin on the back edge of the bench, his strong arm solid against her back. His shoulder brushed hers time and time again as he ate and they talked. When she tried to slow her heart rate, his knee grazed hers under the table as he reached for the steak sauce.

By the end of the main course, she hopped up from the bench, eager to get the cake, eager to make her escape.

"Need help?" he asked.

"Just hold the door," she murmured as she went inside and lit the candles—all sixty-three of them.

Isaac laughed when she set the cake in front of him. "You expect me to blow those out on my own?"

"Give it a try. I'll be right beside you if you need a little help."

From somewhere, Gareth produced a camera, and as she stood beside his uncle, he snapped one picture after another. Isaac had blown out all but three candles when she saw he needed help, leaned forward and puffed the last three out. She heard the shutter click again, and when she looked up, Gareth was studying her with such intensity, she felt her cheeks flush.

"All right, you got plenty of pics of me," Isaac complained. "Now let me take one of the two of you."

"Don't be silly," she protested. "We have to cut your cake. And you have presents to open."

"That can all wait. I want a picture of you two. I'll put it in that frame on the TV to replace the old one."

The one on Gareth's uncle's TV had been taken about three years ago when they'd all gone to the River Walk for the day. Over the past year time had been at a premium. Either Gareth was working, or she was, and they hadn't spent a day with his uncle in a long time.

Feeling regret about that, she decided, "We'll have to go to the River Walk again soon, or maybe to the Alamo and out for dinner."

"Or," Uncle Isaac drawled, "maybe the next time Gareth goes to Tokyo, we could take a vacation and go along."

The silence that fell over the patio seemed to extend to the whole neighborhood. Not a bird chirped. Not a car door slammed. Not a mower buzzed.

Still with a smile on his face, Isaac went on, "I suppose that's a very different life from over here. It would be interesting. What did you see over there? What did you like most?"

Tension had ratcheted up a few more degrees. Gareth said quickly, "I didn't have much time for sight-seeing. I was mostly involved in meetings and putting together reports at night when I returned to my hotel room. I revamped every department in a laptop-computer company."

When they were first married, Laura had gone along on a few of Gareth's business trips. But he *was* working the whole time, and she'd had to sightsee on her own. That was okay once in a while, but she'd missed him. She wanted to be sightseeing with him. So she'd stopped going.

"You can't tell me you didn't see anything!" Isaac pressed.

After a quick glance at Laura, Gareth responded, "I spent some time on the Ginza Strip, that's theaters and restaurants and shopping. I also passed one afternoon at the National Science Museum and the Museum of Western Art." He looked excited about that for a moment, then turned to Laura. "But I missed you."

"You didn't ask me to go with you," she murmured.

"Maybe that's because I knew you wouldn't. Your calendar was booked with catering gigs." Then, as if he knew this wasn't going to get them anywhere, as if he knew this would only make matters worse, he turned to her on the bench, the nerve in his jaw working. "But the Tokyo trip is over now, and I'm home. I'm glad to *be* home."

Gareth might be glad to be home, yet she knew he'd leave again. And after this six-week trip, how long would the next one be? She was afraid their marriage was headed down a dead-end road. She didn't want a child getting hurt if they crashed into a barrier at the end of it.

Although the steaks were grilled just right, and the salad was crisp and the carrot cake had come out well, Laura had just picked at her food. It was that time of day when her stomach was upset and crackers would have made her feel better than carrot cake. She had pushed her food around and made it look as if she were enjoying it.

Isaac was like a kid when he opened his presents. She had bought him a new baseball cap with the Astros emblem and a CD of sixties hits. Those were his favorite.

After he gave her a hug and his thanks, he said, "And Gareth's present arrived this morning."

Laura didn't want to admit she didn't know what it was, so she waited.

"Did you see the lawn mower he picked out for me?" Isaac asked her.

"No, I didn't."

Scrambling from the bench, he motioned to her. "Come on, I'll show you. You, too, Gareth. I want to show you what I got *myself* for my birthday."

Isaac's car had been parked in the driveway when they arrived, and as they went inside the one-car garage, Laura could see why. In a place of honor, smack-dab in the middle, stood a shiny red motorcycle.

"Uncle Isaac! What are you going to do with *that?*" Laura asked, grinning.

"I'm going to ride it!" He took the black helmet from one of the handlebars. "Get a load of this." After he put it on, he beamed at them from inside the helmet. "It's a hoot, isn't it?"

Gareth was already examining the machine and he smiled as he admired the chrome instrument panel, the bucket-type front seat and the metallic red finish. "I bet you've been saving for this for a long time."

"Yep, I have. Wanna take a ride?" He wiggled his eyebrows at Laura.

Normally she would have jumped at the chance to take a ride, feel the wind in her hair and against her body, especially if she could have her arms around Gareth.

Now, knowing she was pregnant, she couldn't take the chance. "I think I'll pass."

Gareth gave her a questioning look.

"I'll clean up supper," she added. "You two take it out." She hugged Uncle Isaac. "But be careful."

"Are you saying I'm too old for this?" he asked with a twinkle in his eyes.

"Not at all. I'd tell Tony to be careful, too," she said in a wry tone.

Gareth laughed. "I guess it's a compliment that she's putting you in the same category as Tony."

"She's about got it right. I feel young again when I'm on this machine." He patted it lovingly.

After Laura had taken a quick look at the mower, which Isaac liked almost as much as his new motorcycle, she cleaned up the remains of supper and put the cake in the refrigerator. Uncle Isaac would be enjoying that for the next week.

The men were gone about half an hour. When they returned, Gareth looked as energized as his uncle. "It handles great. I'd forgotten what it's like to go for a joy-ride."

"Thinking about buying one?" she teased.

"No, but I am thinking about you and I doing something fun for a change."

"Fun?"

"Yes. Like taking a river taxi on the River Walk and sight-seeing like tourists."

Maybe Gareth was getting her message. Maybe there was some hope.

They took iced tea out onto the patio and visited with Isaac for another hour or so. Then, with hugs all around, they left.

Isaac had made conversation easy, and the tension between her and Gareth hadn't been as noticeable while they'd talked with him. But now it was back, and Laura wasn't sure what to do about it. She wasn't sure what to do about anything.

Obviously feeling the strain, too, Gareth switched on the CD player. When he pulled up in front of her mother's house, he flicked off the ignition and unfastened his seat belt, but he didn't make a move to climb out. "Glad you went?"

"Yes," she assured him. "I wouldn't have missed Uncle Isaac's birthday." Unfastening her shoulder harness, she angled toward Gareth. "I'll be cooking at the house tomorrow. I bid on the contract to make desserts for the Spring Fling and got it."

Switching on the light on the visor, he studied her. "That's quite an event. How do you prepare food when you don't know for sure how many guests will turn up?"

"I just guess," she joked, then added more seriously, "They sold tickets, so I do have some idea. But anyone who wants to come can buy a ticket that night, too."

Silence wrapped around them in the car again, until she said, "I'd better go in."

"Afraid your brother will come out here with a flashlight to see what we're doing?"

Laura flushed. Her brother had actually done that when they were first dating. "I don't think that will happen."

Reaching out, he took the ends of her hair between his fingers and slid his thumb over them. "The best part of tonight wasn't the motorcycle ride."

He'd moved closer and his face was very near hers as she asked, "It wasn't?"

Now he ran his thumb over her bottom lip. "No. The best part of tonight was kissing you again."

The deep sincerity in his voice unsettled her. The touch of his finger on her lips made her tremble. All she could do was gaze into his eyes as he bent toward her.

"Gareth—" His name was meant to be a soft protest, but he didn't take it as that.

The next moment, his lips were covering hers. Gareth was virile, with strong needs, and that had always excited her. He liked to kiss, and that had always awakened all of her passion. Now, as his tongue slid into her mouth, as she realized he could still make her world spin, she braced her hands on his shoulders and pushed away.

"What?" he asked with some frustration.

"You're making this harder."

There was an amused twinkle in his eye now. "That's the idea."

Moving even farther toward the door, she responded, "It won't work. We have problems that can't be solved with a kiss."

"Maybe they could be settled in bed."

"No! That's the one really good part of our marriage, and if we don't solve our problems and we take them into bed with us, that will disintegrate too. I don't want that to happen."

His shoulders were squared now, his voice gruff as he asked, "What *do* you want to happen?"

That was the first he'd asked her, and he seemed to be listening, really listening. "I want more time with you. I want you to cut back on traveling. And I want—" Tears came to her eyes. "I want the old connection back. The one we had at the beginning."

He leaned back against the seat. "We're not just meeting for the first time. We've been married for five years, and the novelty's worn off."

"Maybe we should pretend we're starting all over again. Because if we can't feel those old feelings, if we don't want to spend time together, if we can't light up each other's lives, then we don't have anywhere to go."

Silence filled the car until he concluded, "Maybe you want too much."

She shook her head. "I know what we once had, and I want it back."

Because she thought he might ask her to come home with him again, she braced herself. But he didn't ask.

After a very long pause, he inquired, "Will you be at the house all day tomorrow?"

"I don't know. It depends how far I get with the desserts."

"Maybe I'll see you when I get home. If not, I'll be in touch."

There was nothing definite about that. Wasn't that what she wanted? Time apart for them to think? But now Gareth seemed to be withdrawing, and she wondered just what he was going to think about.

When she opened her car door, he climbed out, too. They walked silently up the brick path, and at the porch steps, he didn't climb them with her. He didn't make an attempt to kiss her. He didn't even say good-night. He just watched her use her mother's spare key and go inside.

After Laura closed the door behind her, she leaned against it, wondering if everything she wanted was so different from what Gareth wanted.

If it was—

A tear rolled down her cheek.

Laura's assistant, Corrine Ramirez, who was petite with black, short-cut curly hair, worked with her all day Wednesday, helping her prepare desserts for the Spring Fling. They made everything from cookies to petit fours to cheesecake tarts. Now Laura washed up the last of the cookie sheets while Corrine labeled plastic containers before she stowed them in the freezer.

As Corrine layered the tarts in a container, she remarked, "I'm glad we were working in here today. What's the summer going to be like if it's this hot now?"

Corrine and her husband had moved to San Antonio from northern Arizona so he could take a promotion with a pharmaceutical company. She hadn't yet gotten used to San Antonio's weather. "We survived last summer. We'll survive again this year. I'm just glad the van's refrigerated." Laura turned off the spigot. "Will Joe be coming to the Spring Fling?"

"No, he doesn't like to hang around while I'm working. What about Gareth?"

"I don't know."

"You're still staying at your mother's?"

"Yes."

Corrine gave her a sympathetic look. "Six months after Joe and I were married, we had an argument to end all arguments. I stayed with my sister for a few weeks, and he lived like a bachelor."

"The argument was that serious?"

"Back then I thought it was. He wanted to buy this fancy new SUV. I wanted to use the money for a down payment on a house."

"How did you get back together again?"

"It shouldn't have been so hard," she admitted with a shake of her head. "But when I left, this pride thing happened—to him *and* to me. It was like neither of us could admit we were wrong."

"It's not wrong to want a house."

"It wasn't wrong to want an SUV," Corrine said with a wry smile, "but somehow the issue became a monumental obstacle. It turns out there was more to it than a car or a house. Joe didn't want to go into debt. His parents had had trouble making ends meet and they were always afraid the bank would foreclose. He remembered that."

"How did you find out that's what was behind it?"

"After three weeks of being separated, my sister invited him to dinner. Afterward, she wouldn't let either of us leave the house until we talked. We should have done it the day after the argument."

"Did you compromise or give in?"

"We decided not to buy the SUV *or* the house. Not right then. We knew his truck was good for another couple of years, and our rent was reasonable, so we decided to save for another year at least. It worked out because when we moved here, we had a good-size down payment. Now neither one of us leaves the house when we have an argument. We might need cooling-off time, but we don't leave. And eventually we talk and work out whatever it is."

Laura didn't know if she'd made a mistake by leaving, but it seemed to be the only way to get Gareth's attention. Their marriage had needed a wake-up call, and she was hoping the separation was exactly that.

However, she was about to confide in Corrine about her doubts, when she heard the garage door open. A few minutes later, Gareth was striding through the family room toward the kitchen. "You're still here." He looked surprised, and Laura couldn't tell if he was pleased or not.

"We're just finishing up. We'll be out of your hair in a few minutes."

Corrine emerged from the pantry and greeted Gareth. "I've got to get home and start supper." Turning back to Laura, she asked, "Are you sure you can handle the baby shower yourself tomorrow evening?"

"I'm positive. It's fifteen women, hot hors d'oeuvres, snacks and a cake. I'll make that tomorrow morning. It's a sheet cake and I just have to decorate it with a baby carriage and some balloons. I *will* be going for supplies tomorrow afternoon, though. I need to pick up those new glasses along with everything else. If you need anything, just call me in the morning and give me your list."

"Will do. See you, Gareth." Then Corrine was heading toward the front door to let herself out.

Finding herself alone with her husband, Laura was at an absolute loss for words.

He'd loosened his tie and opened the top two buttons of his dress shirt. His suit coat was slung over his arm. Her pulse sped up as she thought about brushing her fingers through his short hair. Her fingers tingled with desire.

She checked the clock on the wall. "You're home

early." It was only four o'clock, and Gareth rarely returned home before six.

"I thought I'd go for a swim. How about joining me?"

When she considered swimming with Gareth and seeing him in his trunks, she got hot all over. "I don't know if I left my bathing suit upstairs or took it along."

"Why don't you check. Mine's in the mudroom. I took a swim last night."

A swim by moonlight. She wanted to think they might do that sometime in the future together, but she just didn't know.

She motioned to the cookie sheets and the cake pans sitting on the counter. "I really should put all this away."

"It can wait. Come on, let's cool off. If you don't have your suit we can live dangerously and skinny-dip."

"Even with the privacy fence, that's still a little risqué for me."

"Then I hope you find a swimsuit. I'll meet you out at the pool."

Gareth's attitude today had a cool edge to it. Was he withdrawing to protect himself? Was pride going to get in their way on both their parts?

After he set his briefcase on the kitchen table, he tugged off his tie and headed toward the utility room and his trunks.

Laura hurried to the master suite and into her walk-in closet. There she found her bathing suit in the back. Quickly she skimmed off her sandals, shorts, top and underwear and slid into the yellow-and-black one-piece bathing suit. When she stepped into the dressing room, she stood in front of the full-length mirror, running her hand over her tummy. She felt different. Her breasts felt fuller. But at seven weeks, she didn't look different, did she?

Gazing into the mirror again, she wondered if her waist looked just a little thicker.

Thinking this might be the last time Gareth saw her in a bathing suit for a while, she grabbed a towel and went down to join her husband in the pool.

Chapter 3

While Gareth waited for Laura, he swam laps. He wondered if she might decide to go back to her mother's without ever getting in the pool, even if she found a bathing suit. She might decide she didn't want to be with him tonight.

As Gareth's arms sliced through the water, he realized this separation, as well as Laura's pulling away, had made one very huge dent in his ego. He used to be able to predict her every action and reaction. He'd thought the house he'd given her, the life he'd given her, would be enough to make her happy. He'd thought *he* was enough to make her happy. Maybe that had been arrogant. But, damn it, he'd made promises he'd intended to keep for a lifetime.

Last night, when he'd finally realized she was serious about this separation, he'd been more than frustrated by desire he'd wanted to fulfill. He'd been angry that she'd put either of them in this position. He'd been resentful that even his uncle could see the crack in their marriage. He'd been disappointed that she didn't have enough confidence in him and in herself that they could work this out.

That's when a monumental question had stared him in the face. Did she *want* to work this out?

He heard the sliding door open from the dining area of the kitchen to the poolside patio. Stopping his lap marathon in midstroke, he moved to the shallower water and went to the side of the pool. His body responded to the sight of Laura in her bathing suit as she came through the gate. The yellow bands down the side of the suit leading to the high-cut legs drew his gaze first. Then his focus was drawn to the yellow band across her breasts.

When he gave a low, drawn-out whistle, she blushed like a schoolgirl.

"You could enter any beauty pageant and win," he said, meaning it.

In her hand she held something she called a scrunchie. Now she used the white elastic to tie her long hair in a ponytail as she responded, "I think you need a pair of sunglasses. This glare must be distorting your vision."

"There's nothing distorting my vision. You turned my head the first day I saw you and you can still do it now."

She appeared genuinely surprised as she came down the steps into the pool. "I don't think you ever told me that."

"Why do you think I asked you out to dinner that night?"

She shrugged. "While you were waiting for your appointment with Tom Seymore, we started talking about the new movie theater going up and the latest Mel Gibson movie."

"You think I wanted to ask you out because of your taste in movies?" He was genuinely amused by that, and she must have seen it.

"From movies we moved on to restaurants, and we both seemed to have a penchant for Chinese. I thought that's why you asked me to dinner."

Wading into the water slowly, she got used to the cool temperature.

"When I laid eyes on you, my adrenaline rushed so fast I couldn't catch my breath. That's why I asked you out."

"Is that another way of saying you wanted to get me into bed?" she teased.

"It's another way of saying that I was interested on more than one level."

Finally, she sank into the water and swam over to him. "This does feel nice."

"We should take time to swim more often." One look in her eyes, and he knew what she was thinking. He was too busy to swim. Had she really turned to catering because she was lonely?

Resting her arm on the side of the pool, she asked, "How did you really like Tokyo?"

"It was all right. But I *was* working most of the time."

"You said you were in the shopping district. I heard you can buy beautiful jade there. Is that true?"

He didn't even know she liked jade. He hated shopping. Instead of sending that damn letter to the *Red Rock Gazette,* he should have gone into a shop and bought her a piece of jewelry. He'd never brought her a token back from any of his trips. Because he was so work absorbed when he was gone? Because he didn't want to take the time? Because he didn't think it was necessary?

"There was jade," he admitted, "but I didn't pay much attention to it." Suddenly he needed to get away from this subject he'd have to examine more closely later. "Do you want to race?" he asked. They'd done that a few times after they'd bought the house.

"Sure," she agreed with a smile. "But I don't think you'll have any trouble winning. This time of day—" She abruptly stopped.

"What about this time of day?"

"Oh, nothing. I was up early this morning and had

breakfast with Dad before he did rounds at the hospital."

"Does your mother still make him a full breakfast at 5:00 a.m.?"

"Yes, she does. I think she considers it her duty. I offered to cook this morning so she could sleep. But she said after all these years she was awake, so she might as well get up."

Laura's gaze seemed to be fixed to his chest. After she moistened her lips, she brought her eyes back to his. "Tony asked me this morning if you're still coming to his graduation."

Her appraisal of him seemed to make the hot day hotter. "Of course I am. Why would he ask that?" Gareth was fond of Tony and had always felt like an older brother to him.

"Because I'm living *there* and you're living here."

"My friendship with your brother is separate from our marriage, but I guess I'll have to tell him that. Come on, let's push off from the steps. I'll give you a head start."

"You will not. We start at the same time, from the same spot."

The look in Laura's eyes told him that wherever their marriage was headed, they'd be relating to each other as equals. So be it.

They raced back and forth three times. The first two, Gareth won. On their third attempt, however, he slowed, and Laura's hand touched the edge of the pool before his. But she didn't look happy when he came up for air and dragged his hand over his face to wipe away the water.

"You let me win," she accused him.

"Is that so bad?" he asked with a grin.

"When I win, I want to win fair and square."

"There's more than one way to win," he decided, zeroing in on her lips, wanting to scoop her up onto the side of the pool and make love to her right there.

"Don't look at me like that," she murmured breathlessly.

"Like what?"

Her gaze left his, roamed over his shoulders then his chest again.

"Like," she drawled, and then began splashing him, "like you need to be cooled off."

The water hit him full in the face, and when it did, his first thought was retribution. Splashing water back at her, when she turned away he dived underwater, came up beside her and scooped her into his arms.

"Don't duck me," she yelled. "I hate to be ducked."

"Ducking is not what I have in mind."

A second later, his lips were on hers. It was a short, deep, thoroughly wet kiss.

After he ended it, he strode into the shallow end and set her down. "When you're sleeping at your mother's tonight, you remember that first day we met. You remember our first kiss, and also remember every night I made love to you."

Then frustrated with himself, as well as with her and the whole situation, he mounted the steps and picked up the towel he'd laid on a lounge chair. "I'll take a shower in the guest bedroom. The master suite is yours."

Before she got a glimpse of how very much he wanted her, he wrapped the towel around his waist, opened the gate and went inside the house.

As Laura showered and dressed in the master bedroom, she thought about Gareth's words. She did remember their first kiss. She also remembered the first night they'd spent in this bedroom—on the floor because their furniture hadn't been delivered. It had been fun and exciting and they'd laughed as they'd made love, tossed and turned on the hard floor, then made love again. But that was the problem. The fun and the excitement had seeped away.

Until today.

She flashed back to Gareth coming after her when she'd splashed him. That playfulness had been missing for a long time. That was the side of Gareth she wanted their child to know.

As Laura rounded the corner from the bedroom suite into the hall, she heard voices. At first she thought Gareth might be on the phone, but then she realized there was a male voice and a female voice.

When she entered the family room, she frowned. Nancy Caldwell was sitting in Laura's favorite glider rocker. Gareth had hired Nancy when Laura had stopped working with him. She'd had no say in the decision, and she had to admit, she didn't like the redhead.

Nancy was in her mid-twenties and dressed professionally. But her skirt was always a couple of inches shorter than the standard, her blouse usually had one too many buttons unbuttoned. If she wore a jacket it was never boxy, but always fitted closely to her figure. And she had a svelte one. Today she was wearing a red skirt and a white silky short-sleeved blouse. Laura supposed the suit jacket was probably in her car.

Redheads shouldn't wear red, she thought as Gareth saw her and held up the manila folder in his hand. "Nancy thought I'd forgotten these figures, so she dropped them off on her way home."

"You're working tonight?" Laura asked.

"I have notes from a new account to go over. It's great to have a dependable office manager who sometimes manages to read my mind." He smiled at Nancy and she smiled back.

She'd always believed Gareth to be trustworthy. But now she wondered again about all the late nights he worked, the evening meetings, the long hours. It was imperative that she know something.

Forcing a smile, she said, "It's great you make Gareth's life easier. Did you go along to Tokyo?"

Standing then, Nancy shook her head. "No. I offered, but Gareth said he could handle the meetings on his own. I was typing up his notes today." Then she focused a full-blown smile on Gareth. "If you have any pictures of your trip, I'd *love* to see them. Tokyo is a city I'd like to visit someday."

"Sorry. No pictures. I didn't do the sight-seeing tourist routine. But I do have a magazine I picked up over there. If you'd like to see it, I'll bring it to the office tomorrow."

Laura could read nothing from Gareth's expression or body language to tell her if he was attracted to Nancy, but any man would be. At least to the outside package. She wondered if Nancy knew of her separation from Gareth. And if she did, had she been hoping to catch him alone?

Gareth was wearing a pair of black shorts but was still shirtless. Nancy's gaze wandered to his chest more than once, and Laura felt her stomach tighten. This woman *was* attracted to her husband. Considering she and Gareth had been apart for six weeks, she was terrifically uncomfortable with that realization.

"Would you like something to drink?" Gareth asked Nancy, acting the perfect host.

After a glance at Laura, Nancy responded by checking her watch. "No, I'd better be getting home."

"Thanks for staying late and getting a head start on my findings in Tokyo."

"I should finish them tomorrow, then you can make

a formal report to the CEO." She stood and headed for the front door.

Laura said woodenly, "Have a good evening."

Nancy tossed her a perfunctory, "I will."

After Gareth followed his office manager into the foyer, Laura went to the kitchen, telling herself it simply didn't matter how long their goodbye took.

When Gareth entered the kitchen, he laid the folder on the counter. "Do you have plans tonight?"

"I told Mom I'd go along with her and Tony to buy him a new shirt and tie for graduation."

"What about tomorrow night?"

"I'm catering a baby shower."

"Then I guess I won't see you again until graduation on Friday evening." His voice was even, but there was a frustrated edge to it.

She took a step closer to him. "I'll be working here again tomorrow. I have to make salads and bake and decorate the cake."

"Did I hear you say you're going into San Antonio for supplies, too? That's an awful lot in a day."

"I'll get an early start. I might be here before you leave for work."

Although she'd moved toward him, he didn't move toward her. He didn't tell her what plans he might have had for them if she hadn't been busy. She felt as if she was stepping in quicksand any time she was around Gareth now, and a misstep could be dangerous.

Quickly she put away the cookie sheets and other pans she had washed while Gareth watched her. His gaze never left her.

Finally he pushed away from the counter. "I'll be in my office. Give a yell before you leave." Then he walked away without looking back, and Laura had never felt more distance between them.

The following morning, Gareth was gone when Laura arrived at the house. She'd stopped at a local market that opened at 7:00 a.m. to buy fresh meat and bread. She was going to make her own chicken and ham salads, as well as a spinach dip she'd serve with a loaf of sourdough bread. As she put the ham in the oven to bake and the chicken in a pot on top of the stove to boil, she thought about Gareth and their swim, and his office manager's visit. All of it had kept her awake most of the night. Hopefully, she'd get some time to rest after she picked up the supplies in San Antonio this afternoon. She really should stop in at the garage and have the mechanic check her van. It was running rough. But she simply didn't have time for that today.

Gareth hadn't been happy when she'd brought home the eight-year-old refrigerated van. He'd warned her that if it hadn't had problems yet, it was going to have them soon. But she'd ignored his dire predictions. She'd wanted to buy a vehicle with the money *she'd* made. That had been important to her. The man she'd purchased it from was closing his delicatessen business, and she'd thought she'd made a good deal.

But Gareth hadn't praised her negotiation skills. He'd just told her to keep the van on the left side of the three-car garage.

Around lunchtime, Laura craved peanut butter. The cravings she'd had thus far were odd—pancakes at midnight, tapioca pudding, cranberry-orange relish. Weird. She didn't always give in to them, but now, wanting to keep working, she found a jar of peanut butter, slathered some on a piece of bread and munched on it while she cooked eggs to use in the chicken salad. The trouble was, after she ate the peanut-butter bread, it felt like a lead weight in her stomach. Just because she craved something didn't mean she felt good on it.

Hoping the indigestion would wear off, she kept up a steady pace and was putting the finishing touches on the cake for the baby shower, when she heard Gareth's car in the driveway. Checking the clock above the sink, she saw it was 3:00 p.m.

"What are you doing home?" she asked Gareth as he came into the kitchen.

"I thought I'd go with you since Corrine can't. It sounds as if you're picking up quite a few supplies."

"You took off work to help me pick up supplies?"

He looked chagrined for a moment, then he approached her slowly. With each step he took toward her, Laura's heart raced faster. She loved the smell of his cologne. She was excited by the look in his eyes. She could practically feel his body heat from the warm Texas day. When he settled his hands on her shoulders and ran his thumb up and down her neck, her whole body trembled.

"Isn't that what you want? More time together?"

Could things change between them? Was Gareth really going to make an effort to be more available? Was this an overture to show her their lives could change? Or was he simply doing what he thought she wanted in order to get her to move back in again?

She had to give them both the benefit of the doubt.

"It's going to be a quick trip." Her voice was a bit shaky as the attraction between them surged through her. "I need to be at the baby shower by six-thirty to set up."

"You should be able to load supplies faster if I'm along," he suggested with a crooked grin.

Gareth was a swimmer and a runner. His body was muscled and well toned, and there was no doubt he'd be an asset in lifting boxes into the van. He'd taken off his suit jacket, and she longed to run her hands from his shoulders to his elbows, then put her hands all over his body. But she wasn't going to be a tease. If and when they made love again, she wanted to know in her soul that their marriage was going to survive.

"Are you going to change clothes? I'll be ready to go as soon as I box the cake." It was so hard to talk about mundane things when his fingers on her skin made her want to tumble into bed with him.

He dropped his hands to his sides. "By the time you have the cake boxed, I'll be in the van."

His expression was unreadable again, and she could feel his sexual hunger as much as she could feel her own. But sex wasn't the solution. For the past year it had been a Band-Aid that had held their marriage together. She didn't want to use something so precious for that purpose anymore.

Twenty minutes later, as Gareth drove to San Antonio, he asked her about future catering events. They also talked about the odd happenings at the Red Rock Commerce Bank. She'd heard the sirens the other day. Then when she'd read the write-up in the paper, she'd learned Dirk Jenkins, who had apparently been sweet on one of the bank tellers, held up the bank with a squirt gun!

"For some irrational reason," Gareth explained, "Dirk thought he was rescuing Annie Grant. From what I understand, Officer Flynn saved the day."

"Dirk Jenkins was quoted as saying he did it for love."

Gareth glanced at Laura. She sounded so sad. She seemed to want something intangible from him, and he didn't know how to give it to her. But she'd seemed pleased he was going with her, and maybe that would be a start.

They were stopped at a light on the outskirts of San

Antonio when the van coughed and ran rough. Gareth had heard and felt the congested hiccups it had given while he was driving. Now he knew it was going to stall out.

When it did, he tried starting it. It backfired and shook. "Have you been having trouble with this?" He tried the ignition again.

"Only since Corrine drove it last week."

"Did she mention a problem?"

"She said after she filled the tank with gas, it started giving her trouble. But it didn't stop or anything like that."

He wondered if Corrine had put the wrong-octane gas in the tank or if the gas had been dirty.

On the third try, the engine caught and grumbled to life again. The light had turned green and now he put his foot on the accelerator, hoping the van wouldn't stall out again.

When they arrived at the food warehouse where Laura bought supplies, he parked the van at the loading dock, waiting while Laura went inside. Soon the garage door at the dock opened. Her order was apparently ready, stacked on two skids that he and someone from the warehouse packed into the van. Nothing they loaded up was perishable, so Laura didn't have the refrigeration unit in the van running.

Fifteen minutes later, they were headed back to Red Rock. The van started right up this time, and they sailed through lights and San Antonio without a hitch. But when they reached the stretch of road between San Antonio and Red Rock, the van began coughing and running rough again. The whole vehicle seemed to tremble, and then it quit.

Gareth swore, using the vehicle's momentum to guide it to the shoulder of the road.

Laura checked her watch. "I don't have time for this. I have to get the van unloaded and everything packed up before I head out for the shower."

"Let me take a look at it. I have a feeling your problem is the gas Corrine put in it. If that's the case, the van will probably have to be towed."

Laura's face had a drawn look now, and she pushed her hair back with one hand, lowering her window.

She didn't say anything else as he watched for traffic, opened his door and went around front to the hood. At least the road had a wide shoulder and they didn't have to worry about another car hitting them. Raising the hood, he checked the battery terminals, the cables, even the oil. But he couldn't find a problem, and he wasn't going to waste time that Laura needed.

Pulling his cell phone from his belt, he went to her window. "Do you have your membership number for roadside service?"

Silently, she slipped a card from her wallet and handed it to him.

As the minutes ticked by, Laura became more agitated. Because of the eighty-five-degree heat, they'd gotten out of the van, gone to the back and opened the doors. While they sat there, he noticed Laura's face turning a shade pinker. "It will be all right, Laura."

"I don't know it will be all right," she said, her voice pained. "What if the tow truck doesn't come for a half an hour? I can't be late. The mother-to-be's sister is counting on me."

"Accidents happen. I'm sure she'll understand—"

"I have obligations, Gareth. I can't just blow this off as if it doesn't matter. If clients don't know they can depend on me, they won't hire me."

Her voice had risen and perspiration beaded on her forehead. He laid his palm on her thigh. "Calm down. It won't do you any good to get all stressed-out about this."

Jumping out of the van, hands on hips, she faced him squarely. "Would you calm down if you had a business appointment you couldn't get to? Would you calm down if you knew your reputation was at stake—"

Suddenly she stopped, whirled away from him and dashed to a line of brush near the driver's door. When he saw what was happening, he was on his feet and racing to her.

She'd lost her lunch.

Taking a tissue from her pocket, she stayed bent over for a few moments as he held her shoulders. After giving her time to compose herself, he turned her around. "Laura, what's the matter?"

She was perspiring even more now, and her cheeks were much too rosy for his peace of mind. Nevertheless, she said, "I'm fine. Sometimes that happens when I get overheated and stressed."

Sometimes that happens? They'd been married for five years and he didn't even know that.

"How often does this happen?"

She laid her hand on her stomach. "Now and then. Not often. I just got really hot, and I'm worried about getting to the baby shower on time. I don't want to call my client and tell her I'll be late when there's a chance I won't be."

Draping his arm around her shoulders, he led Laura to the back of the van. "Sit in the shade."

She shook her head. "I have a bottle of water up front. I'll get that and—"

Gently, he caught her arm and motioned again to the back of the van. "Sit. I'll get the water."

Before he gave her the water, though, he poured a little into his palm. Then he used his hand like a cloth and held it to the back of her neck under her hair. "I'm sorry if this drips down your back, but it'll help cool you off."

Then he poured another trickle into his hand, and using his fingers, wiped over her face. Her skin was hot, and he didn't think he'd ever touched her exactly like this. With her face turned up to his, he saw worry in her eyes that made his chest tighten. Why was she driving herself so hard? In case they split up? Did she want to make sure she could survive without him?

"You've got to cut back," he decided in a low voice, thinking she was doing too much, rushing too fast, growing her business much too rapidly.

At his words, she closed her eyes. Then she opened them again.

He realized she had probably taken those few seconds so she wouldn't blurt out something she'd regret.

How many times had she asked *him* to cut back?

That was different. His health *wasn't* affected.

A voice in his head reminded him, But the health of your marriage was.

Taking the bottle of water from his hand, she took a few swallows. She was patting her cheeks with more of the water, when a tow truck rumbled up behind them.

"Thank goodness," she breathed and checked her watch once more. "Hopefully I can still make it."

After Gareth closed the back doors of the van, he made sure they were locked. "I can call Nancy to come to the garage and pick us up, but you'll have to leave the supplies in the van."

"Don't call Nancy," she said quickly. "I'll call Mom. Maybe Tony's there. Everything might fit in his car. I hate to leave the supplies in the van at the garage overnight."

"Maybe you should phone Corrine and see if she could take over the baby shower."

While the tow-truck operator hooked up the van, Laura shook her head. "This is my event, Gareth."

"You're not feeling well."

"I'm feeling fine. It's just the heat. Hopefully I can pack the food into coolers, get a five-minute shower and be as good as new."

The tow-truck operator motioned to his air-conditioned cab. "You folks comin'?"

The truck was high, but Laura scrambled inside without a second thought. It was obvious she didn't want his help. It was obvious she might not even want his concern.

But that was just too damn bad. They were still married, and he was going to watch over her, whether she wanted him to or not.

Chapter 4

On Friday night, students, parents and teachers milled about in the high-school lobby. Laura had bought a new dress for her brother's graduation. It was cream, and slim with short sleeves, a royal-blue collar and a royal-blue band around the tight waist. She didn't think it had been that tight a week ago when she'd tried it on, but that could be her imagination.

Her mother was talking to Tony over by the trophy cases. He looked so handsome and grown-up in the navy graduation gown. Their father was speaking to the high-school principal and both men were laughing. During dinner, Vickie's beeper had gone off and she'd had to leave. Now she rushed through the doors of the auditorium lobby, waved to Laura and came to stand beside her.

As always, her sister looked beautiful in a little black dress. "I was afraid I'd miss this. Tony would never forgive me."

Her brother was used to his father and sister being late for family gatherings and special occasions.

"Well, he wouldn't," Vickie repeated after a glance at Laura. "You've never forgiven Dad for missing *your* high-school graduation."

"Of course I have," Laura protested. "He couldn't help it. A patient needed him."

"I saw your face that night. I even saw the tears. And you never mentioned it afterward."

"That's because I forgot about it."

"Uh-huh. That's because you *never* forgot it. I know how that works. I can read you, Laura. We're sisters, remember?"

"I remember." Smiling, Laura changed the subject. "You're the one who saves the world, and I'm the one who feeds it."

After studying her for a few moments, Vickie finally said, "You have this habit of pretending nothing's wrong when something is. Take the situation with you and Gareth, for example."

Her sister had a tendency to lecture, and Laura simply wasn't in the mood for it. "I think I'll go give Tony a hug."

But Vickie caught her arm. "Are you going to stay separated? Are you going to get a divorce?"

Defensively, Laura returned, "I don't know what I'm going to do yet. But it's none of your concern. I'll handle it."

"Well, you'd better handle it soon. I stopped in at Gareth's office this morning after rounds at the hospital."

"You did what?" Vickie had often poked into her life but had never downright interfered.

"I just wanted to check and see how his attitude was running. I wasn't obvious. I made the excuse I wanted to know what he'd gotten for Tony for graduation."

"You could have called him for that."

"He didn't seem to think it was unusual I stopped by. We've always been friendly."

From the first, Gareth had gotten along well with her family, maybe because he didn't have much of his own. Still, this time Vickie had overstepped her bounds. "Just what did you say to him?"

"About you? I didn't say anything. But I got a good look at what was going on there."

In spite of herself, Laura had to ask, "What was going on?"

"His office manager has her sights set on him. It was obvious in the way she smiled at him, looked at him and even worked for him. She wants to please him down to the last comma, and you'd better watch out."

After the other night when Nancy had stopped in at Gareth's house, Laura had pushed her feelings about the woman into the background, believing her own insecurities were making her suspicious. But now Vickie was holding up a mirror, and she couldn't ignore it. "How did Gareth respond to her?" She'd never really seen her husband and Nancy in a working situation.

"I don't think he noticed. Not yet, anyway. He probably just thinks her attention is flattering. You know how men are. But Nancy has more than flattery on her mind."

"I can't control what happens when he's working."

"No, but you can make him happy when he comes home. The problem is—you have to *be* at home."

Vickie, like her mother and the rest of her family, didn't understand how she felt. "If I go home now, nothing's going to change in our marriage. For the past year it's been like we were driving on parallel highways, never meeting. I don't want a marriage like Mom and Dad have. I want more than that."

Again, Vickie studied her for a long time as the rumbles and chatters of many conversations swirled around them. "If you're not careful, you won't have a marriage to go back to."

More than once Laura had thought about confiding her pregnancy in both her mother and Vickie, but now she was glad she hadn't. She didn't need more pressure. She needed to follow her instincts and her heart.

Out of the corner of her eye she noticed Tony broke off his conversation with their mother. A teacher called him over.

"I'm going to tell Mom I'm here," Vickie remarked, then moved toward their mother.

Just then, a deep baritone over Laura's shoulder said, "I didn't think I'd find you in this crowd."

Turning, she gazed up at Gareth. "I thought maybe you got held up."

They were standing very close, and Laura could tell Gareth had recently shaved. His end-of-the-day beard stubble wasn't in sight. His aftershave drew her closer to him. "Tony will be glad to see you."

"How about you? Are *you* glad to see me?"

When she felt her cheeks redden, she spotted Vickie looking at her with interest. "Yes, I am. I wanted to thank you for being so patient yesterday. I didn't have time last night when I had to rush to shower and then leave."

"Speaking of showers…"

His tone said he might be thinking about her naked in one. A teasing smile curved the corners of his lips for a moment, but then he turned serious. "How did the baby shower go last night?"

The talk of babies and the sight of the mother-to-be getting stuck in a chair that was too low had filled Laura with anticipation. She couldn't wait for the whole pregnancy experience. The problem was, she wanted to be sharing it with Gareth. Yet she knew she couldn't right now.

"It went fine. I was fine. The stress and the heat just got to me yesterday afternoon." That was true. She'd had a chance to take a nap this afternoon, and she felt great tonight.

They weren't alone in the midst of the crowd, yet it felt as if they were. Now, however, Laura's mom and dad and Vickie came to join them. Laura knew Vickie had kept one eye on them.

"We'd better find our seats," Janice advised all of them. "The ceremony will be starting soon."

Gareth's hand went to the small of Laura's back to protectively guide her into the auditorium. An usher took their tickets and showed them to their seats.

Beside Laura, about twelve rows back from the stage, Gareth leaned close to her, letting his lips graze her ear. "I brought an extra handkerchief if you need it."

When Laura turned toward him, their lips were almost brushing. "I'm not going to cry. I'm happy Tony's graduating."

Although Laura might not think so, Gareth knew her better than that. Fifteen minutes later when the music started playing, she surreptitiously swiped at a tear that rolled down her cheek. Instead of giving her a handkerchief, he dropped his arm around her shoulders. She didn't lean away, and he felt a great surge of relief. Maybe they could fix what was wrong. If he bided his time, maybe she'd realize again she belonged with him.

After the ceremony he invited Laura to ride with him back to the Bateses' house. Tony was going to spend a short time there with his family, change and then head out to a party.

The drive to the house took only five minutes, but before Laura could exit Gareth's car he asked her, "Did I tell you how pretty you look tonight?"

Her green gaze sparkled as she shook her head. "No, you didn't."

"Well, I'm telling you now."

"Thank you."

To his surprise, he saw her eyes becoming moist. Caressing her cheek, he said, "A compliment isn't supposed to make you cry."

"It's just tonight…Tony's graduation and all…"

She was wearing makeup this evening, and that was rare because Laura liked the natural look. "I want to kiss you, but I'm afraid I'd smear your lipstick, and your family would know we've been making out in the car."

With a small self-conscious laugh, she offered, "My family's a bit too interested in us right now."

"What do you mean?"

Looking sorry she'd brought it up, she murmured sadly, "Vickie thinks our marriage is on the rocks."

"What do *you* think?"

Her gaze stayed fixed on his. "I think we have to work our way back to each other."

That statement gave him pause.

Spotting Laura's parents, Vickie and Tony pulling into the driveway, he nodded toward the house. "We'd better go in."

Although Tony had protested that he didn't want a party, Laura's mother pulled one from the refrigerator. There were trays of meats and cheeses, two cold salads, a vegetable tray and, of course, Laura had made a cake.

Tony grinned at his sister. "I guess it's double chocolate, huh?"

"You guessed right."

"Then I guess I don't mind." When he hugged her, she hugged him back and Gareth heard her murmur, "Congratulations! I'm proud of you."

In spite of Janice's preparations, Gareth knew Tony wouldn't stick around long. He was anxious to be off with his friends and really celebrate. He proved that by diving through his supper.

When he was on his last bite of chocolate cake, Laura placed a present beside his glass of iced tea. It was a square box, and he eyed it curiously. "It's too small for a satellite-radio system." He grinned. Then he glanced at Vickie's box over on the sideboard. "But that's the right size for one."

"As if you hadn't been telling me you wanted one for the past few months," Vickie grumbled.

Gareth saw that Laura looked worried, as if she might not have bought her brother the right gift. However, Tony took the package in hand, unwrapped it quickly and lifted the lid. Then he pulled out a baseball. "Wow! Barry Bonds autographed it. Where'd you get this?"

"On eBay," Laura said with a smile. "Do you like it?"

"It's great." He got up from the table and gave her a peck on the cheek. "Thanks."

While Tony opened presents from his parents and from Vickie, Gareth went out to his car, popped the trunk and pulled out the guitar with the blue bow. When he entered the kitchen, he tried to hold it behind him.

When he finally brought it out into the open for Tony, Laura's brother's gaze met his. "Awesome! This is even better than a new car!" Taking it into his hands, Tony strummed it.

After he handed him an envelope to go with the gift, Gareth explained, "It comes with six lessons. I thought you could get them in before going to college."

"You're the best, Gareth!" Tony gave him a grin that said he really believed that. The boy had wanted a guitar for the past year, but his parents hadn't thought it was important enough to consider. However, Gareth knew Tony wrote music on the side and had been saving up for the instrument.

When Gareth's gaze met Laura's, there was a softness in hers that he hadn't seen since he returned. He knew it had nothing to do with the amount of money he'd spent on the guitar, but rather his thoughtfulness in reading Tony. Maybe that's where he'd come up short with Laura the past couple of years—he'd forgotten to be thoughtful. Or he'd taken for granted that she'd be around even when he wasn't. As long as they'd been married, she'd made him feel special with I-Love-You notes in his wallet, cards on holidays, preparation of his favorite foods. Considering the other person's needs had always been a part of who Laura was. Why hadn't he realized that givers needed to receive, too? He was beginning to see that their careers were part of what had gone wrong between them, but they weren't the whole extent of it.

As Tony went upstairs to change, conversation around the table veered toward the eighteen-year-old's college selection. He'd accepted a spot at a university in Illinois, and Janice hadn't been happy about that.

"I wish he wasn't going so far away," she said for about the hundredth time.

Her husband shrugged. "It's a good school. That's what matters."

"He could be attending the University of Texas," Janice grumbled.

"It'll do him good to see a different part of the country," Vickie interjected. "He wants to see what life is like outside of Texas. I came back after med school. Maybe he will, too."

"Of course he'll come back," Janice insisted. "*This* is his home."

"He might want a life somewhere else," Laura suggested quietly.

"Don't be ridiculous," her mother returned. "He'd miss us all too much, and no place has more to offer than Texas. I just wish he'd settle in his mind what kind of degree he wants. He can't rattle around undecided very long."

"He has a year to make up his mind," Vickie mused. "He ought to opt for a business degree. He'd have the most doors open to him with that."

"He's interested in engineering," Janice put in. "That would be a wonderful career, too."

Throughout the discussion, Laura remained quiet, and Gareth realized now, she was often quiet with her family. Maybe that was because they didn't seem to value her opinion.

He didn't know how that had come about, but he knew that it had. She'd always taken a back seat to Vickie and Tony. Had her family set her up for that with *him?* After they'd married, had she taken a back seat to him because that had seemed the natural thing to do? Had he ignored her feelings because she didn't express them forcefully enough? Why should she have to?

It was a lot for Gareth to think about.

After Tony left, Gareth tested his theory by visiting with the Bates family. Once in a while Laura made a comment, but it wasn't given the weight of Vickie's ideas or Janice's opinions. Was that because Laura hadn't gone to college but rather had become a paralegal? Was it because she was the middle child?

Finally, Gareth knew he had to turn over the whole evening in his mind. When he made a move to leave, saying good-night to everyone, Laura walked him out.

On the front porch he asked, "Are you busy this weekend?"

"No catering jobs, but the Spring Fling's next Sunday."

"A lot of preparation?"

"Yes. Most of it just requires organization. I have to call in orders and make sure I have what I need when I need it."

"Is the van running okay?" He knew she'd gotten it back today because it was parked in the garage again.

"It seems to be. The mechanic said we have to be careful where we buy our gas. I don't want that happening again when I'm on the way to a catering job."

Gareth examined her closely, looking for signs that she didn't feel well. But there were none. She looked beautiful tonight and seemed as energetic as always. The stress and the heat had done a number on her yesterday, and he didn't want to see that happen again. Yet right now, he didn't have any say in what she did or didn't do.

"What's wrong?" Laura asked.

"I didn't say anything was wrong."

"No, you didn't." Unexpectedly she reached up and touched his jaw. "But this muscle is working, and you're sort of frowning."

Laura knew him so well. She could read him so well. But he understood tonight that *he* couldn't always read *her.* Lack of trying on his part? "I was just wondering when I was going to see you again. How about if I give you a call tomorrow afternoon, and we can do something tomorrow night?"

"A date?" she asked, looking pleased at the thought.

"Yes, a date."

Sliding his hand into her hair, he lowered his mouth to hers. He didn't have to coax her into the kiss. She seemed to want to give to him again. She'd been giving to him throughout their marriage, and it was time for him to give back. Now he didn't care about messing up her lipstick, or what her parents might think if she looked "just kissed." All that mattered was the two of them, what they had lost and what they could find again.

His tongue mated with hers, giving her a taste of what their next union could be. His hands stroked through her hair, trying to convey how much he wanted to take care of her. When she softly moaned into his mouth, he broke the kiss, but enfolded his arms around her.

"I can't wait for our date tomorrow night."

She looked a little dazed as she smiled up at him, and he liked that look. He wanted to daze her. He wanted to impress her. He wanted her back home. Maybe tomorrow night he could convince her that was the best place for her to be.

Gareth lay in his king-size bed, staring up at the ceiling with his arms crossed behind his head. Usually he fell asleep and slept solidly. But not since Laura had made herself unavailable to him while he was away…not since she'd decided to stay at her mother's.

When the phone rang, his first thought was of her. Glancing at the clock, seeing that it was 3:00 a.m., he snatched it up. "Laura?"

"No. It's Tony."

It took a moment for Gareth to orient himself to the fact that Tony was calling him in the middle of the night. "What is it? Is something wrong? Has something happened to Laura or—"

"No. No, nothing like that. It's just—" He stopped. "Maybe I shouldn't have called."

"You did, so tell me what's happening."

"I'm in San Antonio."

"Still?"

"Yeah, well, I don't have my car. You know, the guys picked me up."

"What's going on?"

"They're all smashed. We're at a party. I only had a couple of drinks. But the rest of them…they drank down that vodka like it was water. I'm *not* getting in the car with them."

Thank God, Tony had that much sense. "Do you need me to call your parents?"

"No! I mean, that's why I called *you*. Can you come pick me up, and then I can sneak in? They don't have to know."

Aiding and abetting. Gareth didn't know how much he liked that idea. But Tony was a good kid and it had been smart of him to call. Maybe once Gareth had dropped him off at home, he could convince the kid to tell his family what had happened.

"Give me your address and how to get there."

An hour later, with Tony beside him in the car telling him about a girl at the party he particularly liked, Gareth pulled up in front of the Bateses' house. "I think you ought to tell them," Gareth said again.

Tony unfastened the seat belt. "I will, but tomorrow morning, not now. I know Mom will just make a big ruckus. I want to remember how good tonight was, just for a little while longer."

"Do you have your key?"

"I'm going to go in the back door. I can turn off the alarm system there, too, and they won't hear me, I hope."

"I'll go with you, just to make sure you get in okay."

Gareth felt responsible for the teenager now and wasn't going to leave until he was safely inside.

As quietly as they could, they closed Gareth's car doors, went across the lawn and walked around the side of the house. The back-porch light glowed.

"Think they knew you were coming in this way?" Gareth joked.

"No. It goes on automatically at dusk."

However, after he opened the door and stepped inside to punch in the code for the security alarm, Gareth was aware they weren't alone.

A small, dim light glowed above the oven and he supposed the family used it as a night-light. It only took him a second to see Laura sitting at the kitchen table. She stood now as they came in, and everything in Gareth's body went taut. She was wearing a raspberry-colored nightgown of some soft silky material, and on top she'd belted a robe of the same fabric. But they both barely came to her knees, and she looked as enticing as he'd ever seen her.

Now her eyes were filled with surprise. "Gareth! What are you doing here?"

Glancing at the teenager he'd rescued, Gareth responded, "I think Tony should tell you why I'm here."

Silence filled the kitchen until Tony asked, "Mom and Dad still aren't awake, are they?" He glanced anxiously toward the stairs.

"No. I convinced them that all-night parties after

graduation weren't unusual. We thought you might stay over at a friend's."

"I…uh…"

Gareth placed his hand on the boy's shoulder. "She's not going to jump down your throat. You did the right thing."

"Tony?" There was worry in Laura's voice now, and her brother could hear it.

"We went to a party and it got pretty wild. Manuel and Jack couldn't walk a straight line. I knew I shouldn't get in a car with them, so I called Gareth. He came and got me."

"I don't understand. Why didn't you just call us?"

Shifting from one foot to the other, Tony looked uncomfortable. "Because Mom would have made a huge fuss. You know she would have. And Dad has to get up so early… I thought I could just let myself in and not wake up anyone."

"Why didn't you call *me?* You know I have my cell phone in my room."

With an embarrassed shrug, Tony answered, "I just didn't think about calling you."

Her brother's words were like a blow, and Gareth saw Laura take a deep breath. Then she swiftly turned and headed for the refrigerator. "Would anyone like a nightcap? I was going to pour some grape juice."

"No, I'm beat. I'm going to bed." Turning to Gareth, Tony said, "Thanks for picking me up."

After Laura set the bottle of juice on the counter, she crossed to her brother. "You did the right thing by calling somebody. But I want you to know you can depend on me, too. If you ever need anything, I'm here."

When Tony gave her a hug, he said good-night, then headed for the stairs. Crossing to the cupboard, Laura removed a glass.

Early on in their marriage, Gareth had appreciated the fact that Laura wasn't a woman of moods. She was usually calm and even-tempered. But he could usually tell when something upset her—her spine straightened, she did something until she composed herself, and then she blinked fast to prevent tears.

Stepping up behind her, he stood very close, though he didn't touch her. "What is it?"

She shook her head, poured the grape juice and took a few swallows.

With a clarity that hadn't been present before, he understood that if Laura really depended on him, really trusted him, she wouldn't hide her feelings from him. Had she gotten used to just handling situations on her own and not expecting him to notice if she was upset? How many times hadn't he noticed something was bothering her? How many times had he been away when she wanted to discuss something?

As he wrapped his arms around her, he drew her back against him. Her body tensed, but as he rested his chin on top of her head, she relaxed. The silk of her robe was soft and smooth against his arms. The glossy sheen of her hair encouraged him to rub his jaw back and forth over it. Her body, pliant against his, stirred a fire that he'd kept banked for too many weeks.

"Tell me," he requested.

"It hurts that Tony didn't think about calling me."

"Maybe he's just not used to you being here."

"It's not that. Sometimes I just feel like a fixture in this family. I've never been able to compete with Vickie's successes. And Tony, being the youngest and a son—" She shrugged. "Sometimes I just feel invisible, that's all."

Had he taken her for granted for so long that she felt invisible around him, too?

That had to change. She had to know how important she was to him. Although he didn't want to let go of her, he stepped back and nudged her around to face him. "I've changed my mind about this weekend."

"You don't want to go to dinner tomorrow night?" She seemed disappointed, but also almost resigned.

"I'd like to incorporate dinner into something else. I want you to be ready tomorrow morning around 11:00 a.m. Have an overnight case packed."

"Why?"

"Because I'm going to spirit you away. You and I need some alone time, and not just for a few hours."

Now she looked intrigued. "Where are we going?"

"It's a surprise and you'll find out tomorrow. Just tell

your mom you won't be back until sometime on Sunday."

When she gave him a smile, it was the most natural smile he'd seen since he'd returned to Red Rock. A getaway was just what they needed, and maybe on Sunday he'd be taking her back to *their* house.

Chapter 5

Gareth greeted Laura Saturday with a bouquet of pink sweetheart roses and daisies. Her smile made all his planning and shopping this morning more than worthwhile.

"They're beautiful!" She tilted her head to smell the pink roses. "Thank you so much. I'll put them in a vase, then I can enjoy them tomorrow night when we get back. Are you going to tell me where we're going?"

"I'm going to show you." The tone of his voice brought her gaze to his.

"A day away isn't going to fix everything," she said softly.

"Maybe not. But it's going to be a damn good start. This will be a weekend you'll never want to forget."

When heat colored her cheeks, he closed the distance between them and took her hands in his. Lifting her palm to his lips, he kissed it and he felt her tremble. "Are you ready?"

Keeping her eyes on his, she nodded.

"Good. Let's pop those flowers in a vase and get going."

On the road ten minutes later, he drove northeast of Red Rock toward Houston. They'd traveled about ten miles from Red Rock when he slowed and turned off the highway onto a secondary road.

"I think I know where we're going!" Laura said in surprise. "Are you taking me to Las Monedas Resort?"

Now it was Gareth's turn to be surprised. Las Monedas, translated "The Coins," was a five-star resort. "You've been there before?"

"Not as a guest, but I've catered a few events there for the manager, Doug Cinek."

"I thought the resort had its own restaurant."

"They do. On one occasion, I made and set up the cake and cookies for a wedding reception. On another, I catered a private party in one of the suites. Just last week there was a business retreat here, and I made the hors d'oeuvres for cocktail hour before it began."

Laura certainly was getting around. He just hadn't realized how large her client base had grown. "We're lucky they didn't have any conferences booked for *this* weekend or we wouldn't have gotten a suite."

Gareth pulled into a slot in the large parking lot near the hotel entrance.

"A suite?"

"I have lots of surprises planned." He grinned at her. "Come on. Come back to the trunk and I'll show you."

The resort was white stucco with salmon trim. Shade from the building fell over the car as he opened the trunk, and Laura met him there.

Handing her a pretty, gold-foil gift bag with pink paper peeking out over the edge, he explained, "That one you can save to open in the room."

"I can't peek?" she teased.

"You can if you want." He liked the idea she was acting like a kid on Christmas morning.

A pensive expression came over her face, and then, like a kid, she peered in the bag. The pink silk nightie flowed over her hand.

He let that gift speak for itself as he held up a bigger package. "Why don't you check out this one?"

As she did, she pulled out a bottle of champagne. "Wow! You went all out."

"See what else is in there."

A broad smile spread across her face as she spied the gold box. "My favorite chocolates. I can't believe you went shopping."

When her voice broke, he draped his arm around her shoulders. "Believe it. Come on. Let's drop these in the front seat and go check in."

The inside of the resort was elegant and cool, all cream and teal with lush foliage and freshly arranged flowers sitting about. In the center of the lobby was a large glass case holding ceramic pots overflowing with old coins.

When the clerk at the desk saw Laura, she exclaimed, "It *is* you. I noticed the reservation under Gareth Manning and wondered—"

As she broke off, Gareth frowned. What had she wondered? If he was going to bring someone else?

A man in a suit came out from an office behind the registration desk. He had black hair, snapping brown eyes and a smile that was all for Laura. "Well, hello."

With her own friendly smile, Laura said, "Doug, meet Gareth."

Doug came forward to shake Gareth's hand.

Gareth didn't know if he wanted to shake it. There was a look in this guy's eye when he'd spotted Laura that Gareth didn't like. At the same time Gareth was appraising the manager, Doug was giving Gareth the once-over. He wondered again what these people knew...or what they thought they knew.

After the perfunctory shake of Gareth's hand, Doug told Laura, "Mr. McMillen raved about your hors d'oeuvres the whole time he was here. His company will definitely demand your services the next time they're in town."

"I like having satisfied customers."

"We want *you* to be a satisfied customer. If there's anything you need while you're here, just give the front desk a buzz. Do you need a bellman for your bags?"

"I'll drive around to the closest entrance to our room and carry them in myself." Suddenly Gareth just wanted to be alone with his wife, eluding outside distractions.

Doug gave him a nod. "That's fine. Let's get you checked in."

With the manager of the resort himself overseeing the process, the check-in went quickly. As Doug gave Gareth the folder with key cards enclosed, he winked at Laura. "You have a great time."

With her cheeks pinkening, she responded, "We will."

Once they were seated in the car, Gareth drove around to the south entrance and parked. "Does that clerk at the desk know that we're…separated?"

After a short hesitation, Laura turned to face him. "Glenda knows I was staying at Mom's. It just slipped out one day when we were talking. I guess she made her own assumptions from that."

"And then told everybody else on staff, I guess."

Placing her hand on his arm, Laura murmured, "I'm sorry if you didn't want anyone to know. But I was the one who was here and had to answer questions. Sometimes it was awkward."

"If you didn't want the awkward questions, maybe you should have moved back home." As soon as he said it, he realized he shouldn't have.

"Are we going to fight and spoil coming here?"

Six weeks ago Laura would have never asked him that question so bluntly. She would have been quiet and withdrawn. *He* would have wrapped himself in pride and kept silent for a while, too. But that wouldn't have gotten them anywhere.

Now he was glad that she'd put her thought into plain words. "No. We're not going to fight. We're going to go up to our suite, open that champagne and start our weekend."

He saw a little frown play around her lips, but then it was gone, and he thought maybe he'd imagined it.

While Gareth toted his duffel bag and Laura's overnight case, she carried the two gift bags. Setting her tapestry valise on the floor, he used the magnetic key to open the door, then let her precede him inside.

The suite was beautiful with its red and blue motifs, drapes, spread, love seat and sofa. They stepped into the sitting-room area and wandered over to the rich oak table with its two chairs. An archway led into the bedroom furnished with a huge king-size bed. Gareth set their luggage on the bed as Laura peeked into the bathroom, with its double vanities, sunken Jacuzzi tub and double shower.

"I feel as if I'm staying in the lap of luxury," she said with a laugh.

When Gareth joined her in the bathroom, he came up behind her and wrapped his arms around her. "I wanted this weekend to be special. I wanted you to know—"

A loud knock at the door interrupted him.

Laura glanced up. "Did you order room service?"

"Not yet." Reluctantly, he released her and answered the knock. When he opened the door, he found Glenda.

Her arms were full of a large basket. "This is from Doug. I can put it on the table."

Coming to the door behind him, Laura peeked out. "Oh my gosh. Do you treat all your guests this well?"

Entering their suite, Glenda placed the wicker basket on the table. It held a bottle of wine, a bottle of sparkling apple cider, a box of chocolates bigger than the one Gareth had bought, as well as two apples, two pears and two bananas.

"Now we won't bother you again," Glenda concluded as she went to the door.

"Tell Doug how much we appreciate his thoughtfulness," Laura directed the clerk.

Glenda poked her head back into the room. "Oh, and I forgot to tell you Doug said he set up appointments for both of you to have massages at four o'clock. If that doesn't suit, you can call and rearrange the time." Then she saluted smartly and left the room, closing the door behind her.

Shrugging her shoulders in an exaggerated gesture, Laura asked, "What more could a woman want than two boxes of chocolates?"

Gareth had organized this weekend, planning to wow Laura with his attention. But he'd been outwowed. If she'd come to this resort alone, he had no doubt Doug would have still given her VIP treatment. It seemed she no longer needed her husband to buy her chocolates or to show her a good time. As soon as they'd settled in, he'd planned to call to set up massages, but that had been taken out of his hands, too. He knew he was used to controlling the situation and didn't adapt as well to rolling with the punches. Not in his personal life, anyway. But if he wanted Laura to consider moving back home, he knew he had to be flexible.

"Are you hungry for more than chocolates?" he asked her. "We could go down to the restaurant and order lunch, walk the grounds, then get ready for the massages. What do you think?"

Crossing to him, she stood on tiptoe and kissed him on the cheek. "Thank you for bringing me here. Lunch sounds like a great idea."

Her lips left an impression he knew would stay with him all day. His libido was telling him to start undressing her and make use of that big bed. Yet his heart was telling him that Laura needed more than that from him today.

So be it. He'd be patient if it killed him.

Considering she'd only imbibed water flavored with lemon and sparkling apple cider, Laura felt decidedly giddy. In the spa area of the resort, she emerged from the dressing room clad in the long white terry-cloth robe provided for her, and found Gareth waiting, dressed in his. The afternoon had flown by. Over lunch they'd talked about everything from her brother using his good sense the night before, to the band that would be playing at the Spring Fling. As they'd sat under a vine-covered trellis, listening and watching the man-made waterfall in the resort's botanical garden, Laura had almost told Gareth about their pregnancy.

Yet something held her back.

Maybe it was the knowledge they'd be returning to their real world tomorrow, and she didn't know what would happen then. Would Gareth fly off on another six-week business trip? Right now, however, he wasn't going anywhere, and the way he was looking at her made her whole body flush with anticipation.

Suddenly the door to the massage room opened. A man who introduced himself as Sven, and his wife as Elsa, gestured them toward the two massage tables.

Five minutes later, Gareth and Laura were flat on their stomachs, head to head, as the therapists began to work their magic. Laura's awareness of Gareth grew as soft music played nearby. Elsa was working on Gareth, and as she poured oil onto her hands, working it into his shoulder muscles, Laura wanted to be touching him. On his part, Gareth's gaze glanced often at Sven, who was working the tension out of her shoulders at the same time.

Suddenly, Gareth said, "I'd like to give my wife a massage myself."

To her surprise, her husband sat up on the table. "Can you two take a break for the rest of our time and leave us here…alone?"

After Elsa and Sven exchanged a look, they both smiled. Sven motioned to the oils sitting on a small utility cart. "Feel free to use whatever you want. I started with the almond oil."

Then the massage therapists exited the room and closed the door.

Gareth's gaze found Laura's. "I couldn't stand watching him touch you another second. I want to do it myself. Do you mind?"

"I don't mind at all," she murmured.

Her husband had never given her a massage before, and the idea of it made her tingle all over.

Gareth laid the huge white bath towel that had been covering him aside and stood. When he did, Laura's mouth went dry. No man had ever affected her the way her husband did. He was sexy with clothes on. Without them, the sight of his naked body caused a tight curling in her stomach.

As he stepped over to her table, he asked, "Do you want me to continue to use the oil?"

She could hardly find her voice. Finally she managed to say, "That's fine."

Gareth's hands were every bit as large and strong as

Sven's. When he began at the base of her neck and worked outward along her shoulders, she murmured, "That feels so good."

Gareth's massage was much more personal than Sven's. His fingertips seemed to know exactly where she needed to be touched, and his long strokes released all the tension from her body. By the time he removed the towel from her lower half, she was swimming in a lazy sea of relaxation. But then his hands made delicious circles on her buttocks and his fingers sensually lingered on the backs of her thighs. Relaxation transformed into delicious, sexual tension that awakened her awareness of him.

Bending close to her, his tongue rimmed the outer shell of her ear. It was so erotic, she felt her body tremble, and she knew it was time for her to be an active participant. Rolling to her side, she sat up on the sheet-covered table. She was naked. He was naked. No power in the world could have kept them apart.

When Gareth kissed her, she reached for him. Her hunger was as demanding as his. Holding her face between his hands, he pressed his tongue into her mouth where hers played with his as she renewed the joy of touching him. His muscled shoulders were taut under her fingers, and she reveled in his strength. Their frenzied desire burned higher as his hands slipped from her face and cupped her breasts, simultaneously rimming both nipples with his thumbs.

She almost came off the table. Her body was shaking with wanting him, and she could feel the shudder pass through him as she brushed his erection with her knee.

When he broke away, the need in his eyes made her pulse race even faster.

"I want you *now.*" He was breathing as raggedly as she was.

"Sven and Elsa—"

Reaching for the door, which was behind him, Gareth pushed the lock and it clicked.

His hands roamed her body as his kiss seemed to stretch into eternity, fanning her passion to an all-time high. Moments later, he was sliding her to the edge of the table, opening her thighs, urging her closer. With one fast thrust he was inside her and she was clinging to him. His buttocks were sleek and firm under her fingers. She received him with a joy she'd felt the very first time they'd made love. Soon, thoughts of that first time faded, as only now mattered.

Thrusting deeper and faster, Gareth commanded, "Look at me."

When she gazed into Gareth's eyes, the depth of his need claimed her because she needed him just as desperately. Each of his thrusts shook her heart until she knew she'd never love another man. Her orgasm built with a ferocity she'd never experienced before. It was as if the foreplay of the massage, the danger of their making love here, the longing of the past seven weeks, exploded into pleasure so exquisite, no other orgasm could ever be as powerful again.

Gareth muffled his cry of release into her hair. As his body shuddered, she held on tighter, wanting his pleasure to be as great as hers.

Finally, when their breathing became somewhat more normal, Gareth leaned away. After another long, possessive kiss, his voice was husky as he suggested, "Now let's go up to our room and do that all over again."

In full agreement, Laura contracted around him and smiled up at him, playfully asking, "Can we have chocolates first?"

With a chuckle, he wrapped her once more in his arms. "We'll feed them to each other and see where that takes us."

She hoped she knew. She hoped it would lead them home.

As Laura finished showering on Sunday morning, Gareth dressed. He'd showered with her at first, and they'd made love there, just as they'd made love most of the night. It had been the most satisfying sex he'd ever experienced. However, now…

Now he felt as if his life was truly on hold. He'd thought about compromises he might be willing to make. He'd thought about the attention he'd try to give to Laura every day. Yet in the back of his mind a disturbing thought niggled. What if they did get back together? What if he changed his working life? What if he changed the way he related to her?

And then she left again.

He was just beginning to understand how her leaving had impacted him. *He* never would have left *her.* He'd made vows. Come hell or high water, he'd stick to them. That's the kind of man he was.

What kind of woman was Laura? Had she meant her vows? Was she so willing to end their marriage because it wasn't exactly what she wanted? Could he ever forget she'd once left? The questions disturbed him. How could he know for sure that when she came back home, she'd stay?

After he buckled his belt, he drew a polo shirt from a hanger in the closet. He was pulling it on when his cell phone on the dresser beeped. He *could* let his voice mail take it.

Still hearing the shower running, he decided Laura wouldn't be out for a while, and he'd take the call. Fifteen minutes later, he was speaking to one of his Japanese contacts who was based stateside when Laura emerged from the bathroom.

Seeing him with the phone, she turned away quickly, and Gareth had to wonder if she didn't want him to see her expression. As she brushed her hair at the dresser, he wrapped up the conversation and ended the call.

The quiet in the room was too loud. "An emergency?" she asked, her tone much too casual.

To his chagrin he had to admit, "No."

Her soft sigh bothered him more than if she'd told him exactly what was on her mind.

"It's a habit, Laura. My phone rang and I answered it."

Slowly laying her brush on the dresser, she turned to face him. "How would you feel if a call had come in for me for a catering event and I had taken it?"

Backed into a corner, he didn't like it. Instead of making an accusation about how he'd let work interfere with their weekend, she'd simply asked him to feel what she was feeling. That was an effective method.

As he went to Laura, he realized he'd have to put himself in her shoes more often. If he did that, he'd know what she was thinking and feeling. "All right. You've made your point."

She looked so pretty today in navy shorts and sandals and a red knit top. Around her neck she wore a simple pearl, and Gareth knew it had been a gift from her dad when she was a teenager. Little things meant a lot to Laura. Now he let his thumb slip under the pearl. It was warm from her skin.

As he let it dangle again, he gazed into her eyes. "Last night I felt closer to you than I've ever felt. I don't want to let that feeling go."

"Last night meant a lot to me, too."

"Then let's not ruin it by talking about our work."

"We should be able to talk about our work," she said sadly. "If we're both doing something we like that gives us satisfaction, we should be able to share that."

She was right. It wasn't his work that had caused the problems between them, it was the time he spent at it and the trips he took to do it. "That call was about the Japanese contract."

Laura stiffened, and he saw it. But he had to be honest with her. "The CEO received my report and they want me to come back to Tokyo in six months."

"Are you going to go?"

"I told him I'd consider it...that I might not be able to fit it into my schedule. I'd only be gone a week or two at the most. I was thinking if I *did* decide to make the trip, since we know so far in advance, you could make plans to come with me. I'd make sure I wasn't working the whole time."

"In six months?" she asked, as if she was mentally figuring something out. She moved away from him, then packed her brush in the suitcase on the bed. "I'll have to think about it."

He caught her arm. "You don't want me to go at all, do you? Can't you look at the trip as an adventure?"

"I said I'd think about it. But I want you to think about something, too. Maybe that trip to Japan would be an adventure, but what about the other trips? And how many of those would there be until then?"

Exasperated now, he shrugged. "I don't know."

But he did know if they got back together now, he didn't want to face the idea of her not being there again when he returned. If she couldn't make the commitment to stay, no matter what happened between them, what kind of marriage would they have?

She had ducked her head and was rifling through the suitcase for something, and he suddenly knew exactly what was going on.

When he clasped her arm and turned her to face him, he saw tears in her eyes. Now he knew she was really upset.

After he pulled her close, he stroked her hair. "We'll figure this out."

She didn't respond, and he knew what she was thinking. What if they couldn't?

Resting his chin on top of her head, he knew he was going to have to make some big changes or else lose his wife.

Laura pushed herself on Thursday to get everything done on her to-do list. She'd been playing catch-up from the weekend. Today she'd gone over lists for the Spring Fling on Sunday, as well as prepared and frozen two entrées for a wedding reception on Saturday night. Since the weekend, she'd seen Gareth every evening. They'd gone to the movies, played golf and last night...after dinner, they'd spent a few hours in bed.

Staying the night had been a temptation that was hard to resist. But she *had* resisted. At least last night.

This morning she'd seen Gareth briefly. He'd helped her carry fresh supplies into the kitchen and then he'd left for work. Their goodbye kiss had been long and sweet. When she'd asked if he was going to attend the town council meeting tonight at the school cafeteria, he'd frowned and told her he had a dinner meeting in San Antonio. But if he could, he'd catch up with her at the meeting.

She wished she hadn't broken down in front of him on Sunday. But her emotions seemed so close to the surface these days that she wondered if her moods were caused by those pregnancy hormones that she'd read about. Thinking about his trip to Japan when she'd be over seven months pregnant…

But Gareth didn't know she'd be seven months pregnant.

Maybe if she told him about the pregnancy, he wouldn't go. But she didn't want to use the baby, any more than she wanted to use tears, as some kind of manipulative device. She and Gareth had to face their problems and solve them without either of them feeling trapped.

Laura worked all day, only stopping for cheese and crackers and an iced tea at lunch. She had planned to rest a bit before the town council meeting, but everything ran over and she found herself hurrying to get there on time. Tonight the town council was going to discuss school-board recommendations to hire additional teachers for the elementary school. Now that Laura was pregnant, those kinds of issues would be important to her and she wanted to be informed.

As she drove to the school, she couldn't help thinking about Gareth. While they were at the resort, he'd listened to her, looked into her eyes and really communicated with her. What if they could do that all the time? What if they could feel as close all the time as they did when they'd been making love? Then she realized she'd enjoyed having lunch with Gareth on Saturday as well as talking in the garden almost as much as everything else.

When Laura entered the cafeteria, it was three-quarters full, and she sat in a back row near the aisle. If Gareth came in, he'd be able to find her easily.

Mayor Lawrence Danforth was a tall thin man in his forties. His wire-rimmed spectacles sat on his narrow nose. Although his black hair showed no gray, he had a high receding hairline that made his bushy eyebrows seem even bushier. Stepping up to the microphone, he tapped on it for attention. The buzzing in the large room diminished.

"We have several issues on our agenda tonight," he began. "I know hiring additional teachers for our elementary school is important to all of you, and we'll get to that. But there's something else I'd like to discuss first."

"I'm sure all of you have read about, seen or heard about the love letter printed in the *Red Rock Gazette*."

Murmuring went up in the crowd.

The mayor held up his hand. "Unfortunately, the editor, Bill Sinclair, is out of town on a story right now. The letter was printed without names, and there are suspicions from employees at the paper that the editor himself took those names out to create a little ruckus. Well, a ruckus is what we've got. There are too many people in this town who think someone sent that letter to the newspaper for his or her benefit. This town is no stranger to mischief. In fact, the Spring Fling seems to bring out qualities in Red Rockians that they usually keep under wraps. Like the time someone spiked the punch and most of the town wound up skinny-dipping in Lake Mondo. Fortunately, this year, plans for the Spring Fling are going off without a hitch. That's due in part to Laura Manning back there."

Everyone turned to look at her.

Lifting her chin proudly, Laura smiled at the residents of Red Rock.

She was glad when the attention turned away from her again as the mayor continued, "We want to make sure the Spring Fling is the community event we intend it to be. Since that letter was published in the paper, we had a man hold up a bank with a squirt gun because of unrequited love. We had a woman write a scathing letter in response that caused much hard feeling in town.

I want the shenanigans to end. I don't want it spilling over into the Spring Fling on Sunday evening. There's only one way to stop all this nonsense. We need the letter writer to come forward. Or *anyone* who knows anything about the letter."

Laura could still remember what the words in the letter had said. At the time it was printed, she'd wondered if Gareth could have mailed it in. But he'd been in Japan. Besides, he wasn't that sentimental. He never said things like that to her. She couldn't remember the last time he'd told her he loved her. Words were important to women, but they just didn't seem to be as important to men.

Although the mayor had called for the name of the letter writer to be revealed, and although the room buzzed with chatter, no hands went up. No one came forward. No one shouted out, "I wrote it." But this group was only a smattering of Red Rock's population. Maybe when the word got out, the letter writer *would* come forward.

The room was warm now, and Laura felt her stomach turning queasy. She'd gobbled down a slice of pizza at her mother's when she'd stopped there to change. That had obviously been a bad idea. Tony had ordered peppers and onions on it and now…

As Laura took some deep breaths and swallowed hard, the mayor rapped on the podium for silence. "I can't say I really expected anyone to come forward. But

I was hoping. So now I want to give everyone a bit of advice. Forget the letter. If you think someone you know wrote it, ask him or her. If your significant other says no, take his or her word as truth."

After another long look around the room, he said, "I'm going to turn this meeting over to the town council now. They will give you the pros and cons of hiring additional teachers for the district."

Laura felt exceedingly worse as the minutes ticked by. After two of the city council members had spoken, Gareth strode into the room and suddenly appeared in the chair beside her.

"How's it going?" he asked.

"They're almost finished, and I'm..." She waved her hand back and forth in front of her face. "I'm getting hot."

"Why don't we go for ice cream. You can get your favorite, Rocky Road."

At the mention of the ice cream, the thought of the chocolate syrup and nuts and marshmallows, Laura knew she had to get to the bathroom.

"I'll be right back," she told Gareth as she stood quickly and practically ran from the cafeteria to the ladies' room in the hall.

Unfortunately, she heard Gareth coming after her, and she wondered if she could explain *this* bout of nausea any better than she had the last.

Chapter 6

Gareth knocked on the self-locking ladies'-room door until Laura opened it. She looked relatively fine, though her cheeks were a little flushed. "I don't like this, Laura. I think you should go to the doctor's."

"I got hot," she said quietly. "I must have a bug or something. I have a doctor's appointment next week for a checkup."

Gareth slipped his hands into her hair and turned her face up to his. "I want you to come home with me tonight."

"I don't know…."

"Yes, I think you do. I want you to come home and let me hold you. That's all. Just hold you. You're probably not sleeping well at your mother's house. Give me the chance to take care of you."

Her eyes grew very bright.

"You're under a lot of stress. It's not just us, though that's a big part of it. You're thinking about the Spring Fling, too. It's the most important event in this town every year, and a lot of pressure goes with being a part of it. Just look at tonight as a time-out."

He knew he was pressing her hard, but he did want to take care of her, as much as he wanted her to come home.

Determined to convince her, he decided to up the ante. "You won't have to make inconsequential conversation with your mother. Your sister probably won't drop in. And to top off all of that, you won't have to run back and forth to the kitchen. It'll be right there."

The beginnings of a smile played around her lips. "You're making a good case."

"A convincing case?"

He could tell the moment she gave in. Her shoulders relaxed, she let her body rest against his, and then she smiled up at him. "All right. I'll come home with you tonight."

Hugging her close, he decided they were going to take one night at a time.

When they walked into their house together ten minutes later, there was an awkwardness between them that Gareth hadn't expected. Laura had called her mother from the car, explaining she wouldn't be home. The minimal conversation told Gareth that Laura didn't want to answer any of her mother's questions. She didn't have answers yet, and neither did he.

They'd come in through the garage, and now Laura looked as if she didn't know what to do next. "I know it's early for you," she said softly, "but I'm really tired. I'm going to take a shower and turn in."

"It's not too early for me. Would you like something to drink?"

She went toward the refrigerator. "I can get it."

But he placed his hands on her shoulders and stroked his thumb down her cheek. "I'll get it. What would you like?"

"Sprite with ice."

"Sprite with ice it is."

The cell phone on his belt suddenly beeped. When Laura glanced down at it, he said, "My voice mail will take it."

"Gareth, if you need to answer that—"

"I don't." He turned her toward the bedroom. "Go take your shower."

When Laura had left the kitchen, Gareth took the phone from his belt and placed it on the counter. Nothing was going to interfere tonight. Absolutely nothing. He had to get used to the idea of putting business aside so they'd have uninterrupted time together.

A few minutes later he carried the sodas into the

bedroom. Hearing the shower running, he quickly undressed and went into the bathroom. When he opened the shower door, Laura looked surprised, then hesitant.

He knew what was going through her mind, but he didn't get into the shower with her to have sex. "I know you're tired. I just came to help."

After he shut the door, he took her bottle of shampoo from the ledge on the side of the shower. "Did you wash your hair yet?"

"No, I was just enjoying the water."

"Now you can do both." Putting a small dab into his hands, he stood behind her and worked the shampoo into her hair, massaging her temples and her scalp at the same time.

"That feels wonderful," she breathed.

"Good. I think you need to have more wonderful feelings when you're around me."

When she would have turned to face him, he said, "Uh-uh. Just enjoy the water."

After using the shampoo, he stroked conditioner into her hair. Then, dabbing a fruit-scented body wash onto a net ball, he washed her all over. The whole time, he thought about how erotic the experience was and wondered why he'd never done it before. As he smoothed the net ball around her breasts, she breathed in quicker and faster. But tonight, he wanted to give her comfort more than he wanted to arouse her.

As he finished, her gaze ran over his body. His arousal was evident.

"Now I should wash *you*," she said. He knew she would, no matter how tired she was.

"Nope. Not tonight. I'll get my shower while you dry your hair. Your soda is on the nightstand if you want it."

Her eyes were so big, so full of questions, so full of appreciation. She ran her fingers over his jaw that was now stubbled. "Thank you."

He kissed her nose. "Go get ready for bed."

By the time he stepped out of the shower, Laura had already finished in the bathroom. Toweling off, he strode into the bedroom and found her already curled on her side in the big bed.

After he switched off the lights, he crawled in with her, wrapped an arm around her and snuggled her into his chest.

Over her shoulder she said, "If you want to watch TV, I don't mind."

Brushing his cheek against her hair, he said, "I don't need TV. It's been a long time since I held you and just went to sleep."

"Gareth, I know you probably want—"

He knew she could feel his arousal against her. Whenever he'd wanted to make love, she had never denied him. But tonight was about much more than sex.

"I just want to hold you." He kissed her cheek. "Go to sleep."

When she was silent, he realized that's exactly what she'd done. He tightened his arm around her, breathed in her scent and closed his eyes, ignoring the knot in the pit of his stomach that warned him she might not be home permanently.

Whenever Laura thought about how tenderly Gareth had taken care of her on Thursday night, her heart melted. She had never felt so safe, protected and cherished. She stayed with him again on Friday night. Last night, he hadn't just held her, he'd made love to her.

Yet something was different—different from the years she'd spent with him…different from their weekend together. He seemed to be holding back. He'd been quiet at breakfast this morning, too, and she wished he'd talk to her. When she'd asked him if something was wrong, he'd taken a long while to respond and he hadn't exactly given her an answer. He'd just said work had piled up while he was away and he was going into his office for a few hours so that he'd have tomorrow completely free.

Working most of the day on food for the wedding reception tonight, she thought about what she'd wear to the Spring Fling the next evening. Even though she'd be overseeing the dessert table at the event, she wanted to look especially pretty. Hopefully, she'd have a chance to dance with Gareth. Hopefully, they could have some fun along with everyone else.

When Gareth came home around 3:00 p.m., she was loading up her van.

"Need some help?" he asked.

"Sure. Everything on the bottom two shelves of the refrigerator comes out here."

Instead of going into the kitchen to help her load, however, when she turned around he was right there. Tipping her chin up, he pressed an altogether sensual kiss onto her lips. "Never too busy to kiss," he said lightly afterward.

But the look in his eyes wasn't light, and she still had the feeling that something was bothering him.

With his arm around her shoulders, he walked her into the kitchen. She was about to turn into the pantry, when the cell phone in her pocket rang. Pulling it out, she answered automatically, "Delicacies by Laura."

"Laura, it's Corrine."

Her employee's voice sounded thin. "Hi. I'm almost packed up. If you—"

"That's why I'm calling. I'm sick, Laura. I'm sorry. I can hardly lift my head off the pillow. Every time I do, I'm dizzy."

"A flu bug?" Laura asked, concerned for her employee, but with her mind already clicking along, thinking about who she could get to help.

"I guess. I really am sorry. I'm hoping I'll be okay by tomorrow night. I don't want to miss the Spring Fling."

"If you still don't feel well tomorrow, I have plenty of help for that."

"What are you going to do tonight?"

"I don't know. It's a small reception. Maybe I can just handle it myself."

As Laura's mind went over everything she'd have to do, she finished the conversation with Corrine, then turned off the phone.

"Corrine's sick?" Gareth asked, obviously gathering what had happened from her conversation.

"Yes. She's dizzy and can't get out of bed. I'd better get moving. With Corrine not helping, I'll have a lot more to do myself."

"Do you want me to come along?"

Searching his face, she tried to figure out what he was really feeling. Accepting his help, when he hadn't been supportive of this venture to begin with, didn't seem like a good idea. "I'll manage."

"You said that too quickly. Don't you think it's about time I see what you do firsthand?"

"You'll see that tomorrow night."

"Maybe. But I'd like to help tonight."

She thought about it. She'd handle all the food herself. But if Gareth could help her unload, and position some of the trays, as well as let her know when something was getting low…

"You're sure you want to do this?"

"I'm sure. Just let me get rid of this suit coat and

change shirts. Then we'll motor." He kissed her again, and she felt as if they were partners for the first time in a long time.

To her surprise, Gareth was a monumental help to her. He seemed to read what she needed when she needed it. An ice sculpture had been delivered to the social hall attached to a San Antonio church. After covering tables with pristine, white tablecloths, Laura set up the hot buffet and soon had Swedish meatballs simmering in the warmer, sweet-and-sour chicken and rice waiting in another. She unveiled an assortment of cheeses, vegetables and fruit and made sure the wedding cake was positioned exactly right. More than once, she caught Gareth watching her, admiringly sometimes, with questions in his eyes others. Had he figured out she was pregnant? Was he thinking about that?

Tonight she would tell him. It was time.

They were ready when guests started filing in. Laura felt the familiar excitement she always experienced as an event began. Trying to be six places at once, with Gareth's help, she made sure all the guests had their fill. The bride and groom looked so happy, and as they fed each other their wedding cake, Laura remembered her and Gareth doing the same thing. Her gaze met his, and strong emotions seemed to pass between them. She felt connected to him now in a way she never had before.

The little flower girl was adorable in her coral organza dress. She had blond, curly hair and a cherubic smile. Her job had apparently been to spread rose petals for the bride to walk on. Now she still carried her basket around the room, offering them to anyone who wanted some. She looked about three years old, and Laura could easily imagine a child of hers and Gareth's doing the same thing.

As Laura adjusted the flowers on the main table, stirred the chicken and replaced the cover, she saw Gareth near the wedding cake. He was supposed to let her know if she needed to slice more pieces. When her gaze veered in his direction, she spotted the little flower girl running toward the table at breakneck speed. Then suddenly she seemed to trip over her own feet and landed on the floor, rose petals spilling from her basket. Immediately, she began to cry.

Gareth stooped down beside her, murmured something to her, then began scooping her petals back into her basket. Her cries subsided, and when he teasingly let a few petals fall on top of her hair, she giggled and looked up at him.

It was a picture Laura wouldn't soon forget. She and Gareth had never discussed children specifically, just always imagined they'd have some someday. After not getting pregnant for five years, Laura had begun to think she should see a specialist if they truly wanted children. Now they were going to have one. Watching

Gareth with the flower girl, she knew he would be wonderful with children of his own.

The wedding reception began to wind down around 8:00 p.m. The bride and groom had long ago left and only stragglers from their guest list remained. Gareth helped Laura pack up the food.

She was washing a few serving trays in the social hall's kitchen when Gareth rushed in, looking pale, his expression serious.

"What's wrong?" she asked, knowing something was.

"A nurse from the hospital called me. Uncle Isaac was in an accident on the motorcycle. I've got to get over there."

As she thought of Uncle Isaac hurt, she felt a bit dizzy. "I'm going with you. Anything I've left behind, I'll pick up later." Going to her husband she gave him a hug. "It'll be all right. I know it will."

But Gareth's tight hold on her told her more than words that he didn't know if that was true.

San Juan Hospital on the outskirts of San Antonio was a sprawling four-story medical facility. After Laura and Gareth stopped at the information desk off the main lobby, they were directed to the second floor, general patients' wing. Laura could see in the deepening lines of Gareth's face and the tautness of his features that his uncle meant the world to him. He was the only family Gareth had left, and if anything happened to Isaac...

When they found his room, Gareth pushed open the door and preceded her inside.

There were two beds in the room and Isaac Manning occupied one of them. The other was empty. His arm was in a cast and he had a bandage across his forehead. His left cheek was black-and-blue, and there was another long gauze patch on his right arm.

Summoning up a weak smile for them, he announced, "I had a bit of a fall."

The relief on Gareth's face was obvious, since his uncle could talk to him and his sense of humor apparently hadn't been too rattled.

Crossing the room, Gareth stood at his uncle's bedside. "Are you in one piece?"

As Laura bent to kiss Isaac's cheek, he grumbled, "He's never gonna let me on that bike again, is he?"

"I don't know," she joked back. "Seems to me that might depend on if you wear body armor or not."

Isaac's chuckle wasn't as robust as usual. "It was a turn," he said to Gareth. "I took it too fast and too sharp. Next time I'll know better."

Gareth rolled his eyes. "You won't be able to afford insurance on the bike after this. Tell me everything the doctor said."

It was obvious Gareth was still worried, but Isaac continued to treat the whole matter lightly. "As you can see, I have a broken arm, and a few scrapes and bruises."

"Then why are you still in the hospital? Why haven't they sent you home?"

With a frown, Isaac brushed a few wrinkles from his sheet.

"Uncle Isaac?" Gareth prompted.

"Something about a bump on the head. They're gonna watch me 'til morning," he finally admitted.

"A concussion?"

"The doc might have used that word."

Gareth blew out a frustrated breath. "I can see I'm not going to get anything out of you. What's your doctor's name?"

"Don't go bothering him."

"What is your doctor's name?"

"Dr. Garcia. But I'm sure he's long gone."

"I'm going to find out." Clasping Laura's shoulder, Gareth advised her, "Don't let him out of your sight. Don't let him get out of bed until after I've talked to his doctor."

"I'm sure he'll behave while I'm here." She covered Gareth's hand with hers and squeezed, assuring him that she'd keep watch over his uncle.

A few moments later, Gareth was out of the room and down the busy hall.

"The next thing's going to be he won't let me go home when I'm discharged."

"You might be right about that. It wouldn't hurt for you to come stay with us for a few days."

"Us?" Isaac asked with a sly grin. "Does that mean you and Gareth are under the same roof again?"

She was thinking of them as "us" again. As a couple. She'd missed Gareth so. Now he was really listening to her and seemed to understand her concerns about his work. "We're under the same roof."

When Isaac looked away from her, his forehead furrowed and he seemed lost in thought. Finally he said, "I told myself I should stay out of this. I told myself you and Gareth could solve your own problems. But I'm not sure you know what problems you're dealing with."

"What do you mean?"

"Gareth said his work's an issue, and I get that. But do you know why he works so much?"

She had no idea where this was going. "He wants to be a success. He wants to provide for us the best way he knows how."

"That's part of it. But I also think work is his way of keeping up a few walls, a few protective barriers."

She thought about how Gareth seemed to be holding back this week as they spent more time together. When she looked back over their marriage, she realized how little her husband had shared his feelings with her. He shared ideas and schedules and everyday life, but when it came down to what was in his heart, maybe it was those barriers that had kept him silent.

"I'm right, aren't I?" Isaac asked.

She nodded.

"You've got to remember Gareth's background, Laura. He's put it behind him, so that you've probably forgotten that it was there. But his mama left him by dying. After she died, he was desolate, as any child would be. The difference was—he didn't have a father there consoling him in his grief. He might still be my brother, if he's alive, but Stan Manning was an SOB. He didn't care about his wife and he didn't care about his son. I don't know if Gareth ever told you what exactly went down, but Stan left him with me two months after his mama died. He didn't want to be close to his son. He didn't want the responsibility for his son. So he dropped him with me. I didn't know what to do with a kid any more than the next bachelor. But Gareth and I became real friends and we found out we needed each other. Stan gave me a wonderful gift the day he brought Gareth to me. But you've gotta realize how he must have seen it. His mother deserted him by dying, and his father left because he didn't want him."

She'd known Gareth had gone to live with Isaac when he was eight, but she hadn't known his father had left so soon after his mother died. Gareth never talked about it. Her throat tightened when she thought about it.

"I know Gareth left you alone and you have lots of hours to fill. And you love cooking, and the business you've established. But I think Gareth saw your catering business as another desertion of sorts. And then when you left him to go live at your mom's—"

"Uncle Isaac," Gareth said in a stern voice.

When Laura turned toward the door, she wondered how long Gareth had been standing there. But from the expression on his face, it must have been for a while.

With everything out in the open now, she had to know the truth. "Did you feel that way? Did you feel as if I'd deserted you? With the business? With going to my mother's?"

Slowly Gareth came into the room, and his gaze locked to hers. When he stopped at the foot of Isaac's bed, his features looked frozen. "Once you started catering, everything changed. You weren't waiting when I got home. You didn't seem to care if I worked late or not. If I had a dinner meeting with a client and asked you to go along, you were busy."

She tried to absorb all that but most of all the pain underneath his words. Yet she had pain of her own. "Don't you understand I was tired of sitting alone at night? I was tired of going to bed alone? It seemed all I ever did was wait for you. I decided that was no way to live. If you were going to be busy, so was I."

"So then, we were never waiting for each other."

"You never even considered *not* going to Tokyo," she accused. "You acted as if six weeks was nothing."

"I was mistaken about that," he admitted. "I didn't realize our marriage was ready to break apart. But to tell you the truth, Laura, when I got home and you weren't there, I wondered what our vows meant to you."

"I just needed some time-out. I just needed—"

"You needed to make a statement. I get that."

Maybe he did. But she also saw something else. He *had* seen her leaving as a desertion. She realized now she'd broken a thread of trust between them, and he might never be able to forgive that. If he couldn't…

"Can you forgive me for asking for the separation?"

He didn't respond. She could see he didn't intend to, because he didn't *know* the answer. He might love her, but forgiveness was something else entirely. She had wanted space, and a little distance to see if she could get perspective on the two of them. But that space and distance might have caused an irreparable rift.

Tears stung in her eyes and she didn't want to break down in front of him and his uncle. "I'm going to call Tony to come and pick me up. That way you can stay as long as you want."

Leaning down, she kissed Isaac. As she passed Gareth on the way to the door, she wished he'd stop her. But he didn't. And he didn't ask her where she was going because he knew. They had a lot to sort out, and she might never be going home again.

Chapter 7

When Tony picked up Laura at the hospital, she was crying.

"What's going on?" he asked. "You sounded awful on the phone."

"Let's just go home," she said now, brushing away her tears.

Although they made the twenty-minute trip in silence, she could feel Tony's gaze on her every now and then. Finally in front of the house where she'd grown up, he said, "At least tell me why you were at the hospital."

After she explained about Gareth's uncle, Tony shook his head. "So he was in an accident and Gareth was worried. And what happened to you?"

What happened to her? She felt as if her world had exploded. Now she thought about exactly what had happened to her. "I've messed up everything."

"Between you and Gareth?"

She nodded as tears filled her eyes again. Somehow it was easier to talk to her brother than any other member of her family. "I don't know how to fix this, Tony. I hurt Gareth badly."

"By leaving him?" Tony asked, cutting to the chase.

"I never intended it to be that…exactly. I didn't know how to get him to listen to me. I guess I just wanted to shake things up and see how much he loved me."

"I don't get it, Laura. When the two of you are together, anyone can see that he loves you. It's the way he looks at you."

"Well, I guess I couldn't see it."

"Why couldn't you just tell him what you wanted?"

"Because telling anyone what I want isn't easy for me."

After a long silence, Tony insisted, "You've gotta stop sitting on the sidelines."

Her gaze jerked to her brother's. "What do you mean?"

"You always sit on the sidelines. You never get into the ruckus. We can't shut Vickie up. Mom talks loud, so we all hear her. Dad says exactly what he thinks. But you…you never get in there and push for what you want. It's as if you don't think you're good enough to be listened to. It's as if you don't think you're as important as me or Vickie or Mom or Dad."

Was her own insecurity the root of all of this? Had she never felt worthy enough to demand Gareth's attention? To stand up for what she wanted? To tell him she was afraid they were drifting so far apart? She'd never had confidence with her family. But in her marriage…

It finally dawned on her that she hadn't had enough confidence in herself and in her marriage to believe that she and Gareth could work things out. She never would have left if she'd believed in her love for Gareth and his love for her. That's what had hurt him so terribly. That's what he couldn't forgive.

"I guess I've never been courageous enough to fight for what I wanted, except for the catering business, and that was the wrong fight."

"Why?"

"My preoccupation with it led Gareth to believe I didn't want to be with him anymore, that I didn't appreciate the life he was trying to provide."

"What's going to happen now?"

What *was* going to happen now? She'd made one mistake after another. Having Tony pick her up was the last one she was going to make. She loved Gareth Manning, and she was going to prove that to him, one way or another. Somehow, she'd make amends. Somehow, she'd show him she didn't break her promises or her vows.

"Can you spare me another hour?"

"If it's for a good cause," he bargained with a small smile.

"I'm going to pack. I'd like you to take me home."

"To your house and Gareth's?"

"Yes." She never should have left Gareth at the hospital alone tonight. She never should have run out. She wasn't going to run out again. She was going to wait for him in their house, and somehow convince him to give her another chance.

Since Isaac asked Gareth to go to his house and make sure it was locked up, Gareth decided to stay the night. He had no reason to go home. Laura was at her mother's. If all went as planned, in the morning Isaac's doctor would discharge him. He'd make sure his uncle was settled tomorrow before he drove back to Red Rock. He knew Laura needed the van for the Spring Fling, but he had to be ready to see her again. He had to be ready for whatever came next.

After Gareth made sure his uncle's house was secure, he stretched out on the couch. He thought about the conversation he'd overheard between his uncle and Laura, and how it had pinpointed exactly how he'd felt. Only, he hadn't realized it until that moment. He hadn't realized he'd felt abandoned by Laura. Except, he didn't think she'd really meant to abandon him. He knew now she simply wanted to get his attention.

When she'd asked tonight if he could forgive her, why hadn't he said, "Yes, of course. I love you. I can forgive you."

Because he'd wanted to make her hurt the way he'd hurt when she wouldn't take his calls? Because he wanted her to understand they couldn't solve anything when they were apart? Because he was a bastard just trying to salve his own ego?

That made him sit up, stare into the darkness...and wonder exactly what he'd done.

Laura returned home after church Sunday morning and found her van in the garage as well as all her supplies from the night before unloaded in the kitchen. But Gareth was nowhere to be found, and his car was gone.

When she'd realized last night he wasn't coming home, she'd cried herself to sleep. This morning she'd been frantic with worry.

Finally, her gaze spotted the note on the refrigerator. She slipped it out from under the banana magnet.

Laura—I knew you'd need the van, so I brought it home. I have to drive back to San Antonio again. The doctor wanted Uncle Isaac to have two more tests and he won't be discharged until this afternoon. I called one of his poker buddies and he said he'll come over and spend the night with him. So as soon as I buy some groceries and get Uncle Isaac settled, I'll be home. I don't know what time it will be. I don't know when I'll be where this afternoon, but I want to talk to you tonight. If I don't make it to the Spring Fling, I'll stop by your mother's house. —G

Automatically, Laura went to the counter and picked up the phone to try to call Gareth. She wanted to tell him she'd be at *their* house, not at her mother's house. But when she dialed his cell-phone number, voice mail picked up right away, and she knew he had the phone turned off. Then she remembered—no one could use cell phones in the hospital. She didn't leave a message. What she had to say was too important to leave with a message service. Hopefully, he'd get to the Spring Fling. If not, she'd have Tony tell him she was back home where she belonged.

When five high-school girls arrived to help Laura prepare for that night, Laura tried to push her anxiety and nervousness aside. But that was impossible. Late in the afternoon, when the girls left, promising to meet her at six in the town square, Laura took a half-hour nap. Afterward she showered, dressed in a gauzy rainbow dress that she'd been saving for a special occasion, slipped on some flat shoes because of all the running she'd be doing tonight, then packed the van.

Three hours later the Spring Fling was in full swing. The circle of traffic that circulated around the parklike square was blocked off. The thousands of twinkle lights arranged on the trees glowed in the dark. The park lights illuminated the paths where residents of Red Rock mingled, conversed and joined the serving line. Laura tried to be everywhere at once, but found the girls she'd hired to be efficient and responsible.

Ever since she'd arrived she'd been watching for Gareth. In the crowd of people, she was afraid it would be impossible to find him. The mayor had welcomed everyone. Now, he and his wife were dancing on the patio under a crescent moon. A band, set up on a small stage, played faster songs for the younger folk, ballads for couples in love, and oldies for anyone who could remember the jitterbug and twist.

Laura was making sure the fruit-salad bowl was still filled, when the hairs on the nape of her neck prickled, right before a deep voice complimented her. "Everything looks wonderful. You've done a great job."

Her breath caught and she was almost afraid to turn around. But fear and insecurity had dogged her for too long. Now she was going to be the courageous woman she knew she could be. Turning, she faced her husband. "Are you going to sample any of it?"

"I have more important things on my mind right now than eating."

Trying to push words past the lump in her throat, she finally managed to ask, "How's Uncle Isaac?"

"He's hurting some. But his friend, George, is with

him, and I bought him plenty of ice packs. They've got food for at least a week and enough old westerns to last them almost that long. But I don't want to talk about Uncle Isaac."

Although there were people milling about everywhere, she looked into Gareth's eyes, and they were the only two people in the world. "Gareth, I'm so sorry." Her voice cracked.

Taking her hand, he drew her toward the white gazebo that for the moment was empty. Tugging her up the two steps, he pulled her into a shadowed corner. "No. *I'm* sorry. Last night…" He shook his head. "I handled that like a man full of pride and no love. I love you, Laura. I want a life with you. Uncle Isaac was right, that I've had walls up all my life. And they're just going to have to come down. I understand now I can't have a good marriage just because I want to. I have to work at it, just as you've always worked at it. I've taken entirely too much for granted. And I've taken *you* for granted. If you'll let me, I'll renew my promises to you, and this time I'll keep them differently."

She was looking up at him now, seeing everything in his eyes she had always wanted to see—passion, tenderness, commitment and so much love she could never doubt what he felt again. Still, she had to ask, "Can you forgive me for leaving?"

"I can forgive you anything, as long as you'll stay and make a life with me."

Tears were rolling down her cheeks, and she didn't do anything to stop them. "Yes, I'll make a life with you. I'll renew my vows to you. I'll show you in every way I know that you're the man I want to be with for the rest of my life."

She'd hardly finished when his mouth came down on hers. His kiss was hungry and possessive and claiming.

When he broke it, she had to tell him her secret right now. "I'm pregnant."

He looked at her as if he couldn't possibly have heard her correctly. "What did you say?"

"I'm pregnant. *We're* pregnant. What do you think?"

With a whoop of laughter, he picked her up in his arms and swung her around. "I think that's the most wonderful news I've heard in at least five years. Oh, Laura! How do you feel about it?"

"I feel wonderful."

He pulled her close for another hug and kiss. Then he murmured in her ear, "Would you like to dance?"

Laughing, she answered, "Yes, I would."

Leading her to the patio, he enfolded her in his arms. Then he leaned slightly away. "We still have a lot to talk about."

"We have the rest of our lives to talk."

"I know. You've really done a wonderful job here tonight. Do you want to keep your business while we have a baby?"

"I don't see how I can."

"You can. You can hire competent help, maybe even franchise your hors d'oeuvres and desserts. You can run the business from afar until you want to become a hands-on manager again."

"You really think I can do that?"

"I think you can do anything you set your mind to."

"But…will you mind? I know how you felt about me starting this…"

"We're starting fresh, Laura. I know now you have to be your own person, too, not a shadow of me. While I was waiting for Uncle Isaac to be discharged this afternoon, I made a few calls. I've got lots of options. For one thing, I'm definitely going to curb the traveling. For another, I might not have to travel at all. I can take a job as a permanent management consultant at Ludlow Industries in San Antonio. They're a computer-software company that has grown large, fast. They don't need someone to reorganize their departments…they want someone there to make sure they don't make mistakes. I can take the job and have plenty of time for a family."

"But is that what you *want* to do?"

"Actually, it is. It's the same work I've been doing. In the past, I think I kept up the traveling and working for independent companies because I was running from us and the intimacy we could have. I don't want to do that anymore."

"Oh, Gareth."

"Don't look at me like that. I might have to take you home right now."

"I wouldn't mind at all."

As they gazed at each other and held each other tight, he smiled. "If you want to work full-time, maybe I'll learn to be a stay-at-home dad."

When she laughed, he kissed her again. Their kiss seemed to go on as long as the dance. Just as the music ended, he leaned close to her ear. "Remember that love letter in the newspaper? I'm the one who wrote it."

"You?"

"I hoped it would tell you everything I couldn't say."

Leaning slightly away from him, she ran her hand down his jawline. "I'm glad you told me yourself to-night."

Although the music had stopped, they didn't notice. They were too busy kissing…lost in each other…lost in the future they were going to have.

Soon, everyone around them was applauding. They broke apart, but Gareth kept an arm tight around her.

Loud enough for everyone to hear, he declared, "Just so you all know—*I'm* the one who wrote the love letter in the newspaper. But I advise everyone else not to try it. If you have something important to say to your wife, say it in person."

Then he kissed Laura again, and she knew they were truly starting their happily-ever-after.

Everything you love about romance...
and more!

Please turn the page for Signature Select™
Bonus Features.

Bonus Features:

Signature Select™

BONUS FEATURES

Secret Admirer

Getting to know the
CHARACTERS

Isn't it great when you read a book, and you've been so pulled into that world that you want more of the characters you've grown to love? Here are some more character tidbits to satisfy your curiosity.

Matthew Harper

People see Matt as an intense guy with a wicked streak. But what few know is that Matt was the school goody-goody in the eyes of his teachers. In seventh-grade science, Matt used to hand in extra credit, to the point where it was called "extra, extra credit." Matt's tireless efforts certainly made him seem like a golden boy, but his extra credit created more work for his teachers. Finally, after handing in a thirty-page report on the life of a tiger shark, his teacher told him he should concentrate on having fun doing other activities. Matt was confused by this mandate but figured he'd focus on improving his grade in English. Of course, after writing an extra-credit term paper on Ernest Hemingway, Matt received praise from his teacher—and encouragement to go play kickball with his friends. His diligence is legendary and helped build the confidence to succeed in all aspects of his life. Well, convincing Jane Snow that she loved him was harder than writing any term paper!

Jane Snow

Jane is a successful businesswoman who found her true love in both business and pleasure. But when she first went to college she majored in creative writing, thinking that she would become a famous writer—like Virginia Woolf or Jane Austen. She'd always had a dreamy quality about her, so she put some of her thoughts to paper. Somehow, her attempts at prose shortened to poetry, but she felt awkward sharing her work with the class. Jane exuded confidence and poise while crunching numbers and making presentations to her peers. It seemed natural that she would switch to a major more in line with business. Still, she has never lost her love for poetry and to this day, Jane will write a verse or two in her secret journal. She hasn't shown this creative side to Matt yet, but she knows that it's only a matter of time before she shares her talent.

Mindy Snow

After watching her sister find Mr. Right, Mindy Snow is on the lookout for her own true love. She enjoys her job as a hairstylist, but years ago she dreamed of bigger things. She wanted to become a stylist to the stars and even practiced on her sister, Jane, before she realized that Red Rock is where she belongs. Mindy still scours magazines for the latest trends on the Hollywood fashion scene and replicates these hairdos for her clients. While she is happy where she is,

Mindy knows she might have to satisfy her long-held dream one of these days....

Greg Flynn

Greg is one of the best policemen in Red Rock, Texas, and seen as the town's peacemaker. Women went wild over his quiet and seductive ways until they realized he was in love with Annie Grant. Back in middle school, Greg was one of the shyest guys in school, especially when it came to girls. Puberty proved a torture for Greg because he wasn't brave enough to converse with the opposite sex and developed a mild stutter. For one painful year, Greg watched Clint Eastwood movies and tried to mimic the actor's speech and movement. Over time, Greg began to walk with more self-assurance, and when he felt nervous, instead of stuttering, he would simply scowl and wait for something brilliant to emerge from his mouth. It wasn't until he got to high school and started to fill in to his height that he became comfortable with his female peers.

Annie Grant

One of Annie's greatest wishes is to quit her job at the bank and open her own florist shop someday. But this wasn't always her desired career. For one brief period at age thirteen, Annie wanted to be a model. As a result, she tried to dye her hair blond. She ended up spending two months with pink hair, a perfect match for the pink roses in her parents' garden. Her older brother, Hank, had taken pictures of this bad hair job and threatened to have them published in the *Red Rock Gazette*. For revenge, Annie went into Hank's bedroom while he was asleep and applied makeup, a blond wig and earrings to her slumbering brother. She took pictures of her own. Because Annie was a redhead, she felt like an outsider in her youth. But since her stint with pink hair, she's come to appreciate her copper tresses.

Dirk Jenkins

Holding up a bank with a squirt gun isn't the only crazy thing Dirk Jenkins did in Red Rock.... Everyone knows someone spiked the punch at the Spring Fling a few years ago. How could they forget, with the infamous photo at Lake Mondo to remind them? No one ever found out that Dirk was one of the men responsible for making Red Rock the laughingstock of Texas. Until now. Dirk used to maintain that he was the reincarnation of Evel Knievel (despite the fact that the math was a little off) and did random stunts to impress a crowd. His most famous stunt was to line up several barrels and a ramp on the shore of Lake Mondo. He claimed that he would jump the barrels while riding backward on his motorcycle. At the appointed time, Dirk appeared in full Evel Knievel regalia and spent several moments revving up his motorcycle. He then accidentally went forward instead of backward and rammed into a tree. The only injury Dirk sustained was hurt pride and a sprained ankle.

Gareth Manning

Successful businessman Gareth Manning has it all, a beautiful wife and a baby on the way. But not everyone knows that Gareth has an addiction to sugar. As a child, Gareth was the first to chow down on cake, candy and cookies. During his adolescence, he regularly spent his lunch money on ice-cream bars and chocolate cupcakes instead of a healthy meal. Despite this habit, Gareth grew strong and healthy and eventually learned better eating habits. Now Gareth tries to keep his intake of sugar under control, but if one were to rummage through his desk, one would find several candy wrappers. His wife has an inkling of his penchant for sweets, which is why once a week, she'll make him a special pie. This dessert will usually disappear by the next morning.

Laura Manning

Laura is blissfully happy with her husband and looking forward to the birth of her baby. She didn't always know that she wanted to be a caterer; in fact, she stumbled into it when she planned a friend's bridal shower, and the rest, as they say, is history. Perhaps Laura's natural abilities in the realm of food and parties developed in her teens when she organized slumber parties. She was the first to gather a group of friends together and plan the food and girlie activities (dress-up, Truth or Dare, etc....). As she grew up, Laura never lost her flair for bringing people together and having fun. In fact, some are even encouraging her to write a book detailing her culinary secrets. Could she be the next domestic diva?

Ryan Fortune

After so many years, Ryan is now happily married to his true love, Lily. But there was a time when he had nightmares about his second wife. He couldn't forget her murder and would often wake up in the middle of the night. Ryan went through a period of insomnia where he would walk through his lavish home and find projects for himself. He built bookshelves, retiled a bathroom and reupholstered a set of chairs. Lily knew Ryan was going through a phase and so she waited patiently for him to work through his grief and feelings of guilt. After several months, Ryan seemed to have recovered and took Lily on a trip around the world.

Lily Fortune

While Lily was content with her first husband, Ryan has always been the love of her life, which is why she is so happy that they got their second chance at love. Lily is a hopeless romantic and enjoys reading romance novels in her spare time. She withstands Ryan's teasing with a smile and knows that Ryan has a romantic streak that equals her own. He brings her flowers and chocolate for no reason except to show that he loves her—and to make up for all the years they were apart.

Bill Sinclair

Ol' Bill knows everything that goes on in Red Rock and delights in pulling pranks on the good citizens of his town. The love-letter prank isn't the first one he pulled. Back in his younger days he was known for stirring up trouble. In 1950, Bill put up a banner across the high-school gymnasium, that read, Will you marry me, Susan? and created a mess that put the letter fiasco to shame. At the time, there were forty-seven Susans at his school.

A conversation with
ANN MAJOR

Ann Major is the bestselling author of fifty novels. Nora Roberts has described her work thusly: "Engaging characters, stories that thrill and delight, shivering suspense, and captivating romance." Sandra Brown says, "Her name on the cover instantly identifies the book as a good read." Recently, we spoke to Ann Major about life, writing and romance.

Tell us a bit about how you began your writing career.
When I was twenty-six I had my first child. Since I was home all day, I figured I had lots of time to pursue my dream of writing novels. So I just sat down at a manual typewriter and began writing. I wrote two books that went up to page 150 and then I didn't know what to do, so I stopped.

I wrote another book that was very complicated. For example, the heroine was insane. I wrote a brooding gothic I never even tried to sell. I wrote a romantic adventure set in Cornwall, England, in the Tudor period. Five years later, lively voices started talking to me in my head. I thought, "Voila!—characters!"

I went back and rewrote the Tudor adventure-romance for the fifth time, sent it to Dell without even putting an editor's name on it and sold it to Vivian Stephens, the founder of RWA. A week after selling that novel I sold a partial to Silhouette.

What's your writing routine?
I used to have a much more regular routine. I work at something all the time—not necessarily writing. I have three grown children. I take care of my eighty-one-year-old mother and her various businesses. I have grandchildren. I have three homes. I have lots of girlfriends. I travel a lot. I am married and I cook for a husband. So, I simply have to work anywhere and everywhere. I have two laptops and another sort-of-laptop—I can't remember what it's called—but you can write on it in the yard for twenty hours before the battery goes down. So, I can and do work anywhere. I work on planes, trains, in cars, in libraries, etc....

When I'm writing first draft, I like to get EVERYTHING ELSE DONE, AS IF THAT IS EVER POSSIBLE, and then I usually go off and work eighteen-hour days at one of my homes or at a nearby ranch. It really helps me to totally get away from my hometown. There are simply too many things to manage at home as I tend to be compulsive. So I need to go to a boring place so I can really concentrate. On second draft, I usually stay home and write. If I'm writing at home, I usually get to my office around 10:00 a.m. and stay until 6:00 p.m.

How do you research your stories?
I interview people. I eavesdrop. I use the Web a lot. I check books out of the library. I immerse myself in the activity somehow. I subscribe to periodicals that have to do with this subject.

When you're not writing, what are your favorite activities?
I do yoga. I cook. I kayak. I work out EVERY DAY. I read, garden, hang out with my cats. I go dancing. I party. I listen to music. I visit my children or grandchildren. I entertain. I hang out with my mother, who is very frail. I sail. I lunch with girlfriends. I wish I were more of an introvert like writers are supposed to be.

Could you tell us about your first romance?
The only romance that counts with me is the ongoing one I have with my husband. He came to my birthday party when I was three years old. I know this because my mom kept a baby book and wrote that down. He was ten. We met again when I was seventeen and he was twenty-four. I had a big crush on him, but our parents were first cousins, so he was forbidden as a boyfriend.

Forbidden or not, we hung out for a year. When I was twenty-two and he was twenty-nine he came home from Vietnam. We were both sort of engaged to other people, but went out together because we were "just" cousins. Well, that soon changed. I broke my

engagement, and here we are, happily married
thirty-five years later.

Do you have a favorite book or film?
I have too many favorites to name. I like
Mary Higgens Clark's books and Nora Roberts and
Sandra Brown and Mary Lynn Baxter. I've been read-
ing Nancy Mitford lately. I liked the film *Dirty
Dancing*. I loved *Master and Commander* and am
looking forward to seeing *Troy*.

Any last words to your readers?
Write to me anytime at www.annmajor.com.
I am always happy to hear from readers. I write for
you, just for you!

Ann Major's book, COWBOY AT MIDNIGHT,
launches *The Fortunes of Texas: Reunion* continuity series in June 2005

A conversation with
CHRISTINE RIMMER

Before Christine Rimmer began her writing career, she'd been everything from an actress to a salesclerk to a waitress. Since the publication of her first book, a Harlequin Temptation, in 1987, Christine has written over fifty contemporary romances for Silhouette Books. Recently, we spoke to Christine Rimmer about life, writing and romance.

Tell us a bit about how you began your writing career.
I began my writing career as a playwright. Then I tried poems, short stories and novellas. Took me several years to figure out that writing romance was the way to go for me. Once I did, though, I never looked back!

What's your writing routine?
Writing is my job and I treat it that way. I start work at eight in the morning and usually call it a day around four-thirty or five. A disciplined daily routine has made it possible for me to write fifty-plus romances.

How do you research your stories?
I do a lot of research on the Internet now, but I still use the library, newspapers, AAA maps and tour books, personal interviews and a number of other resources. Whatever it takes to find out what I need to know for the book.

When you're not writing, what are your favorite activities?
Reading, reading, reading! I also enjoy Trivial Pursuit with friends and family, a good barbecue and travel.

Could you tell us about your first romance?
My first romance, *The Road Home*, came out in 1997 from Harlequin Temptation. I chose my favorite all-time setting for that book, a tiny town in the Sierra Mountains where I spent every summer of my childhood.

Do you have a favorite book or film?
I was completely swept away by Audrey Niffenegger's debut novel, *The Time Traveler's Wife*.

Any last words to your readers?
Best always and thanks for reading my stories.

Christine Rimmer's next book, *Lori's Little Secret*, will be on sale in May 2005 from Silhouette Special Edition.

AUTHOR INTERVIEW BONUS FEATURE

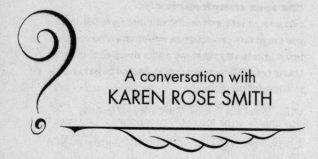

A conversation with
KAREN ROSE SMITH

A former English teacher and home decorator, award-winnning author Karen Rose Smith has sold over fifty books since 1991. Recently we spoke to her about life, writing, and romance.

16

Tell us a bit about how you began your writing career.
My writing career began with the desire to express emotion with words. In high school, I wrote poetry and was lucky enough to have one published in the school's literary magazine. When I was bored in class, I created scenarios in my mind to accompany songs on the hit charts. In college, my cousin and I wrote a script for *The Monkees* TV show and sent it to their concert venues. However, I began writing seriously in my thirties when back surgery interrupted my lifestyle and I needed an outlet. I began with short stories that kept getting longer. I'd read romances since I was a teenager, so that was the genre I chose to try when I decided to write a full book.

What's your writing routine?

My writing routine varies. Now I usually work on more than one project at a time. In the morning I do "raw" writing and meet my quota of pages for the day. After a break of cooking or exercising, I work on polishing whatever manuscript will be turned in next. I also work promotion into that schedule, and if I get insomnia or drink too many cappuccinos, I do raw writing again at night. Those are bonus pages that give me time off later!

How do you research your stories?

I research plotlines and characters in many different ways. My favorite is traveling. To be honest, I've only been doing that for the past few years. There are special settings that draw me to them. The Santa Fe, New Mexico, area is one. This year I hope to visit Montana and Wyoming. Actually being there and drinking in the setting can give a book an extra sparkle. If I can't visit an area, I find a contact there to answer my questions.

Occupations are an area of constant research. I use the Internet, contacts and friends of friends. When I write a cowboy story, I like to visit a farm or ranch to make the smell of hay and leather real. If I write about a businessman, I watch CNBC network and read financial papers. I use everything I can see, touch, feel and hear!

When you're not writing, what are your favorite activities?

My favorite activities are playing with and caring for my two cats. My husband and I try to have date night once a week. I love visiting with my two-year-old niece and family. The telephone keeps me connected to my critique partner almost daily, even though she lives half a state away and we visit face-to-face every year or so. And when I take a break from writing, I listen to music...or shop!

Could you tell us about your first romance?
My husband and I met in college. After a first meeting among friends, we gravitated toward each other and have been together ever since! We were married the summer of our college graduation and will celebrate our thirty-third anniversary this year.

Do you have a favorite book or film?
My all-time favorite movie is *Ghost*. One of my favorite books is *Fear Nothing* by Dean Koontz.

Any last words to your readers?
Often I am asked—Why do you write? I write because when I do, I tap a place inside me that connects me to something that is much bigger than I am. For me, writing is equivalent to standing before the ocean, watching a sunrise or sunset, or listening to deeply moving music. It's mysterious and glorious and always an adventure!

Karen Rose Smith's next book, *Cabin Fever,* will be on sale in May 2005 from Silhouette Special Edition. In addition, her book, *The Good Doctor,* which is part of *The Fortunes of Texas: Reunion* continuity series, will be available in October 2005.

You won't want to miss
Signature Select's new twelve-book series
THE FORTUNES OF TEXAS: REUNION,
which features your favorite family!
Ann Major launches the series with
COWBOY AT MIDNIGHT—
available June 2005.

For a sneak peek, turn the page!

Here's a sneak peek...

COWBOY AT MIDNIGHT
by
Ann Major

PROLOGUE

The Double Crown Ranch, Texas

Somebody was going to die!

Rosita Perez *knew* this as she sprang forward in her bed and threw off her sheets and cotton quilt; she *knew* it by the swift darts of pain that made her left breast ache.

The room felt as icy as a meat locker. Even so, her long black hair with its distinctive white streak above her forehead was soaking wet, as was her pillow. Hot flashes, her gringo doctor would say.

Smart gringo doctors thought they knew everything. She *knew* better.

Somebody was going to die. Somebody close at hand.

Rosita was descended from a long line of *curanderos.* Since birth she'd been cursed, or blessed with the sight. Like her ancestors, who'd been natural healers, she saw things; she felt things that other people didn't feel.

Life wasn't lived on a single plane. Nor was the world and its machinations entirely logical, much as her bosses, Ryan and Lily Fortune, might like to think. She'd learned to keep her visions to herself because most people, even her beloved husband, Ruben, didn't believe her.

After pulling on her robe, she tiptoed out of the bedroom and down the hall, taking care not to wake Ruben. A light from outside beckoned her and she headed for the front windows of her living room.

The red glow in the sky above the ranch made her shake even more. Sensing evil, she felt too afraid to go out on her front porch.

Which was ridiculous. She'd faced cougars and bobcats and convicts on the loose while living out alone on ranches. Despite her misgivings; no, because of them, she opened the front door and forced herself to pad bravely out onto the porch of her ranch house.

Help! The cry was silent and it came from nowhere, and yet from everywhere. The plaintive wail consumed her soul. Sensing death, she sucked in a breath and stared at the dark fringe of trees that circled her home like prison walls.

"Who are you?" she whispered.

A bloodred moon the exact shade of the skull in her nightmare hung over the ranch. Circling it was a bright scarlet ring. She stared at the moon, expecting it to turn into a skull. She stared and stared, aware that the dense night smelled sweetly of juniper and buzzed with the music of millions of cicadas.

Summer smells. Summer sounds. Why did they make her tremble tonight?

She kept watching the moon until it vanished behind a black cloud. She wasn't feeling any easier when a bunch of coyotes began to hoot, and she heard a man's eerie laughter from beyond the juniper long after they stopped.

"Who's out there?" she cried.

The cicadas stopped their serenade. A thousand eyes seemed to stare at her from the thick wall of dark trees.

Had someone heard her? Stark fear drained the blood from her face.

With a muted cry, she raced back inside her brilliantly lit living room with its dozens of velvet floral paintings and comforting overstuffed furniture. Not that she felt comforted tonight.

Slamming the door, she stared unseeingly at the sofa piled high with her recent purchases from a flea market—mirror sunglasses, towel sets, children's clothes and toys, all in need of sorting. Breathing heavily, she triple-bolted the door and sagged against it.

Maybe the moon hadn't been a human skull, but one thing was for sure—she'd never seen anything like that bloodred moon circled with a ring of fire before. Never in all her sixty-six years.

And the laughter… That terrible, inhuman laughter…

Someone was out there.

Rosita could trace her blood to prehistoric civilizations in Mexico. She knew in her bones that such a moon meant things didn't bode well.

The Fortunes were in trouble—again.

She'd worked for them for a long time. Too long, Ruben said. He wanted her to retire so she could focus on him. "We'll move away, not too far, but we'll have a place of our own."

Ruben had always wanted his own land, but she loved Ryan Fortune and his precious wife, Lily, as if they were members of her own family. She couldn't leave them. Not now! Not when she knew they needed her more than ever. In the morning she would try to warn them as she cooked them eggs and bacon and tamales and frijoles. She cooked frijoles with every meal.

They would probably laugh at her and tease her as they always did. They'd waited so long to realize their love. They wanted to be happy, and she wanted that for them, too. With the sun high in the sky, maybe she would be able to laugh and hope all would be well.

She made a fist. "I have to tell them anyway! First thing, when I go to the ranch house!"

When she finally stopped shaking, it was a long time before she felt safe enough to switch off the light. Even then she was still too restless to go back to bed or to sort through her flea-market purchases, so she curled up in her favorite armchair and let the rosy-tinted darkness wrap her while she waited for the sun to come up and chase her ghosts away.

24

If only she could wake Ruben and tell him about the skull and the laughter.

But he would only think her stupid, tell her it was nothing and order her to bed.

"*Ya verás*. You'll see, *viejo*. You'll see," she whispered.

Then she shivered as the shadowy forms of the tall furniture in her living room shaped themselves into snakes and cougars and alligators.

Someone was going to die!

...NOT THE END...

Look for the continuation of Cowboy at Midnight *by Ann Major in June 2005.*

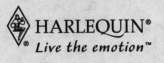

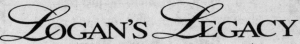

Signature Select™

ANN MAJOR

Ann Major considers life, like her writing, to be one great adventure. Her motto is Have Laptop—Will Travel. Besides traveling, she enjoys reading, sailing, swimming, ocean kayaking and hiking. She's even tried her skill at white-water rafting.

Ann delights in the "little rituals" of everyday life: time spent with her husband of thirty-five years, their children, their grandchildren, their cats too many to count and her mother. Ann was born and raised and lives in Texas.

CHRISTINE RIMMER

A reader favorite whose books consistently top the Waldenbooks romance bestseller list, **Christine Rimmer** has written more than fifty novels for Silhouette Books. Her stories have been nominated for numerous awards, including Romance Writers of America's RITA® Award and the *Romantic Times* Series Storyteller of the Year Award.

Christine has written for a number of Silhouette imprints, including Silhouette Special Edition, Silhouette Desire and Silhouette Single Title. Look for her latest book, *Lori's Little Secret*, out this month from Silhouette Special Edition.

KAREN ROSE SMITH

Karen Rose Smith, award-winning author of over forty-five published novels, loves to write. She began putting pen to paper in high school when she discovered poetry as a creative outlet. Also writing for her high school newspaper, intending to teach someday, she never suspected crafting emotional and romantic stories would become her life's work! Married for thirty-three years, she and her husband reside in Pennsylvania with their two cats, Ebbie and London. Readers can e-mail Karen through her Web site at www.karenrosesmith.com or write to her at P.O. Box 1545, Hanover PA 17331.